Heart of Gold

Random House
New York

Heart
of Gold

Russell H.
Greenan

The English words to Luigi Denza's *"Funiculi, Funicula"* (pages 271, 272)
are by Edward Oxenford.

Library of Congress Cataloging in Publication Data
Greenan, Russell H
  Heart of gold.
  I. Title.
PZ4.G7982He [PS3557.R376]   813'.5'4   74-23865
ISBN 0-394-49495-4

Manufactured in the United States of America
9   8   7   6   5   4   3   2
First Edition

*For Margaret
and Bill Greenan*

Heart of Gold

1

The house was on Marlborough Street—a three-story brownstone whose intricately tailored cornices, consoles and pediments had all been ravaged by the abrasive onslaughts of a hundred Boston winters. While standing on the stoop, waiting to be admitted, the Reverend Dr. John Matthew Lenox again wondered what Amos Cavanaugh had in mind.

Earlier that day at the coffee hour, when the ladies of the congregation were volubly complimenting him on yet another inspired sermon, the old man had appeared from nowhere and whispered hoarsely in his ear, "Come to dinner tonight, Reverend. Come at six-thirty. Don't forget. It's important."

Lenox had automatically smiled and nodded. As he did, he saw his own plans for the evening—which included a visit to a fancy new Turkish restaurant on Park Drive—evaporate like breath on a windowpane. But under the circumstances, what else could he have done? It had been more of a command than an invitation. And one couldn't snub a rich parishioner, in any case. Besides, Lenox was filled with curiosity.

Cavanaugh himself opened the ponderous door. Beneath the mellow saffron glow of the vestibule light, the wrinkles in his vulpine face resembled cramped writing on parchment.

There lies his autobiography, the minister reflected—the whole sad story, neatly inscribed. Each of those lines represents a crafty scheme, a hard bargain driven, a mean and miserly satisfaction. How eloquently they proclaim his innermost secrets!

The aged man led him into the dining room. Though he lived alone, he had for the occasion hired his cleaning woman to come in and cook. Sparkling crystal glasses, fine decorated china and heavy sterling flatware were arranged upon the long oval table. The sight of these luxuries reminded Lenox of the tales Geraldine Gargan told—of how Cavanaugh bought out bankrupts for a penny on the dollar, foreclosed on widows and orphans, swindled young heirs and generally practiced the most pitiless kinds of usury. It was from such sources that the well-set table probably derived, he thought glumly.

Despite the elegant utensils, however, the meal was a dreary one. The cleaning woman—an untidy creature with pink-rimmed eyes—served them limp celery, sweet gherkins, tomato juice, sliced white bread, lukewarm canned consommé, and an insipid stew of leeks, carrots, string beans, soggy potatoes and gristly beef. Once, while the lady was absent from the room, Cavanaugh criticized her petulantly.

"Why isn't this confounded soup hot? That simpleton can't do anything right," he grumbled. "Last winter I had her living in for a couple of weeks, and it was a catastrophe —an absolute catastrophe. Believe it or not, Reverend, she spent ten dollars a day on groceries, just to feed the two of us. And the kitchen was never warm enough for her, no matter how high I raised the thermostat. Then she actually had the gall to say she was getting chilblains—can you imagine? As for hard work, she didn't do a lick of that. Oh no! The floors didn't get scrubbed, the silver didn't get polished, the windows didn't get washed, the furniture wasn't dusted—nothing got done at all. From morn till night she lolled out there in the kitchen with the kettle on, pretending she was brewing tea, but the truth was that she was only burning gas to make the room like a hothouse. And she thought she was pulling the wool over my eyes—the ninny. I gave her the bum's rush. Told her to pack her bag and get out. I can manage better alone, and a good deal more economically, too."

Beyond this single acrimonious outburst, there was little else in the way of mensal conversation. The few affable gambits that Lenox attempted were either squelched or ignored by his dour host.

A barely congealed lime gelatine concluded the dinner. After that, the two men went into the living room across the hall to drink their coffee.

Why has he asked me over? the minister wondered for the tenth or twelfth time, glancing at Cavanaugh, who was staring morosely at the fireplace fender. Could he be contemplating a gift to the church? Him? It wasn't likely. Miracles occur only in the Bible.

"Inheritance tax," the old man suddenly muttered, as if to himself. "They won't get it, by golly! Legal larceny— that's all it is." He turned and faced his companion. "My money's in Switzerland, Reverend—in a fireproof, burglar-proof vault. I'm not a dunce. Maybe you've noticed that I have less furniture now, and fewer paintings. Have you? Yes—well, I've been auctioning off the better stuff, at Louis

Small's gallery. Then I send the cash straight to Geneva. I'm seventy-nine, you know. At the Harvard Medical School they say I don't have long to live—but I'm not scared of death. Why should I be? I've led a useful life. No, sir! I'm not frightened a bit. It's just that I don't want to be cheated out of what's rightfully mine. I suppose you'll think I'm crazy, although I've always believed in God and said my prayers—haven't I, my boy? Haven't I?"

Lenox nodded encouragingly, pretending he understood the meaning of the other's cryptic words.

"Absolutely!" said Cavanaugh, his mouth shaping a meager smile. "Oh, I might be clutching at straws—sure. But what if it's really true? What if it's all exactly as the fellow claims?" Inserting two fingers in his vest pocket, he drew forth a slip of paper—a newspaper clipping—and passed it to his guest. "Let's have your opinion," he added, squinting one eye in a conspiratorial wink.

Lenox unfolded the clipping and read as follows:

CAN WEALTH BE TRANSFERRED TO THE HEREAFTER?

Prof. Rupert Hofbauer, internationally famed physicist, will send interested parties a brief treatise on this vital subject. To cover costs, forward twenty-five cents to Prof. Hofbauer, 194 Blagden St., Boston 02116.

"It was in the Sunday *Tribune*, among the classifieds," Cavanaugh said. "I might have missed it, if a friend hadn't pointed it out to me." He smirked. "A lady friend—an attractive and sensible woman that I met one day at an auction. But this article, Reverend—what do you make of it?"

Still mystified, Lenox hesitated. Had the sly old scoundrel actually been taken in by this drivel? At last he replied tentatively, "It sounds bogus, Mr. Cavanaugh—like some sort of confidence game."

"Yes, yes. That was my impression too—in the beginning. After all, I'm no fledgling. However, you have to consider the marvels of modern science. Can't hide your head in the sand, these days. No, sir! Why, fifty years ago if you suggested men could fly to the moon, they would have flung you in the booby hatch. To the moon—imagine! Even now that it's happened, I can hardly believe it. But, science aside, what are your feelings about the idea as a religious man? The hereafter is a real place, is it not? It isn't just a superstition. Well, then it ought to be feasible for material things to be transported there, I should think. And the Lord is just . . . and justice means that a man is fully entitled to keep all the property that belongs to him—doesn't it, Reverend?"

Meeting his host's ferocious glare, Lenox pondered this question. "Perhaps," he conceded finally.

"Perhaps? Perhaps nothing! Absolutely! And who deserves a man's inheritance more than the man himself? Nobody!" Cavanaugh had begun to slaver at the corner of his mouth and this, together with the truculent look in his eyes, gave him a slightly lunatic appearance. "By gosh, when I think of inheritance taxes, it makes my blood boil. And then these other fools—the ones who claim money is evil, vulgar, poisonous, corrupt. I can't suffer them."

The miser licked his thin dark lips, drank some coffee and set his cup on a nearby table. "Tell me, where in the Scriptures does it say that money is wicked?" he continued. "Oh, the Good Book often condemns the evil use of money—certainly—but never the money itself. No sir! Doesn't Ecclesiastes state that 'A feast is made for laughter, and wine maketh merry: but money answereth all things'? Doesn't he, Reverend?"

"Yes, to be sure. Still, the Bible also reminds us that the Lord giveth and the Lord taketh away."

"I agree. I agree. Eventually, he'll take it away—sure. The question is—when? The instant your heart stops beating? Bushwah! Anyhow, in the United States your money doesn't go to God after you die. It goes to the Internal Revenue Service—which is more like the devil, if you ask me. No, my boy. Listen to me—I've done some deep thinking about this and it's my conviction that though the Lord is going to take everything back, all right, he won't do it till the Judgment Day. Isn't that the Day of the Last Reckoning? It wouldn't be fair, wouldn't be justice, to repossess a person's goods before the end of the world. That's how it seems to me."

The logic of his argument caught Lenox by surprise. Dotty as Cavanaugh was, he had succeeded admirably in shoring up the flimsy structure of his avaricious dream. The minister, deciding to humor him, said, "I guess it could happen that way. It's plausible enough, Mr. Cavanaugh. And if you're right, then the advertisement in the news-paper—"

"Exactly!" the old man broke in, his gray eyes now as hard as nailheads. "It becomes more credible, doesn't it? Well, I sent for that little pamphlet. A quarter was all it cost. Naturally, I didn't entertain extravagant hopes. Like you, I figured this Hofbauer for a bamboozler who was spreading his net to catch a fish. But I really didn't have anything to lose. Just the week before, the specialist at the Medical School warned me I might be dead in six months, so my options were limited. Tell me, Reverend—have you ever heard of anti-matter?"

Lenox raised his eyebrows and regarded his companion curiously. "Anti-matter, did you say? Yes, I've heard of it. It's a term in physics—atomic or nuclear physics. Why do you ask?"

"And is that all you know about the stuff—only that it's a term in physics?"

"Let's see. I've read about anti-matter in the *Times*. I believe it has electrical charges that are the opposite of those in ordinary matter. A fantastic theory."

"Fantastic? Maybe—but it's more than just a theory. Anti-matter has been created in the laboratory, though it disappears almost instantly. The electrons are positive instead of negative, and the protons are negative instead of positive. They're backwards, which is why they can't survive in our universe. Regular atoms cancel them out."

Cavanaugh sniffled and wiped a bead of saliva from his bluish lips with the veined back of a scrawny hand. "Did you know there are reputable scientists who contend there's another universe—an anti-matter universe—existing right alongside our own?" he asked. "They say there are black holes out in space—tunnels leading to that other world. Years ago a huge forest in Siberia was annihilated by a gigantic explosion, and the physicists claim it was caused by an anti-matter meteor that got into this universe by mistake. Trees were knocked down for twenty miles in all directions. They know it was anti-matter because they couldn't find any trace of the meteor. It had been canceled out. Yes sir!

"Well, in the pamphlet Hofbauer describes these things very clearly. Then he goes on to tell of his own work, and what he's learned from it. I found it fascinating. He maintains he has positive proof that when a person dies, his spirit is reversed and translated to the anti-matter universe.

Over there, it enters another body—a young but mature body, an anti-matter body. He says the spirit or soul is just as indestructible as matter and energy, and so it can never actually die. It simply flies off to this place—which you or I would call heaven, although the professor refers to it as the Otherside of Existence—and when it arrives there, commences a whole brand-new life. The civilization over on the Otherside is way in advance of ours, you understand. Instead of being born, their people are produced in laboratories, and because they don't want to be bothered with infants and children, they manufacture only adults. Isn't it astounding? But for each person they produce, naturally, they have to have a soul, and these souls come from our universe. I think it makes sense, myself. What's your opinion, Reverend?"

Lenox blinked. Good Christ! he thought. The old boy must be soft as a soap bubble! Yet, even as he drew this conclusion, a picture began to form in his mind, and in this picture he could faintly discern his own image. Cautiously he replied, "I don't know, Mr. Cavanaugh. It's certainly a novel conception and, I suppose, not too inconsistent with Christian belief. Still, if the Otherside is heaven, where is hell?"

"Now, now—don't question me on fine points," said Cavanaugh irritably. "Heaven and hell, God and the devil, Jesus and salvation—these matters are sure to be settled eventually. What's important is that for the first time, science confirms the existence of a life after death."

"Confirms? Is there demonstrable proof?"

"Ah, you're skeptical for a theologian, my boy. Not that I blame you. But we'll get to the proof later. Let me finish. Where was I? Oh yes. After I got the pamphlet I waited, thinking that if Hofbauer was a bamboozler he'd soon be around to see if I swallowed the bait. He never came, though, and I waited two weeks. Well, I didn't want to waste any more time, so I went over to see the man.

"This Blagden Street runs out of Copley Square, near the library. I found the house, all right, but he wasn't home. Believe it or not, I dragged myself down to that place three times before I finally caught him in. And when I introduced myself, the fellow was as stand-offish as one of those Brahmins from the Hill. But, by golly, he thawed out a bit after I mentioned money."

The old man raised his coffee cup in a trembling hand and drank from it. He licked his lips, crossed his legs at the shanks and then went on with his story.

"An odd, foreign-looking gink, Hofbrauer is. Talks like that Baron Munchausen comedian who was on the radio years ago. He said he was a teacher at M.I.T. and though at first I didn't believe him, it turned out to be true. He's on the faculty, all right, because the next day he drove me over to the school and gave me a little tour. Ever been through the Massachusetts Institute of Technology, Reverend? A fascinating place. We visited the Hayden Library, the MacLaurin Building and the Guggenheim Library. We even had some tea in a cafeteria, with a couple of his colleagues. It was a grand experience. He wanted to show me his own lab in the High Voltage Research Building, but he couldn't. The projects there are hush-hush; you need a special badge to get in, and I didn't have one. Anyway, I was pretty well exhausted by then.

"Getting back to that first day though—he was awfully cagey. Later on he told me that he thought I was from the government. It seems the government knows the professor is working on something tremendous, and they've offered him a generous federal grant if only he'll give them progress reports. But he doesn't trust politicians—and I can't fault him for that. My dad used to say that when politicians die, they have to be screwed into their graves. Ha! Because they're so crooked, you see? Well, that's why Hofbauer was distant. It was a week before he let me see his invention, the Charge Translator. A marvelous machine, it is. It's in his basement. With this Charge Translator, he's able to communicate with the Otherside of Existence."

Lenox had often wondered how con men could flimflam otherwise sensible people, could make them agree to the most outlandish proposals. Now he had an inkling of the way it was done. The method was full of intricacies and subtleties. It called for patience, psychology, timing and all the skill of the thespian. At first the "professor" acted aloof and suspicious, compelling the dupe to beg for information. Then, when the "professor" opened his heart and delivered his spiel of mumbo jumbo—liberally laced with plausible scientific details—the poor dupe was overcome with gratitude. After that, the chummy tour of M.I.T. was granted, including the "chance" encounter with a couple of "colleagues." It was a masterly production—a real operetta. And once the stage was set and the overture finished, that indispensable prop, the "marvelous invention," made its predictable appearance. Shades of money mills and orgone boxes! Still, how could this canny man fall for it? He must be further gone than he looks, mused Lenox.

Blandly the minister asked, "Communicate with the Otherside? How does he do that, Mr. Cavanaugh?"

The miser grinned, and the wrinkles in his leathery countenance were like knife wounds. "The process is simple," he answered smugly. "A message is placed in the Charge Translator and a switch is thrown. At the speed of light the paper is changed to anti-matter. Now, since anti-matter is alien to our world, it vanishes. Where does it go? Why, off to the anti-matter universe—to the Otherside. Over there they read the message and send back a reply, using their own highly advanced scientific instruments."

It took Lenox a moment to digest this rough morsel of science fiction. Hoping his face hadn't betrayed the skepticism of his thoughts, he said, "That's clever. But do they speak English on the Otherside?"

"Certainly they do!" snapped the old man querulously. "And German, French, Chinese and the rest. Haven't I just explained that the people there came from this world originally? In the anti-matter universe, they live pretty much the way we live here. That's why I want to translate my capital. I don't want to start my new life as some ragged pauper.

"Before, you mentioned proof. Well, listen. I saw Hofbauer put an orange in his machine and it disappeared right in front of my eyes. Yes sir! It could have been a trick, I guess, but I don't see how. The Charge Translator is made out of titanium and molybdenum, and it's loaded with wires, cathodes, electromagnets and other things. Anyhow, this orange was in a compartment that had a glass door, so you could see it plain as day. There was a flash of light—not a blinding flash, either—and then the orange was gone. Instantaneously! He said it went from this life to the next, and I'm inclined to believe him. I'm old, but my eyes are sharp, Reverend."

Somewhere in the house a clock with a tinny chime tolled nine. Cavanaugh sniffled, hunched forward in his chair and regarded his guest closely. "And if an orange can make the trip, so too can my money," he said, his features quick with cunning and avarice. "Only, to arrange it I require the help of an honest man, which is why I asked you here tonight."

A keen tingle of joy went through Lenox and he felt suddenly very warm, but he said nothing.

Wagging a bony finger at him, Cavanaugh continued, "I've known you since you were an infant, and you've always been straight as a line in a ledger. Yes sir! And your father—well, he was a saint on earth. Good trees bear good fruit. Remember, too, this is a religious matter. You will help me . . . won't you, my boy?"

"Naturally, Mr. Cavanaugh, in any way I can," said the minister, almost too quickly. "Your faith in me is very flattering. But wouldn't Mr. Tilbury be—"

"Tilbury? Don't say a word to him! Oh, he's a good banker, Reverend—sure. It's just that this isn't his kind of deal. He'd raise a lot of nonsensical objections. No, you're the only one I've taken into my confidence because you're the only one who can handle the job."

"I see. And what exactly will I have to do?"

"Hardly a thing. After I die you'll fly to Switzerland and fetch my money. Then you'll make the arrangements with Hofbauer so he can ship it over to me. That's all there is to it. I'll give you a power of attorney."

"But can't the money be transferred to this country through regular banking channels?"

"No, no!" said Cavanaugh in alarm. "Those Internal Revenue bandits keep track of large transactions. Big checks are microfilmed. They'd want to know where the funds came from. They'd confiscate them. They'd tax the money till there was nothing left. The Internal Revenue! It should be called the Infernal Revenue!" He paused a moment to compose himself before adding, "But don't misunderstand me, Reverend. It's not against the law to bring money into the country. I'm not asking you to do anything illegal. I'd never do that. Anyway, being a parson, you won't be too bothered by customs men."

Lenox restrained a smile. "It seems a strange business," he said. "I don't know much about financial dealings, but are you sure this is what you want to do?"

"I'm fairly sure—not a hundred percent. I want to talk with the professor some more . . . ask him a few questions. In fact, I'd like you to go over to his house with me one day and see the machine operate. Who knows? If there's a trick, you might be able to spot it. I haven't given the fellow a nickel yet. All I'm saying is that so far, the proposition sounds pretty solid to me. That's why I'm making plans. If I decide to go through with it, which will probably be the case, I'll give you written instructions—all the details. The only complication might be the gold. That's a nuisance."

"Gold?" Lenox echoed. "What gold?"

"Oh, I didn't mention the gold, did I?" Cavanaugh mumbled. He looked slightly confused. "Well, the American dollar isn't negotiable on the Otherside of Existence. It's too bad, but I guess you can't have everything. So you'll have to exchange the cash for gold, which is what they use there. It won't be a problem, though. I know an honest dealer on Bromfield Street, and I'll speak to him about it beforehand. You'll have to get Mexican gold pesos; they're the best ounce-for-dollar bargain nowadays, though the gold price has gone up shamefully. It would be cheaper if we could buy bullion, but the politicians won't let you any more."

"About how much gold will there be, Mr. Cavanaugh?"

"What?" asked the miser, peering at him blankly.

"The gold coins. Will there be a lot of them?"

"Certainly. A dozen bags, maybe—and they'll be heavy. You'll have to make several trips. For the love of God, don't lose any! Don't tell anyone what you're doing, either. The greatest safety lies in secrecy. And above all, make sure Hofbauer actually sends every penny's worth over to me. Don't let him pull any fast ones, Reverend. Mexican pesos. Yes, they'll be best. The bank is in Geneva. Oh, you'll handle everything perfectly. Absolutely! You were always a bright, trustworthy boy."

A dry chuckle, like the rasping of badly meshed gears, broke from the old man's small mouth. His eyelids drooped wearily, and spittle dribbled down his chin.

The cleaning woman poked her head in the room to say that the dishes were washed and she was going home.

When she closed the door again, Cavanaugh started to retell the story of the disappearing orange, embellishing it this time with more scientific terminology and louder attestations to the sharpness of his vision. As he went on, however, his enunciation became poor and he commenced to ramble. Irrelevancies, unfinished sentences, redundancies and fits of sniffling completely garbled the tale. At last he seemed to be unable to continue at all. Struggling from his chair, he stifled a yawn.

"I'd better get to bed," he said. "I get up at five in the morning, you know. Yes, Reverend, every morning I'm up at five. I'm an early riser. Of course, being old, I don't sleep like I used to."

On wobbly legs he saw Lenox to the door, where, after a last warning to keep what he'd heard to himself, he bade him good night and let him out.

2

The Volkswagen was in the alley behind the house. Lenox
unlocked it, climbed in and lit a cigarette.

By God! he thought, smiling obliquely. I always knew
that someday I'd get a break, but never in my wildest
dreams did I imagine Amos Cavanaugh would be the one to
give it to me. Isn't the world a paradoxical place?
Anti-matter . . . explosions in Siberia . . . the Otherside
of Existence . . . people produced in laboratories. I wish I
had it all on a tape recorder. What an after-dinner
conversation! Titanium and molybdenum . . . the Judgment Day. Does he really believe it? I bet he does. He has
to. For a tightwad like him, the idea of keeping his money
after death—of having pockets in his shroud—must be
positively irresistible. And those bags of gold. That was a
nice touch—a little finesse to make the fantasy that much
more credible. It's just the kind of thing Amos would
understand. Yes, this rascal Hofbauer has chosen his pigeon
well. Cavanaugh would cheerfully endure eternity in the
lowest pit of hell if only Satan let him bring his strongbox
along. Having cheated everybody else, the old bastard now
wants to cheat the Grim Reaper too. But will he go through

with it? Will he actually plunk a fortune in my lap? He really does seem to trust me. Jesus! There must be some virtue in religion, after all, when even pretended piety attracts such blessings. But will he actually go through with it? And just how much money does he possess?

Lenox frowned and gazed pensively into the darkness.

Arousing himself at last, he tossed the cigarette out the window and took off his coat, his clerical collar and his dickey. From a canvas satchel on the seat beside him he pulled a mulberry turtleneck sweater and a fashionable mauve felt hat with a wide floppy brim—both of which he donned. Then he folded the coat and shirt, stuffed them in the bag, started the engine and drove out of the alley.

Not many minutes later he parked near the juncture of Massachusetts Avenue and Boylston Street, locked the car, put on a pair of gold-framed dark glasses and entered a large, brightly lit cafeteria. He went directly to a table in an alcove where a frail man in a green flannel shirt sat huddled over a tabloid newspaper.

"See anything with class, Cheeks?" Lenox asked.

The reader glanced up. "Hey, Johnny!" he said. "How you doing? Naw—they got a bunch of giraffes running tomorrow. What's happening? I was down to Raynham last night for them sprints and got wiped out. Handicapping a dog is worse than playing the numbers. It hurt, too, because right now I ain't got much income coming in. These smart-ass kids with their crappy electric guitars! Even at weddings! Nobody wants a good saxophone player no more. Lou Ardoise just left ten minutes ago. He's beefing about Francis Dupont burning him for a hundred and a half. You know Dupont—the gimpy character. He copped a breeze back to Bangor, they say. Ardoise had to be soft to take markers from that clown. With a glass eye you could see he was phony. Anyhow, good ribbons to bad rubbers is what I say."

Completing this outburst, the man called Cheeks rolled up the tabloid and shoved it in his hip pocket. From the aluminum ashtray on the table he snatched a cigar stub and stuck it in his mouth. Its charred unlit end looked as belligerent as the muzzle of a gun.

"I lent Francis twenty dollars on Thursday," said Lenox ruefully.

"Cheese and rice! That wasn't smart, John. When you started hanging out here a year ago, what was the first thing I told you? Don't lend money to people you don't know, right? Lend a friend—sure! But a casual stranger? You might as well throw the dough in the garbage. You paid Dupont's plane fare, I bet."

"Probably," Lenox said, smiling. Then he shook his head and asked, "What happened to Silk Duchesse?"

"Faded in the stretch."

"How did she lose, Cheeks? The race must have been fixed."

"At Suffolk? Naw! She lost because them mares just don't have the strength," the frail man replied brusquely. He had the round face of a baby, but an unhappy baby—one with colic. It was to his full, ruddy cheeks that he owed his nickname. "Hey, see that dude over there, Johnny? That's Cliffie Coogan."

Turning casually, Lenox saw a broad-shouldered, fat-jowled man talking to a busboy by the door.

"You don't know Coogan, huh?" Cheeks asked. "The guy's famous. He was in on the Plymouth mail job. Yeah. A couple of million they got. Biggest score in history. Cliffie was the one dressed up like a cop—the one who stopped the truck. That's what I heard. The Feds tried to pin it on him, but they never could. For about a year, every place Coogan went there was two postal inspectors standing in his shadow. They can't do nothing now, though, because the statue of limitations ran out. He's home free." Cheeks shifted the cigar butt in his mouth and grimaced. "I knew the slob when he was nobody—just a dumb bouncer in the Leitrim House in Scollay Square. Them days, I played with the Frank Terry Trio."

"Since he's got money, how come he stays in Boston?"

"A good question. If it was me, I'd be living in Florida or Vegas. Puerto Rico ain't bad neither, with that El Comandante race track. One winter I stood there at the Hotel Miramar. They had some great Spanish flamingo dancers in the floor show . . . What have you got for tomorrow, John—anything?"

"It's supposed to rain."

"Showers, only. It'll keep the dust down."

"I like Betty's Boss in the fifth."

"You do?" Cheeks asked, raising his eyebrows.

"Yes, I do," said Lenox testily. He drew two ten-dollar bills out of his pocket. "Here, put these on his nose. Are you going out?"

"Tomorrow I can't. Got to see a guy. But I'll give it to Ardoise. Twenty on Betty's Boss. If that gee-gee comes in, you'll be rich like Coogan over there."

The minister thought of Amos Cavanaugh. "Nothing wrong with that," he answered, his expression unfathomable behind the sunglasses. "Who knows? One day I might be rich."

"Yeah? You got big hopes. The real estate business must be getting better."

"It hasn't been bad—no, not bad at all."

"So maybe you can lend me a sawbuck. After them frigging greyhounds, I'm a little low on fuel."

From his pocket Lenox readily fished another ten and handed it across the table. "Lucky for you you're not a casual stranger," he said, laughing. "I'm getting a cup of coffee, Cheeks. You want anything?"

"Naw," said Cheeks, slipping the money into his breast pocket. "I just had a couple of eggs and a ration of bacon. It was a disaster. I must be a feeb to keep eating in this place. You could've patched a tire with them eggs. I couldn't swallow them hardly. They kept getting stuck in my upper glottis. Emil Green says the cook is a hit man for the Mafia." He rolled the cigar from the right side of his mouth to the left. "Thanks for the ten, though. You got a good heart, John."

Lenox went up to the counter to get his coffee.

It was a mistake to tell him I'm in the real estate business, Lenox ruminated, standing in the cafeteria doorway. That's much too prosperous a profession.

The night was mild. Wily-faced people loitered in small bands on the paper-strewn sidewalk. Above their heads the amber streetlights glowed like eerie celestial phenomena. Through the broad intersection an endless column of obstreperous automobiles charged, head lamps gleaming.

"Bags of gold. Bags of gold," Lenox murmured as he left the doorway and sauntered to the phone booth near the corner.

He dropped a coin in the box and dialed a number. When the connection was made, he said, "Crystal? Hi! This is Johnny Matthew. Remember me?"

"I sure do," a sultry voice replied. "You're that handsome refined gentleman who likes a good time. Ain't that right? How you doing, baby?"

"I'm doing great. Can I come up?"

"Well, not this exact minute—no. But if you was to arrive in about an hour, then I could fit you in real nice."

The minister laughed. "One hour. I'll be there," he said.

"Lovely. Lovely. Bring a bottle of Chivas, why don't you? I can't get out of here before the stores close, and all I got in my cabinet is some funky gin. Hey—and maybe you could buy a little ham and Swiss cheese someplace, too. That would be dandy grand. We could have a picnic in my boudoir. Get pastrami if you can find any. You like hot pastrami, baby?"

"Love it. It sets me aflame."

The sultry voice giggled. "Okay, honey man. You know my number and all?"

"Better than my own name," Lenox answered.

"See you, baby."

3

At breakfast the next morning, with a mind somewhat blurry from his late revels, Lenox considered and reconsidered the bizarre conversation at Cavanaugh's home the previous evening—and the more he did, the brighter his future seemed. By so much did the arguments of his hopes outweigh the opposition of his misgivings that he could feel—in his imagination, at least—the miser's cash already bulging his trousers' pockets.

Oh, the things he'd do with such a fortune! Complete freedom would be his, and a life of comfort and pleasure. Once and for all he'd discard his little stiff white collar— that damn albatross he'd worn so long around his neck— and go out and live like a human being.

Yes, and he would treat the money royally, far better than the old man ever did. He would liberate it from that dank Alpine vault, resuscitate it, give it a chance to exercise, encourage its circulation. Into the best society he would introduce it, take it to the finest restaurants, to the track, to the casinos, on a tropical cruise. And he'd arrange for it to be fondled by the most beautiful women—Aphrodites, Helens, Delilahs.

Toward the end of his meal these intoxicating reveries were suddenly interrupted by a ringing doorbell, and a minute later his housekeeper, Mrs. Keller, came to announce that one of his parishioners, Mr. Gingerich, was waiting to see him in the office. Lenox sighed, drank the dregs of his coffee and left the table.

He found his visitor standing in the very center of the room, gazing raptly up at the small brass chandelier that hung from the ceiling. Gingerich was a florist, and wherever he went he seemed to carry with him a faint fragrance of blossoms and plants. In appearance he resembled his minister. Both were tall and slender, with fair complexions and even features. They differed chiefly in their expressions. While Lenox had an easy, good-natured look about him, Gingerich's aspect was usually enigmatic, wary and vaguely hostile. Nevertheless, the florist was a willing kind of man—a man who could always be counted on to volunteer for the less attractive of the congregation's many enterprises.

Hearing the minister enter, he brought his eyes down from the chandelier and said, "That used to be a gaslight. We had one like it in Maine when I was a little boy."

"Did you? Have a seat, Jerry," Lenox replied.

"I won't be staying long, Reverend. I just came for the old clothes. They have to be sorted and hung on the racks. The sale is Saturday morning. Do you have much this time?"

"No. A couple of pairs of pants, some shirts. But Mrs. Keller brought a bundle of things from her home."

"Fine, fine," said Gingerich. He smiled artlessly, sidled to the oak bench by the fireplace, wavered there for a second or two, and then sat down. "We're doing pretty well with this bargain-basement idea, aren't we? Every time we run them, we set a new record for profits. Three hundred dollars we made in March. That's more than they took in at the white-elephant jumble."

"I know, Jerry. Your clothing sales have been a tremendous success—a real windfall for the charity funds. I don't know how you do it, frankly."

"It's easy, Reverend Lenox. First you collect the stuff, and afterwards you put little posters in the neighborhood stores. It's legwork, mostly."

"I'm always amazed by the turnout. The housewives come in droves. How's everything else, Jerry? Been feeling okay?"

"Pretty good," the florist answered. His eyes, which were large and round, wandered back up to the chandelier. "Last night I slept six hours—a long time, for me. Of course I had to take my pills, but that's all right."

"Are you still seeing Dr. Lifkin?"

"Lifkin? No, haven't been to him for a while."

"Then those little fantasies have stopped finally?"

The man on the bench dropped his eyes from the light fixture to the minister's face. "My impulses, you mean? No, I still get them . . . off and on."

Lenox nodded, his expression sympathetic. "But are they like the others? Are they as strange and—"

"Yes. They're as crazy as ever," said Gingerich. "Saturday, for instance, I was walking with my two boys in the Public Garden, and all of a sudden I got this urge to climb a tree—a big old elm, near the Arlington Street gate. I wanted to climb it in the worst way. I don't know why. My mind was blank for a minute, and I got an impulse. Funny."

"Yet you didn't act on the impulse, did you?"

"No . . . almost, though. I actually went up and touched the trunk. Then Joseph, my oldest, said, 'What are you doing, Dad?' And I snapped out of it. But if he hadn't spoken, I'm sure I would have started climbing."

A note of bewilderment had crept into Gingerich's voice. He bent his head and contemplated his hands, which were folded together and dangling between his thighs. At his temple a vein throbbed. It looked like a tiny blue worm struggling to reach the surface.

With a show of cheerfulness Lenox declared, "Our brains and our nervous systems often play strange pranks on us, Jerry. I can assure you that you're not the only member of the church who has wild fancies. One of our ladies developed a dread of telephones, believe it or not. Claimed that every time she put a phone to her ear she received an electric shock. And a year ago a young man just out of college confided in me that he had a morbid fear of automobiles. The poor fellow was so terrified of being run down, he'd walk miles out of his way to avoid busy streets. It was a real problem for him, but he underwent treatment and now he's much improved. Part of that treatment, I might mention, was a lengthy stay at a country hotel in Vermont. Rest, relaxation, fresh air, a change of scene— they're the best medicines for nerve disorders."

"I suppose," said Gingerich doubtfully. "The thing is, I don't feel nervous—not really. What I feel is more positive . . . deeper."

"But neural attacks don't always manifest themselves in a case of the jitters. What did Dr. Lifkin say? He called it an anxiety neurosis, didn't he?"

"Yes, he did. I think he's making a mistake, though. It's too fierce for anxiety, Reverend, and too . . . too unpleasant. I wish I could describe the way it is. If I could, you'd see what I mean. It's like some criminal walks into my head and takes over the operation of my mind—the way a thief might jump in your car and drive off with it. That's what it's like."

The florist moved restlessly on the bench, lifted his head, glanced vacantly around the room and then resumed speaking. "I get other kinds of feelings, too, besides the impulses. You're right about the brain playing tricks. Some of the ideas I get are so unusual, I wonder if anybody in the world ever had them before. You wouldn't believe—" Gingerich abruptly abandoned this sentence. After a second's thought he began a new one. "They say it's like a computer—the brain, I mean. They say it's tremendously complicated, that it's made up of millions of cells and strange little switches and gadgets. They say it can store no end of memories, good ones and bad. They say it has an almost unlimited capacity and potential. When you stop and think about the brain—about how powerful it is—and then you think about the way people act, you realize that everybody is only walking down a very narrow road, and that on either side of that road there are miles and miles of . . . of unexplored territory. Of course, as long as the brain is working all right, a person will never wander off that narrow, narrow road; but with a tremendously complicated instrument, full of tiny components, an awful lot of things can go wrong—can't they, Reverend?"

"Certainly. However, you're not in that bad a state, Jerry, not at all," Lenox responded a trifle impatiently. "When a person's mind goes, he can no longer cope with life. People in that condition—psychotics—can't work, can't perform simple tasks, can't even take care of themselves. When the human brain goes awry, it doesn't assume new functions, it loses old ones. It becomes feeble and ineffective."

"Sometimes it's like that, and sometimes it's not," said

Gingerich quickly. The throbbing of the blue vein in his temple was now markedly more pronounced. "You have to remember, the mind always has complete control. No matter who you are, you have to do what your brain commands. And the brain can command anything . . . anything it wants."

"Have you discussed all this with Dr. Lifkin, Jerry?"

"Many times."

"What advice did he give you?"

"He told me not to work so hard."

Lenox shrugged. "Well then, why don't you do as he tells you?"

"Because I can't, Reverend. If I were to slow down, I'd be out of business in six months. Everyone thinks being a florist is an easy job, but it isn't. There are worries and pressures like in any other profession. A lot of times the weddings, funerals and holidays all come at once, and the pieces have to be ready just the same. I was up half the night making that spray for the Brickley boy because of a sudden rush. And there are unexpected losses, too—like the power failure from the hurricane last summer costing me a thousand dollars in wilted orchids, gardenias and roses. No, being a florist isn't easy."

"But you have a couple of assistants. Why not leave them in charge and go on a vacation?"

Gingerich laughed, but there wasn't much humor in his circular eyes.

"I'm serious," Lenox said. "Take Vicki and the children to Florida—swim, fish, have a few drinks, go to a race track, get some sun. A couple of weeks of that, Jerry, and you'll be a new man again."

"Oh, don't worry about me," the florist replied, getting to his feet abruptly. "I'm not in such bad shape, really.

Most of my trouble comes from drinking too much coffee, I think. It's what gives me the insomnia and . . . and the nightmares. Isn't it funny the way your mind goes on working even when you're sound asleep? I keep dreaming about the kitchen . . . the kitchen in our house. Crazy. Well, I better be going. Have to drive to Weston and pick up a box of Madonna lilies. Then I have to drive back to the flower shop and make two wreaths and a big blanket. It's sure been nice talking to you, Reverend. Just the sound of your voice seems to cheer me up. I told Vicki that, and she said it's because you're such a good man. She said you have a heart of gold." Gingerich laughed self-consciously. After a moment he added, "That bundle of clothes, though. Do you have it handy?"

"I'll have Mrs. Keller get it for you, Jerry," the minister said.

As he left the room to fetch the housekeeper, he thought to himself, *Narrow is the way which leadeth unto life, and few there be that find it.*

4

A parishioner, Alice Drake, was at the Peter Bent Brigham Hospital recuperating from a gall-bladder operation, and that afternoon he went to see her.

Lenox did not like hospitals. When he was nine years old, his mother had died of pneumonia in one, and since then the smell of medicine and the sight of white rooms, capped nurses and curtained beds filled him with revulsion. Even while he entertained Alice with tidbits of gossip, disturbing memories scratched at his mind. Behind his eyes he saw the slender body of his mother under the oxygen tent, saw the wan, contorted features, the gasping, the coughing of blood. And again he experienced the raw ache of despair—now diminished by time, but unchanged in quality—that had so oppressed him on that long-ago day.

He might possibly have overcome his dread of such places if his father, only a few years later, hadn't begun dragging him along on visits to the sick and dying. The idea was to nurture his compassion, to acquaint him with suffering—handy stuff for a future minister—but it had quite a different effect on him. Never did Lenox feel so ill at ease, so frightened, as when he entered the minatory precincts of a hospital or sanatorium. In many ways his father had been an idiot. If he hadn't been so chary of spending the congregation's money on coal, his wife would never have contracted pneumonia. Concern for his damned flock was greater with him than concern for his family.

After leaving Alice, Lenox went to Geraldine Gargan's for tea. He was glad to find the old woman alone.

"New china?" he asked, inspecting a fragile cup.

"Heavens, no," said Geraldine. She had ivory-colored hair and an aristocratic face. "It's Sèvres. The service was a wedding present, though I seldom use it. My Aunt Edna gave it to us. She lived in Paris—on the Quai d'Orsay."

"Ah, Paris!" Lenox murmured, smiling.

"Pshaw! Men invariably say, 'Ah, Paris!'—and I really don't know why. It can't be because of the women. The Parisiennes are all rather scraggy, I think. You lived there a year, didn't you? Your father told me you had hopes of a literary career—that you were a bit fed up with theology. He was quite dejected about it, as I remember—which was understandable, considering the many years you spent at the divinity school. It takes so long to acquire a doctorate. If he hadn't died, John, would you have remained in France? Would you actually have abandoned the ministry?"

"I don't know. Probably. But I couldn't have stayed very long. I had nothing to live on."

"It's just as well you returned," she asserted, offering him sugar from an ornate bowl. "Preaching in Boston is a much better life than tramping the boulevards with a pack of raffish artists and tipsy intellectuals. The bohemian mode of existence is romantic but shallow. It's fortunate that the young rarely have money, I'm inclined to believe."

"Perhaps you're right," said Lenox. "Speaking of money . . ."

"Oh, yes—that earthquake in Sicily. I haven't forgotten," Geraldine declared, fussing with a plate of variegated cakes. "Only this morning I saw some photographs of it in *Time* magazine. How frightful it must be for those poor people! They're living in caves—and typhoid is rampant." She shook her head in dismay. "I'll give you a check, of course, Reverend. It's a Christian duty. Nevertheless, I hope you won't expect me to carry more than my share of the burden. Remember what I told you the last time. I'm not the only member of the congregation who has a sound financial position."

"True. However, you're one of the few who have both money and a social conscience, Geraldine."

"Oh dear! You want a sizable amount, don't you?"

"One thousand dollars. That's all."

"That's all? Really, John! Do you consider a thousand dollars a moderate donation?" the woman protested, though without exhibiting either surprise or resentment. With a cup of tea in her hand, she sat gracefully on the edge of a blue satin upholstered chair. "When I was a girl, such a sum might buy two automobiles or a cottage on Lake Winnipesaukee. Half that was a year's wages for some men."

"It doesn't buy much now, I'm afraid, but it could save someone's life," Lenox said. Then he added slyly, "Mr. Cavanaugh recently explained to me how valuable money used to be. Before long I'll be an authority on the debasement of American currency."

"You, young man, will have much less difficulty in bringing me around to your point of view if you refrain from making ghastly personal comparisons," she said severely. "Amos Cavanaugh and I have nothing whatever in common. He is an individual totally devoid of human feeling. His father suffered from the same deficiency, so apparently it's an ingrained familial trait. Do you remember the father?"

"Faintly."

"Clarence was his name, and he too was a money-lender. An odious creature. His whole character was permeated with greed. Toward the end of his life his face came to look like a mask of the devil. Really! He was the final evil distillation of the venom of usury."

"Nicely put, my dear. Are these ladyfingers?"

"Thank you. Yes, but they're not as fresh as they could be. Clarence Cavanaugh was a pawnbroker—a swanky pawnbroker, but a pawnbroker nonetheless. And quite sanctimonious about it, too. 'My business is helping the unfortunate,' he used to crow, but his clients were never so unfortunate that a deal with him didn't make them more so. His specialty was newly bereaved widows."

"I suspect you're magnifying the man's shortcomings," declared Lenox, taking a yellow cake from the tray.

"Not by an iota. During the thirties he had liens on half the house furnishings in the Back Bay. People actually queued up at his front door on Marlborough Street, seeking to borrow money. They got it too—but at what terms! Wilfred Drever told my husband that he'd once done business with Clarence, and that before he'd do it a second time he'd make a compact with old Lucifer himself. He said that the interest on his loan equaled the principal before the ink had dried on his signature."

"The ladyfingers aren't stale at all, Geraldine. They're delicious."

"Thank you, Reverend," the elderly woman said. "Have another." She drank some tea and then set the cup and saucer on the tray. "Yes, he was an acquisitive rascal, but though he got money, he got very little else. His wife, Adele, ran off with Robby Fletcher, leaving Clarence with the two children. It was a huge scandal. Years later Robby returned, but Adele never did come back. Her sister said she remarried after getting a Mexican divorce, and that she was living in Kansas. There were rumors, however, that she ended up on the Bowery in New York. Amos didn't seem to miss his mother much—he was too like his father for that—but poor little Martha was quite shattered. A sweet girl she was, too. From then on in that mean household she lived the life of Eugénie Grandet. Eventually she eloped, like her mother. Sneaked away with an Italian immigrant from East Boston—can you imagine? I heard, not long afterward, that she had a child by him."

Geraldine made herself more comfortable on the satin-covered chair. "Did your dad ever tell you about Clarence's last rites, John?" she asked. "No? Well, I shall. He was riddled with cancer, Clarence was, and he'd been unconscious for hours, but when the silver crucifix was pressed against his lips he opened his eyes and stared at it. Then, glancing up at your father, he mumbled something. 'What was that he said?' the physician asked. And with the greatest reluctance, your poor father answered, 'Mr. Cavanaugh said, "Twelve dollars, sir. That's the best I can offer." ' "

Lenox burst out laughing. "A great story," he said, "but it's too good to be true. It sounds like an anecdote out of Pepys."

"I was present when it happened. So was Cecily Harper-Jones, and she'll verify my every word," said the lady regally. "Then, after making that sharp appraisal with his last breath, Clarence closed his eyes again and passed away. Have a *madeleinette*, why don't you?"

"Thanks," Lenox replied, helping himself to another cake. "But why are you so down on the Cavanaughs?"

"Because they're an evil bunch, that's why. At the risk of sounding uncharitable, I must say the world would be better off without their sort. They produce only misery. Clarence ruined whole families, John—transformed fine, proud people into broken wretches."

"Still, old Amos has always been religious."

"Religious? Pshaw! He's like the Scotsman in the joke—the one who took a keen interest in the sermon but only a passing interest in the collection plate. However, let's not talk of the Cavanaughs any more, shall we?" Geraldine's patrician features illuminated in a charming smile. "I was speaking to Angela Bosquet after church on Sunday, and do you know what she told me?"

"I haven't the least idea," said Lenox.

"She said her eldest daughter, Rowena, finds you extremely attractive. What do you think of that?"

The minister's face became grim. "Rowena's a fine young lady," he answered, "but I have no desire to marry her."

"My, you're quick off the mark today, aren't you? That she finds you attractive, John, isn't quite the equivalent of a proposal. I only mentioned it because I thought it interesting. But what have you against marriage? After all, you're not a papist priest—and you're thirty-two now. The Bosquets own tracts and tracts of Wellesley, you know." Geraldine sighed softly, then stood up. "I can see I'm annoying you, though. Very well, I'll write that check."

"I couldn't endure their kind of life," said Lenox.

"Why? They're perfectly normal people."

"Perfectly—yes. But perhaps I'm not. I could never

stand the routine, the . . . straitness, of such an existence. To me, it's hardly like living at all."

"Really? What a strange remark! I think you should remember you're a minister, young man, and that you should set a good example for those in your charge. However, I do not wish to interfere." She moved easily to an elegant rosewood secretary, sat down at it and opened a large checkbook. In a pigeonhole she found a gold pen. "Shall I make it out to you or to the church?" she inquired.

"To me," he said. "The church account is still in a muddle. I was an idiot to let two people as haphazard as Cecily and Leonard manage that last fund drive."

"You can't stay single forever. That would be bizarre," said Geraldine Gargan as she scribbled in the book. "Rowena's a bit tall, but she's pretty and far from unintelligent."

The telephone rang then. Before she could answer it, Lenox told her he had to be going. Unhurriedly she signed the check, tore it from the page and handed it to him.

As he let himself out of the apartment he could hear her chattering away on the phone.

5

Wednesday of the following week, Cavanaugh brought him to Rupert Hofbauer's house, and there they were shown into a vast, overfurnished parlor. As soon as they were settled, Lenox commenced a covert study of his new acquaintance. The professor had a slight frame, an incipient potbelly and bandy legs. His eyes were black and almost devoid of sheen, while his nose was as thin and straight as a sundial's gnomon. From his upper lip a small yellowish-gray mustache sprouted. It looked like a tiny truss of moldy hay.

Though he did not welcome the minister enthusiastically, or even cordially, neither did he seem frightened by his presence. Evidently, Lenox mused, the rascal thinks himself capable of selling anybody on his ridiculous scheme. There must be many gullible people in the world.

"Frankly, Reverend Doctor," Hofbauer began at once, his voice gruff, "it astonishes me that Mr. Cavanaugh brings a religious gentleman into this scientific enterprise. Church and laboratory—they are not such close comrades."

"Ah now, Professor!" Cavanaugh responded jovially. "The Reverend is a bright lad, with all sorts of university degrees. He'll understand you—and he keeps an open mind."

"Perhaps, but why is the interview necessary? You know I am a busy scholar, that I do not have time to waste on little things. *Ach!* And what about secrecy?"

"Well, how else can it be handled, sir?" countered Cavanaugh. "He's my agent. As to his discretion, I'll guarantee it. Remember, he's a man of the cloth."

Hofbauer wiggled his mustache. "Always people think you are a crook or a gangster," he muttered barely audibly.

"I don't think that, Professor," Lenox declared, flashing his most engaging smile.

"Of course not, and neither do I," said Cavanaugh in an aggrieved tone. "Would I be here if I did? Sound business procedure, that's all it is. The Reverend is going to represent me when I'm dead and gone. How can he do that without knowing the setup?"

But Hofbauer raised fresh objections, and the miser, his face wrinkling and unwrinkling like the bellows of a concertina, was obliged to refute them with more arguments.

While they niggled, Lenox appraised the parlor. There was plenty to see: an ebony grand piano, some Queen Anne chairs, a lacquer screen, a pair of monstrous Art Nouveau lamps, a wrought-iron music stand with a violin case resting against one of its legs, oil paintings, potted plants, an ancient-looking cuckoo clock on the wall, and similar marvels. There was a good deal of small bric-a-brac, too—mostly busts of famous men. A bronze Mozart sat on the piano, a milk-glass Goethe on the mantel, an alabaster Julius Caesar on a side table, and a silver-plated Sir Isaac Newton in a niche. Other celebrities peered out of corners or glowered from the tops of bookcases. The largest member of the collection was a Parian-ware Wagner. This had its own pedestal—a slender column of green marble—and being larger than life-size, quite dominated the room.

Substantial and genteel, thought Lenox—the perfect setting for a confidence man. That cuckoo clock is so homey. And he's even got a violin, just like Albert Einstein.

". . . an imposition to bother the people on the Otherside, sir," the German was saying. "I think it is not considerate."

Cavanaugh, trembling slightly from the exertion of the debate, managed a tight-lipped smile. "But it's only this once," he said. "Why is it inconsiderate? If my representative can't witness a translation, I really don't see how we can proceed. There's a tidy amount of money involved. I would hate to abandon the whole proposition over so minor a detail."

Acknowledging the threat by raising and lowering his pallid eyebrows, the professor said frigidly, "To keep a scientist from important work—that is not a minor detail." Then, sighing, he stood up on his bowed legs and added, "*Ach!* However, you give me no choice. The Reverend Doctor is already here, is he not? Very well. I will allow it this one time only. Come, gentlemen, come. Let us accomplish it quickly. For me, every minute in the day is valuable."

Lenox and Cavanaugh got to their feet also, and followed their inhospitable host past the bust of Wagner and out into the hall. They trooped toward the rear of the building to a cellar entrance, descended a flight of wooden stairs and arrived in a dingy room jammed with boxes and crates. Through this maze Hofbauer guided them to a second and more brightly lit room, where the rough walls were whitewashed and the concrete floor was covered by spinach-green carpeting.

There, two objects immediately caught Lenox's eye. The first was a slate blackboard on a steel tripod, the surface of which was crowded with numerals, Greek letters and other mathematical symbols. The second resembled a kitchen stove designed by a megalomaniac. It was a large glittering metal cube on four squat legs. Rows of knobs, dials, buttons and switches embellished the top of the thing, while from its back a pair of thick red cables, like surreal serpents, emerged and crawled up the stone wall to a fixture near the ceiling. Other wires, in a variety of colors, shot out of one of the side panels and described a rainbow arch as they made their way to a fuse box bolted to the floor. In the front of the cube there was a rectangular door fitted with a gray-tinted glass window, and under that, an imposing range of gauges.

The minister regarded this bizarre appliance with unfeigned admiration. Beside him, Cavanaugh was making snuffling sounds of glee.

Wasting not a moment, the professor strode directly to the contraption, yanked open a boiler plate on its top, scrutinized the complex circuit that came into view, slammed the plate shut, examined the external wiring and methodically adjusted several of the dials.

"One bad connection and we would be nothing in only a microsecond," he explained gutturally. "There would be left a few pions, maybe. The power is not imaginable."

Adopting a somber expression, Lenox nodded.

The German then threw two switches and pressed a blue button, and the machine responded by producing a low hum, like the drone of a dentist's drill. From an aluminum bin nearby he obtained a net bag of oranges, took out one of the fruits and held it up for them to inspect.

Cavanaugh cleared his throat noisily. "If you don't mind," he said, "I'd like you to translate something different this time." He extended a bony hand; in it was a large oval stone. To Lenox it looked like the kind of rock a cave man might have bound to a stick to make a war club. "I want you to send this over instead," declared the miser, an obstinate set to his features.

Hofbauer glared at him. "You are suspicious," he growled. "It is just as I said upstairs. You do not trust me."

"Now, that's not true!" Cavanaugh exclaimed. "I only want to convince myself that the Charge Translator can cope with a solid article. An orange, you'll have to admit, Professor, is not as substantial as a bag of gold."

"Atoms, Mr. Cavanaugh, are atoms."

"Absolutely! And that being so, it shouldn't make any difference what we send, should it?"

Hofbauer grimaced like a man in pain, but he dropped the orange back into the bin. "Have I not said I can translate the heaviest elements—mercury, lead, uranium? My honest words do not satisfy you, eh?" he grumbled. "All right. Give me that—what you have there."

With an angry flourish he opened the see-through hatch. Behind it lay a ceramic compartment the size of a shoe box. In this he placed the stone. Then he shut the door, turned around, fixed his black-olive eyes on Lenox, who all this time had been hovering at his shoulder, and said none too graciously, "I will explain. I hope you will understand."

He paused to gather his thoughts while the machine carried on with its monotonous buzzing.

"You have heard, Mr. Cavanaugh tells me, of anti-particles. That is good," he began, folding his hands over his tumid belly. "Have you heard also of Heisenberg's uncertainty principle? No? I did not think so. Therefore you do not know Schrödinger's wave equation, either. That, Reverend Doctor, is bad. Without such elementary knowledge you cannot comprehend the Charge Translator, except in a most general, unclear way. But I will do my best.

"You know, of course, that an atom has a nucleus of positively charged protons and uncharged neutrons, and that around this nucleus fly like little airplanes the electrons, which have a negative charge. That is schoolboy stuff. Now, an Englishman named Paul Dirac used the discoveries of Heisenberg and Schrödinger to predict there existed such a thing as a positron. What is a positron? It is an electron that has, instead of a negative charge, a positive charge. Later, positrons were actually found—in cosmic rays. So! All this is ancient history. However, not too, too long ago, negative protons also were discovered. Yes, and if one has positive electrons and negative protons, one has exactly the opposite of natural atoms. One has anti-matter, Doctor. This made the physicists think and wonder. Science, you see, looks always for regularity, for symmetry, for equilibrium. Suppose, they hypothesized, for every atom in the universe there is an anti-atom in another universe—an anti-universe—to make things balance? Fantastic, eh?"

Rupert Hofbauer nodded sagely. "I, too, made these speculations," he continued, a note of pride in his voice. "In my office at M.I.T. one day, I read about an experiment that was performed at Serpukhov by the Russians, and like sudden lightning I received a big new conception. That night I stayed up the whole time, doing calculations, and in the morning I went on a plane to Batavia, Illinois, where is situated the National Accelerator Laboratory. Many, many people I asked questions out there, and the more answers I got, the more sure I was that I had found a revolutionary explanation of atomic structure. After three days I came back here, sat down with my pencil and worked like a man who has an inspiration. Ideas in my brain floated like music. That's true, gentlemen. It was like composing a symphony.

"When I was finished and I had verified my figures in the computer, I began to realize it might be possible to make a machine—a sophisticated instrument—that could actually convert matter into anti-matter, and do it under controlled conditions. Well, do you know what that would mean to the world? It would mean an unlimited fountain of power. Yes, exactly. Why? Because if anti-matter combines with natural matter, they disintegrate—both of them. They get mutually annihilated. But when they disappear, Reverend Doctor, they leave something behind. They leave energy—a great, great amount of energy.

"You are following me? Excellent! So, I constructed the machine you see here—the Charge Translator. It was difficult and expensive to do. Then, when it was finished and the day came to test it—ach, I got all jittery and jumpery. I knew if there was a small mistake in my computations, I might blow to pieces the whole neighborhood and kill many poor people. But I am a true scientist, and for a true scientist danger must always be only an abstraction—is it not so?

"In the conversion chamber, where is now the stone, I put a tiny piece of silver—silver because the components are not too tight and not too loose. After that, I took a deep breath into my lungs and closed the switch.

"What was I expecting? I was expecting the silver atoms to change a few at a time into anti-silver atoms. I was expecting these anti-atoms to bump into the regular atoms and cause at once reciprocal destruction. I thought there would be a series of microexplosions which would liberate a quantity of radiant energy. I was expecting to observe a dull, constant glow. According to my calculations, I would be able to modulate this process of decay, to speed it or to slow it, by means of an electromagnetic field. The silver, you understand, would get smaller and smaller—so gradually that you would hardly notice it—until, after some days, it would be gone totally. But its annihilation would generate power. Ha! That was what I expected. What happened in reality was that the entire piece of metal disappeared immediately. Pouf! It was gone—gone, like a magic trick."

"Absolutely amazing," murmured Cavanaugh.

"Incredible!" Lenox said ambiguously.

"Quite so. Ah, gentlemen, you do not know how I felt," Hofbauer declared, his wayward mustache twitching with emotion. "I was stunned, like somebody who falls down on his head. I did not any more believe my own eyes. By the laws of quantum physics, if that silver disappeared completely, then an explosion like a hydrogen bomb should go off. And there was nothing—a sparkle of light only. What was the answer? It had not been converted into energy, the metal. Where did it go to, therefore?

"I thought and I thought. I inspected, top to bottom, the whole machine. I recalculated my figures. I looked in all my books and I squeezed my brain for some idea, but nothing came to me. After three or four hours I was starting to believe that the only way I could solve this mystery was to construct a much bigger Charge Translator—one so huge a man could fit inside it. I myself then could travel off to where the piece of silver had traveled.

"As I was thinking that idea, however, I looked again at the machine and noticed an astounding phenomenon. What do you think, sirs? In the conversion compartment, unbelievably, there was an object—a blue cylinder! Before, there had been something, and then there was nothing. This time, there had been nothing, and now there was something. I asked myself if my mind was sick. How could this be? Am I crazy?

"So! All right. I opened the door up, and pulled out this object. It was a scroll of thin paper, written on with strange marks I did not recognize. In little groups these marks were arranged, but each group was different from the other ones. It was something like a papyrus. I unrolled it carefully and found it was many meters long. Soon I saw what resembled Cyrillic printing on the paper—and after, letters that were actually Roman! Spanish it was. Yes. In that tongue I am not fluent, but I was able to figure out the meaning of the paragraph, and what it said was that the silver had been received and that the one who received it would like very much to communicate with the one who sent it. Inspecting the rest of the scroll, I discovered this same statement in English, German and many other languages. The writer, it was evident, did not know to where his message was going, or who would read it."

Hofbauer grimaced impatiently. "I will not describe the correspondence which followed. It is enough to say that the man—or anti-man, actually—who sent the scroll was a chemist named Billings. Years ago Mr. Billings had been an instructor at New College, Oxford, but during the Great War, while experimenting with a Mills bomb, he unfortunately blew himself up. It was he who told me of how men's spirits continue to live after their bodies die, and how those spirits are transported to the anti-universe, or Otherside of Existence. And that, gentlemen, is the only part of my whole story you are really interested in, eh?"

Cavanaugh, grinning like a happy child, nodded.

"I was prepared for marvels," said Lenox, maintaining an artless expression on his face, "but what you've related has simply put my mind in a whirl. These spirits—do they live on the Otherside forever?"

A subtile glint burgeoned in the professor's dark eyes. "Ah, Reverend Doctor, please do not ask me to reveal every detail," he replied. "All will be published soon, and when it is I will have a Nobel prize for my labor. Yes, but now I must be silent like a mouse. The United States would pay much money for my information, and although I need money, I do not take any from them. Why? Because it is not the kind of knowledge only one country should have. It is too dangerous. Instead, I do services for discreet, respectable people like Mr. Cavanaugh, and charge them small fees."

"The fees aren't that small," Cavanaugh complained.

"Bah! Considering the magnitude of the service—the universe I am rearranging for you, remember—they are infinitely small." Hofbauer laughed inharmoniously. "But enough chitter-chatter, gentlemen. You will see now the phenomenon I saw that day. Excuse me if I do not explain how it happens. Of all my secrets, that one is the biggest."

He smiled serenely. Then, bending over the metal cube, he turned a red knob and closed a green toggle switch. The hum grew louder. "Your eyes keep on the window," he said. "It takes only several seconds."

This advice was unnecessary, however, as both men were already staring fixedly at the tinted glass pane and the gray, striated stone clearly visible behind it.

A good quarter of a minute elapsed. Just as Lenox had

begun to fear that the highly touted apparatus was going to mortify its designer, the humming stopped abruptly and there was a puff of yellow light in the little compartment. It was not a particularly bright flash, certainly not strong enough to befuddle the eye; yet when it was gone, so too was the oval stone. The ceramic-lined chamber appeared exactly as it had before, except that now it was empty.

"Miraculous, by golly!" Cavanaugh cried out rhapsodically. "What do you say to that, Reverend?"

The minister blinked, shook his head and blinked again. How had the bastard done it? he wondered. It was as if the rock had evaporated. Finally he turned to the old man. "I really don't know what to say, Mr. Cavanaugh. It's the most remarkable thing I've ever witnessed," he declared truthfully.

6

As soon as they were in the automobile, Cavanaugh asked, "Did you hear a thump or anything when it happened?"

"No," Lenox said, starting the engine. "Did you?"

"Not a sound, and I was listening as hard as I was watching. If that rock fell through a trap door, one of us would have heard it. Isn't that so, Reverend?"

"Yes. There'd have been a noise of some sort."

"That's the real reason I made him use the stone."

"Very shrewd," the minister said, while thinking it would have been shrewder still to have insisted on transmitting a few surprise questions to the Englishman (or anti-Englishman) Billings, just to see what answers (or anti-answers) they might have evoked. But doubtlessly the glib Hofbauer would have managed, one way or another, to forestall any such gambit. Aloud he added, "The whole business was uncanny, Mr. Cavanaugh. If it was an illusion, he brought it off flawlessly."

"An illusion? How could it be? You saw it with your own two eyes. What about the professor, though—do you think he's honest?"

"I can only say that he sounded authentic. His

knowledge and his scientific fervor seemed quite genuine."

"Yes, he's probably on the up and up. Anyway, I won't be trusting him blindly," the old man said, smiling craftily. "When the time comes to make the deal, I'll have an insurance policy. I'm no infant with milk on my chin."

Lenox, guiding the car into the traffic, wondered what his companion meant, yet he hesitated to ask.

Cavanaugh giggled. "There's a way to play it safe, you know—a precaution that will guarantee I don't get rooked or bamboozled. My friend put me on to it."

"Oh? Which friend is that?"

"The one I told you about—my lady friend. I was feeling poorly the other night, all aches and miseries, and she came by and gave me an alcohol rub. She also gave me a crackerjack idea. What I need to protect myself against being swindled, she said, is a secret sign." Cavanaugh tittered again. "Don't you get it, Reverend? Well, if you and I arrange a password between us, after I'm dead the professor can only learn what that password is if I communicate it to him from the Otherside. And if there is no Otherside, if the whole thing is bunkum—I won't be able to communicate it to him, will I? And if he can't tell you the password, my boy, then you won't give him a thin dime. No sir—not a penny!"

Lenox grasped the stratagem at once. "A very clever idea," he said, shaking his head in admiration. "It's foolproof. It means he can't possibly cheat you."

"Of course! I'm no babe in arms. Mind you, I don't really believe it will happen that way. This last demonstration just about convinced me. If Rupert Hofbauer isn't bona fide, if he isn't legitimate, then I'm a poor judge of men. He'll know the password, all right—wait and see."

Arriving at Marlborough Street a few minutes later,

they left the Volkswagen and climbed the steps of the flaking brownstone house. The moneylender unlocked the heavy door and led his guest inside. They went at once into the study, where Cavanaugh dug a bundle of papers from a desk drawer and began a meandering explanation, sheet by sheet, of what they signified. One supplied the name, address and telephone number of the Geneva bank, and the name of the man Lenox should speak to there. Another described the account and gave its code number, while a third provided incidental information—where to stay in the city, where to eat inexpensively, and so on.

However, it was the fourth page that interested Lenox most, for from it he finally found out just how much the account contained. Scribbled in unequivocal figures beneath a serpentine column of deposits was the grand total: eight hundred and eighty thousand dollars.

A sudden feebleness infected the minister's legs, compelling him to lean for a moment against the heavy desk. Nearly a million! The sum addled his senses. A million! He never dreamt it would be so much. Not a million!

"Get it all in five-hundred-dollar bills. They're the certificates with McKinley's portrait," Cavanaugh was saying in his arid voice. "Don't get any thousands, because banks make records of the serial numbers on thousands. The whole thing should fit into a large cookie box—and if you gift-wrap it, no one will give it a second look. Think of all that wealth in such a small bundle! Keep it in the hotel vault until you leave, then stick it in the bottom of your suitcase. As for the customs inspectors—they won't harass a member of the clergy. And once you reach Boston, don't waste any time getting it into a safe-deposit box. Is everything quite clear, Reverend?"

Lenox, still bemused, nodded mechanically.

Additional papers divulged the procedures to be followed from that point on. The name and location of the gold dealer on Bromfield Street were furnished, as were the current prices of Mexican pesos. A complicated chart converted amounts of money into corresponding quantities of coins, and then listed the weights of these portions. From notes under this chart, Lenox learned that he was expected to make six trips to Bromfield Street, and each time haul eighty pounds of pesos away with him—or, altogether, close to five hundred pounds of gold. He had, of course, no intention of executing this part of his mission, his own plan being to remain in Europe with the cookie box of cash, to never come back, to disappear like smoke—yet he thought with keen regret how exciting it would have been to actually handle so substantial a treasure.

Cavanaugh now instructed him to be on his guard against bandits, and to make absolutely certain that neither the dealer nor Hofbauer short-changed him in any manner.

The professor's fee was twenty thousand dollars, but he was not to get it until every last coin had been translated. Lenox, too, was to receive a generous reward: one thousand dollars for the Church Maintenance Fund.

"It's more than you expected, isn't it? Oh, I can be open-handed, Reverend, in spite of what people whisper behind my back," the miser declared, grinning and screwing up his face until it resembled a crumpled paper bag, out of which, inexplicably, two gray agate eyes leered. Then the grin faded and he went on, "These notes explain what's to be done if Hofbauer can't give you the password. In that improbable event, all the money must go to the Harvard Medical School. I hate acting the role of Santa Claus—hate it because it's unbusinesslike, you see—but what else can I possibly do?" He stared appealingly at Lenox, his mauve nether lip aquiver. "And those fellows did keep me alive for twelve years, which has to be worth something, don't you think? Anyhow, here's the covering letter."

Gravely the minister accepted the various papers.

"What else?" Cavanaugh asked himself. "Oh yes, I'm leaving the house to my niece, my dead sister's daughter. Lucia is a strange child—weak in the head, I suspect—but I promised my dad I'd keep the place in the family, and she's the last blood relative I've got. Tilbury will handle that, though. In fact, it's the only thing he will handle. I intend to destroy all the records that deal with our secret transaction, Reverend—including the statements and letters from Switzerland. You can't be too careful with those tax gougers. Now, the next item is the power of attorney."

From a vellum portfolio he drew two forms. Each man read them over and then signed both copies. It was easily and swiftly done. Cavanaugh, after sealing the documents in an envelope that was already addressed and stamped, insisted on mailing them immediately.

"Think what a bad joke it would be if I flew off to the Otherside before this business was properly settled!" he said. "Not that I feel like I'm dying. The truth is, I feel fine. Maybe I'll outsmart those doctors and go on to live another dozen years. Ha! Wouldn't that be something?"

Lenox was appalled by the thought, but he smiled and nodded.

Leaving the house, they walked to the corner and dropped the envelope in the mailbox. "That's that!" the old man said happily. "Do you have any questions about anything?"

"There's one bit of information I'm lacking, Mr. Cavanaugh—the password you mentioned."

"By golly, you're right! The password! Well, it's simple enough, my boy. The password is 'Rupert Hofbauer.' "

"Rupert Hofbauer?"

"Absolutely! Isn't that a dandy? Rupert Hofbauer. His own name. He'd never guess it in a million years!"

"Ingenious," said the minister. "And easy to remember."

They parted at the brownstone stoop.

7

He read the sentence again: *Whoso sheddeth man's blood, by man shall his blood be shed: for in the image of God made he man.*

"Gibberish!" he muttered. "Shed a man's blood, and someone will shed yours. Then, presumably, a third individual will happen along and spill his blood, too—and so on, ad infinitum. Why? Because man is made in God's image! There's more nonsense in a chapter of the Bible than there is in the whole of Lear, yet a thousand generations have gulped down its hairsplitting logic—lumps and all."

The quotation occurred in a 1935 sermon of his father's that Lenox was updating for delivery at the next Sunday's service. He himself had not composed an original sermon in well over a year, having then decided that life was too brief for a man to expend even a couple of hours of it writing pithy lessons for his fellow creatures.

But wasn't it odd that this business of shedding blood should so easily take hold of his attention? Often, of late, his mind dwelt on such things. The notion of murder, like a bit of jetsam from one of his cruising daydreams, kept bobbing around in the dark sea of his consciousness.

Murder. There were reasons to ponder it. Cavanaugh

never should have said, "Maybe I'll . . . live another dozen years." That was imprudent—almost insolent. He, Lenox, would be middle-aged in another dozen years.

Murder. Surely the rewards outweighed the risks. As to morality—the scoundrel was seventy-nine. He had no right to twelve more years. Did he want to live forever? Even good Geraldine Gargan had said the earth would be a better place without him, had she not? And she'd known him a long time. What's more, he was ill—close to death. A single nudge and the affair could be neatly resolved.

Nor was murder, despite popular belief, one of those exacting enterprises that an inexperienced man might be wary of attempting. Inept and ignorant folk performed the sly deed every hour on the hour, and damn seldom were they caught. Why, the daily newspapers were sodden with gore: cadavers in rivers, automobiles, alleys, in tenements and penthouses, in lovers' lanes, in gunnysacks and steamer trunks. It was a thriving recreation.

Murder—yes. He had the nerve to accomplish it, too, though it would have to be arranged in a coldly impersonal way. Amos need not see his assassin. There was no reason for him to learn, in the final seconds of his life, that his pious minister—the boy he'd known from infancy—was to be his pitiless executioner. Lenox felt quite squeamish about this. To face his victim, to reveal his identity under those circumstances, would be an excessive hardship for both of them, he was convinced. He must strike him down from behind. Let the old devil imagine that he died at the hands of Nemesis.

Suddenly he tossed the pencil he'd been holding onto the sheets of the sermon. Christ, he thought in disgust, I'm getting as bad as Jerry Gingerich. Mad reveries. What the hell do I have to worry about, when all that's required is a little patience? Cavanaugh is on his last legs. He'll be gone in a matter of weeks.

At this juncture the doorbell rang, and since Mrs. Keller was out shopping, he was obliged to answer the summons himself. Standing on his front steps was a shabbily dressed woman of about forty. Her face, though pleasant, bore signs of a sensual and intemperate disposition.

She tendered a winning smile and said, "Ah, Reverend, I really hate to disturb you but I've had a string of misfortunes—a whole clothesline of them—and being in the neighborhood and knowing your grand reputation for good works and munificence, I thought I'd try my luck, so to speak, by paying you a visit in the hope and modest expectation that you'll be able to provide me with a little spiritual comfort and temporal succor. May I come in? I won't consume more than a minute of your time."

The minister, who hadn't much liked the peculiar emphasis his caller had put on the word "succor," nevertheless stood aside and bade her enter. As the lady passed, he noticed two things: one, that she was limping, and the other, that she reeked of sweet wine. Finding her way into the living room, she sat down on the Empire sofa, sighed, rubbed with her left hand her right ankle, which was swathed in an elastic bandage, and glanced curiously at her surroundings.

"Tasteful appointments," she pronounced graciously. "But do have a seat, Reverend. No need to stand."

Lenox took an easy chair and said with mild irony, "Thank you." Then, in his professional tone, he asked, "What is the nature of your trouble?"

"The nature of it? It's ill-natured, I'd have to say—like most trouble. Only rarely do I have any good-natured calamities." She threw back her head and laughed heartily at her joke. Her bosom—two mounds of Himalayan proportions—wobbled seismically. After a moment of this, she regained her composure and went on, "The Charles River embankment—that's where it began. While down there the other evening for a promenade, I stepped in a gopher hole or some such orifice and turned my ankle. The agony, believe you me, was indescribably excruciating. I had a bitch of a time—I beg your pardon, Reverend—getting home, and never would have made it at all if I hadn't been lent an arm by a gallant gentleman who was out airing his whippet. Men of his stamp are rare these days. A perfectly charming, cultivated, chivalrous, noble old lecher he was. When we finally reached my apartment I presented him with a mug of rum and one or two other tokens of my appreciation, though we'd best not go into that part of the story."

She winked at Lenox twice, once with each eye, and gave a girlish shrug that again set her breasts in rolling motion. "But that's neither hither nor yon," she continued. "It's the sprained ankle that's the hub and nub of the thing. Because of it I lost my waitressing job at the Casa Toledo, and although ordinarily I could manage fine, just this month I blew the rent money on a rug for my bedroom—a darling piece of work that I picked up in Filene's Basement. It's from Tabriz, in Persia, and I adore it—I really do. When I sit naked on it, Reverend, I feel feverishly romantic, like Scheherazade—even though she was from Baghdad and that's not in Persia, is it? Of course, I usually have spare cash in the ginger jar, but part of that I gave to the doctor who wrapped my injury, and the rest I spent on diaphanous lingerie—see-through underwear, you know— that I got at Raymond's, to cheer myself up. So now I'm impecunious—flat-busted, in a manner of speaking. The only food left in the house is wheat germ and a jar of chutney, and even Brillat-Savarin couldn't make a meal out of that. 'Penury and woe'—as the poet sings. And there's another mouth to feed besides my own."

Lenox managed to follow this narrative, but not without difficulty. Wondering vaguely what the woman would look like in diaphanous underwear, he inquired, "You have a child, do you?"

"Me? God, no! The other mouth belongs to my Pekingese, Ogadai. You can't feed dogs wheat germ, I've discovered. Healthful though the stuff may be, they just won't eat it. Must be something to do with their little glands. I've got a check coming from the Casa on Wednesday, but I'll never last till then unless some great-hearted person bails me out. Will you lend me thirty dollars, Reverend?"

At once the minister assumed a severe expression.

"I could get by with twenty," she said quickly, taking her cue from his change in countenance.

A pause ensued then, during which each regarded the other. Lenox thought that he had never before seen anyone dressed in such threadbare clothing. The collar and cuffs of the lady's white blouse were badly frayed, while her jacket was so worn that individual fibers stood out in it like the lines of a crossword puzzle. And her skirt was, if anything, in worse condition. There were numerous areas in the woolen fabric where either the woof was deprived of its warp, or the warp was bereft of its woof—and in some places, indeed, neither had survived. Even the elastic bandage on her ankle was limp and tattered.

At length he asked, "What's your name?"

"Urquhart," she responded readily. "Mary Urquhart. Mrs. That's a Scottish name—Urquhart. Sounds like a rude noise, doesn't it? I was quite a while getting used to it. But my husband, Andrew, was a stalwart lad and a very good provider, especially between the percales. Insatiable, nearly—a genuine ogre. I referred to him sometimes as 'Pubic Enemy Number One'—a nickname he adored. Ah, Andrew! We met one Monday morning in a South Boston tavern, and truth to tell, I thought he was a dim-witted lummox at first. It wasn't until he'd downed five or six nobblers of bourbon that he finally blossomed. His character gradually underwent the type of metamorphosis Dr. Jekyll made so famous. He snuggled up to me at the bar and began asking me riddles. To this day I remember a couple of them. Reverend—why did the traffic light turn red?"

"What? Oh. I don't know . . . why?"

"Well, wouldn't you turn red, too, if you had to stop and go in the middle of the street? Ha, ha! Terribly droll, Andrew was. I suppose if I had to, I could manage with ten. I'm not a heavy eater, but Ogadai loves his beef liver."

"Yes . . . yes. All right, Mrs. Urquhart," said Lenox, striving to preserve his dignity, "I'll give you twenty dollars. However, please don't come and ask for such aid again. Our church is by no means a wealthy one. Is that clear?"

"Perfectly. And don't you worry, lamb," she answered, grinning, "I'll return every penny of it, the minute I get my check. Cross my heart and hope to die." Accepting the money he handed her, Mary folded the bills adeptly, stuffed them in her jacket pocket and rose languidly from the sofa. "Thank you, Reverend. You're a darling fellow—*un vrai chevalier.*" She reached out and chucked him under the chin. "Didn't I say it wouldn't take more than a minute? Now I'll leave you to your matins and orisons."

While hobbling after him into the vestibule, she

persevered with her chattering. Lenox, when they got to the front door at last, opened it, and gently but firmly steered her out of the house.

Returning to the living room, he shook his head and scowled. And more terrible still did this scowl become after he looked out the bay window and saw the articulate Mary Urquhart hurrying along Pinckney Street at a remarkable pace. All evidence of her limp had vanished completely.

"Why, the crafty old boozer!" he exclaimed.

Then, catching the reflection of his startled features in the glass pane, he laughed softly and turned away.

8

One night, while sitting with Cheeks in the smoky Massachusetts Avenue cafeteria poring over the charts of the next day's races, Lenox came upon a long shot named Five O'clock Phil and remembered with a start that five o'clock was the bizarre hour at which Cavanaugh got up each morning. The detail lodged in the forefront of his mind.

On the following day, just before dawn, Lenox dragged himself from the comfort of his bed, dressed in casual clothing, drank some strong coffee and drove to Marlborough Street. Wreathed in a dewy mist and gilded by the first beams of the sun, the miser's house had a fairy-tale appearance. The weathered brownstone looked like gingerbread, and the slate roof and green copper trim might well have been frosting.

He went by without pausing, turned the corner at Clarendon Street and entered the alley, where, after threading his way through ranks of overflowing garbage cans, he stopped the Volkswagen alongside the brick wall that enclosed Cavanaugh's backyard.

It was pleasantly tranquil there. He lit a cigarette and regarded the wall with a calculating eye. Because of its great height it was a formidable barrier, but what made it even worse was that its concrete coping bristled with embedded pieces of broken glass. In the soft horizontal sunlight the keen shards glinted like jewels in a giant tiara. He would need two ladders and a suit of armor to scale such a palisade, he decided. The lone interruption in the brick wall's blank surface was a horseshoe-shaped doorway. This, however, was sealed by a reinforced wrought-iron gate that was secured by a double length of thick chain.

"No invitation to burglars here," he grumbled. "It's a wonder there isn't a goddamn moat!"

Above the menacing coping, treetops were visible. Years ago the yard had been a pretty garden, he recalled, but then the ancient Irishman who had tended it died, and Cavanaugh, rather than pay a replacement a higher salary, had allowed the area to grow rank with weeds.

Wriggling around in his seat, Lenox saw that an ocherous brick building stood on the opposite side of the alley. The entrance to this house was on Clarendon Street. In the flank that he was looking at, there were just two windows—both up near the roof—and a single, evidently rarely used basement door. He realized with no little satisfaction that the spot was an admirably secluded one, particularly at that time of day. Any number of crimes might be committed in such a setting, and as long as they were committed quietly, the neighbors would be none the wiser.

Hurling his cigarette away, he drove from the alley, made two consecutive right turns, found a space on Marlborough Street less than twenty yards from Cavanaugh's front door, pulled into it and parked the car. By his watch he saw that it was five-fifteen. Birds were twittering in the trees, while from Commonwealth Avenue, a block south, the intermittent hum of traffic could be heard.

He waited patiently.

At five twenty-four a light came on in the large Palladian window to the left of the stone stoop, and an instant later the bent figure of Cavanaugh drifted into view. Instinctively Lenox slumped down in the seat, but there was no need to; the old man never looked his way. He was puttering with dishes on a small dining table that stood by the window.

For the next quarter-hour, the minister watched his parishioner munch bread and sip steaming coffee from a china cup. At the end of that time the miser finished his breakfast, left the table and disappeared into the shadows of the room.

A few minutes later Lenox started the Volkswagen and returned to the rectory.

9

In a speech that seemed as endless as time, Mr. Spears proposed that they sponsor a baked-bean-and-brown-bread supper for one of his friends, a politician who was going to seek the office of state senator in the fall. Good old Spears, thought Lenox gratefully. He could always be counted on to deliver the requisite supply of suffocating boredom at every meeting.

The other church elders were reacting to his palaver in their usual fashions. On the Empire sofa Mr. Sanders and Mr. Delorry had escaped into catatonic trance, while Mr. Tilbury, ensconced in the easy chair, was fast asleep and whistling like a thrush. The remaining member of the group, Mr. Bosquet, was striving determinedly to keep his eyes open, though it was obvious from the periodic twitching of his fleshy face that he couldn't hold out much longer.

What would I do without Spears? Lenox wondered. When it came to audience-lulling, the fellow had no peer. Not only was he blessed with a voice as monotonous as a metronome, but he also had a positive genius for selecting the drabbest themes imaginable for his monthly oratory. He was the sandman himself—the answer to an insomniac's prayer.

At last Bosquet, like a stricken swimmer going down for the third time, cried out in a sharp and anguished tone. It was a moment before the minister understood that he was calling for a vote. Tilbury was duly nudged into wakefulness, and a show of hands was made. The baked-bean-and-brown-bread-supper proposal was soundly defeated, five votes to one. Spears grimaced crossly, lit an enormous umber cigar and rapidly filled the room with swirling yellow fumes.

While they were all still somnolent, Lenox raised the subject of the Sicilian earthquake and easily obtained their unanimous approval of a thousand-dollar contribution—to be drawn from the Charity Fund—for its victims. It was so easy, in fact, that he immediately regretted not having asked for fifteen hundred.

Sanders then got to his feet and declared that he'd noticed there was moisture seeping through the church walls. The bricks needed to be pointed, and he happened to know a good masonry man in Charlestown who'd be glad to inspect the building and submit a cost estimate for the job. Everyone but Spears, who stoutly denied there was any seepage, agreed to this suggestion.

Before any further business could be introduced, Mrs. Keller—a stocky, plump-cheeked woman—came in with coffee and cake. The elders greeted her warmly, their aged countenances aglow with boyish smiles.

During the serving of these refreshments, Delorry said to Tilbury, "Hey, Ed—have you seen Amos lately?"

"Cavanaugh? Just at church," Tilbury answered. "Why, Bert?"

"He sold some land I was interested in, last month. I don't understand why he didn't mention it to me. I would have paid him a better price than the other fellow."

"Land? What land?"

"A couple of small lots over in the South End."

"I'm afraid Amos' intellect is failing," said Tilbury, accepting a cup of coffee. "He's been selling everything he owns, I hear—even his furniture. Says he's getting ready to die, though what the connection is I can't see. And believe it or not, he hasn't made his testamentary dispositions yet."

"Is that so? Hasn't made a will?" Delorry asked, lifting his eyebrows.

"Not a proper one. The house he's left to his niece, but I'll be hanged if I can figure out what he plans to do with the rest of the estate. You can't get much sense out of the man these days. Death is all he has on his mind. Actually seems to enjoy talking about it. The funny thing is, he looks better now than he did a year ago. It's as if the old galoot has taken a new lease on life."

"If he has, Ed," Delorry replied, "I hope it's a more equitable lease than the ones he used to force on his tenants."

Both men chuckled.

The cake was passed around and the conversation became general. Lenox drank his coffee meditatively.

When the break was over, Spears tried to deliver a second address—this time on the matter of social activities for teen-agers—but the others quickly headed him off. The minister then gave his financial report. He did it glibly, and no embarrassing questions were asked.

By now they were all restless and anxious to depart. He held them there, however, by talking for another ten minutes about summer camps for the underprivileged children of Roxbury, intending to follow this up at the next meeting with an appeal for a donation.

As soon as he finished, Sanders moved for adjournment. A moment later they all filed out.

10

In the course of the following weeks Amos Cavanaugh attended every Sunday service, and there was no denying that he appeared remarkably healthy. Other parishioners commented on it. His gait was steadier, his face bore fewer wrinkles, his hard eyes scintillated, and the color of his thin lips had magically changed from purple to a shade that was almost red.

Lenox stared down at him from the pulpit. How much longer was the stubborn bastard going to hang on? Even a couple of years would be an eternity. Twenty-four more months of childish rituals and maudlin sermons; of births, marriages and funerals; of trite confidences and silly confessions; of white-elephant sales, picnics, committee meetings and raffles; of sickrooms, mortuaries, hideous psychiatric wards and nursing homes for incurables—while all that idle money awaited him impatiently in Switzerland!

No, he couldn't endure another two years of being a so-called man of God under those circumstances. Far better to be a minion of the devil!

What would it matter to the world if the miser died a

bit prematurely? What, indeed, would it matter to the old man himself?

One morning Lenox went to the Morgan Memorial Goodwill store and bought some used clothing—a raglan raincoat, a scarf, gloves, a cap and a pair of dungarees. He hid them in a battered satchel in the cellar of the rectory.

Less than a week later, during a chilly afternoon at Lincoln Downs, he lost four hundred dollars playing two-horse parlays. Driving home dispiritedly that evening, he stopped for gas at Attleboro, and while the tank was being filled, went to the restroom. There, standing in a corner like an emissary of fate, was a two-foot length of galvanized iron pipe. Lenox picked it up, weighed it in his hand and took it with him under his coat when he returned to his automobile.

11

Though it was still dark, a strip of light like a wisp of yellow silk now lay on the eastern horizon. Lenox had not realized how windy it was until he got out of the car. On the ground little dervishes of dust danced, while overhead a vast elm creaked and rustled eerily.

"Christ, it'll blow them away!" he whispered as he tugged the ill-fitting secondhand cap down on his forehead. "I'll need something—pebbles or stones."

He hurried to the tree, and by the wan glow of the street lamp examined the patch of earth at its broad base. In among the debris of leaves and paper scraps were pieces of rough gravel. He collected as many of these as he could find and dropped them in his pocket.

The rumble of a distant automobile caused him to glance around then, but Marlborough Street was reassuringly empty. Its houses were unlit and apparently dormant.

He put on his gloves and walked across the road, coming to a halt directly under Cavanaugh's Palladian window, where he bent over and laid a dollar bill on the brick sidewalk. Quickly, before the breeze could snatch it away, he anchored it with gravel. Three yards farther on he placed a second dollar, similarly secured, and beyond that a third. Around the corner he went on along Clarendon Street and into the alley, making certain, however, to mark his progress at regular intervals with more green bills. This task completed, he went back and sat in the Volkswagen.

A heavily overcast sky was delaying the dawn, and although Lenox was glad of the protective gloom, he feared it might start raining. If that happened, he'd have no choice but to drive straight home and return to his bed.

In rapid succession two cars rushed by, their headlights carving swaths in the night. Toward the other end of the block a husky man emerged from an apartment house and strolled off in the opposite direction. The minister watched this early riser closely, until he vanished around the corner of Dartmouth Street.

Stillness now prevailed. The wind had fallen measurably, and the elm tree, no longer buffeted, had ceased its keening. It was nineteen minutes past five.

So far I've done nothing, he thought calmly. At any point, if I want to, I can drop the whole scheme. What would I lose? Only a few measly dollar bills.

For a while he sat there listening to the sound of his own breathing, then he said aloud in a bitter voice, "Yes, a few measly dollar bills. Not quite a goddamn million of them. That's what I'd lose. That's all. That's all."

Hardly had he finished muttering these words than the light flashed on in the Palladian window, and Cavanaugh, dressed in a bathrobe and holding a coffeepot, could be seen hovering beside his little breakfast table.

John Matthew Lenox did not hesitate. He knotted the scarf around his neck, thrust the galvanized pipe inside his coat, stepped from the Volkswagen, raised his collar, and with his head down and his face averted, made for Clarendon Street.

A half-minute later he was in the alley, standing in the doorway across from the high glass-encrusted brick wall. On the pavement at his feet, fixed with the last of the pebbles, was a crumpled five-dollar bill. Furtively he surveyed the scene. Only the windows of Cavanaugh's upper floors overlooked his position, and from these he had nothing to fear.

But suppose a police car came cruising through the alley, as police cars so often did through the alley behind the rectory? What then? A spasm of panic jerked his body, and the length of pipe nearly slipped from his gloved hand.

Still, no crime had been committed yet, and perhaps none would be. It was entirely possible, notwithstanding all his claims to sharp vision, that Amos would never notice the critical first dollar—that he might just sit there in his window, gnawing his toast and swilling his coffee. And when he was finished, he'd get up and wander off to the bathroom for his morning shave. Yes, that's exactly how it would all turn out.

Birds began to chatter somewhere. Were they sparrows or starlings? he wondered vaguely. Above the slate roofs of the slumberous houses, the sky was growing florid with auroral light.

How long had he been waiting there? Five minutes? Ten? How long should he continue to wait? A futile, ridiculous business—skulking in a niche in a back street at this surreal time of day! Could he be serious? It was nothing but a farce, a vaudeville skit.

These speculations, however, were brought to an abrupt end by some shuffling noises that came from the direction of the alley's entrance. Lenox quickly pulled up the scarf over the lower part of his face and yanked the cap farther down on his forehead.

After a short period of silence there was a sound like a gasp. This was followed by a second and more prolonged flurry of scraping footfalls. Again the noise died, but a moment later it resumed, and it was now extremely close by.

At last Cavanaugh tottered into view. He wore bedroom slippers and a lavender-colored woolen robe. Tightly clutched in his hand, and looking like a bunch of fresh parsley, were the dollars that the minister had set out for him. An expression of rapturous greed was deeply imprinted on the old man's face, while his nose, like a quivering compass needle, pointed directly at the five-dollar bill on the ground before the doorway. When he stooped to pick it up, Lenox hit him on the head with the iron pipe.

The blow was a hasty, backhanded one, but though it didn't land squarely, its force was sufficient to send the miser sprawling in the gutter, where he managed almost immediately to squirm around onto his shoulder and stare up at his assailant with blinking, frightened eyes.

"You!" he cried shrilly. "You!"

In that instant a strange irrational notion took possession of Lenox's mind. He wanted to throw the pipe away and clasp the injured man in his arms. It was like a mad revelation. He wanted to get on his knees and put a handkerchief to the blood that had begun to ooze from beneath his victim's grizzled hair. He wanted to comfort him, to assure the frightened old fellow it was all a terrible mistake. Words of apology actually rose to his lips. "I didn't . . . I . . . didn't want . . ." he stuttered in confusion.

But even while Lenox was experiencing this odd

transformation, Cavanaugh grabbed the rim of a garbage can and struggled to his feet. His small mouth opened and from it issued a vociferous lupine howl. For what seemed an eternity to Lenox, the strains of this plangent wail echoed and re-echoed from the surrounding buildings. At once the humane intentions that had burst into flame in the minister's heart were doused by a tidal wave of apprehension. He looked about wildly. Then, to prevent his parishioner from producing a second such bellow, he jumped out of the doorway and hit him again, this time with greater accuracy than before.

A crimson gout of blood flew from Cavanaugh's nostrils. His eyes, suddenly devoid of expression, bulged in their sockets. He took a step back, shuddered violently and fell sideways across the tilted lid of the garbage can. Thrice more, Lenox struck him. Under these ferocious blows the old man's head lost its symmetry, becoming as eccentric as a head reflected in the roiled surface of a fun-house mirror. Blood trickled down his temples to flood the creases in his leathery cheeks. He rolled slowly off the garbage can, landed on his face on the pavement, wriggled convulsively onto his back, straightened both legs as if to make himself more comfortable, and then was perfectly still. In each of his hands he held money: in his left, the cluster of one-dollar bills, and in his right, the single crumpled five. With the blood now running into his gaping mouth, he gazed blankly up at the clouded sky.

Down the alley a dog barked fretfully. Lenox flinched. As quietly as possible he laid the length of pipe on the ground. Then he quickly wrenched the bank notes from his victim's grasp and crammed them in his trouser pockets.

The dog did not bark again. Only the prattling of the

birds disturbed the silence—that and the harsh, hollow sound of his own breathing.

I must get out of here, he warned himself. That goddamn howl—surely it was heard by somebody. I must get away.

His eyes, in the course of a frantic reconnaissance, darted aloft to the top floor of the Cavanaugh house, and when they did he received a jolt that almost deprived him of his senses. For there, in the lower pane of one of the windows, he saw—or thought he saw—a pale, grim human face looking down at him.

His stomach turned over. His powers of orderly reasoning seemed to evanesce like smoke, leaving at the very bottom of his brain a residue of fluttering terrors.

He stared and stared until at last his vision blurred. Then groggily he shook his head, blinked several times and stared some more. However, what he now observed was subtly different from what he'd seen a moment earlier. The details of the room were more distinct than before, yet among those details he could no longer make out the livid face. Through the arch formed by the drapes he discerned a crystal chandelier, and to the left of it a picture in an ornate frame. There was also a large keyhole-shaped clock sitting either on a mantel or a high piece of furniture, and beside it a candelabrum.

But where had the face gone to? It couldn't have disappeared in the second that he'd closed his eyes.

Even as he pondered this mystery he noticed that a pair of spherical drops dangled from the chandelier directly in front of the big clock. He squinted. The outlines in the murky interior grew vague, suggestive.

"My God, that's it!" he muttered hoarsely. "The dial

of the clock—that's the face. And the crystal drops are the eyes. It's an optical illusion. It was only a trick of my imagination."

Relief swept over him, and the normal functioning of his mind gradually resumed. After a last swift glance at the inert figure at his feet he turned around and—half walking, half trotting—fled from the alley.

Marlborough Street, its shadows dissipated, appeared even more deserted than it had before. In the Palladian window the light was still burning, while the heavy-paneled front door of the brownstone stood slightly ajar, as if patiently awaiting the return of the master of the house.

Lenox scrambled into the Volkswagen and peeled off his gloves, but when he put up his hands to untie the scarf that should have been masking his face, he found to his dismay that it had slipped down under his chin. He remembered then Cavanaugh's shrill words, "You! You!"— and the dreadful look of recognition that had accompanied them.

"Ah," he sighed. "I understand now. But it's over— finished—so it doesn't matter any more."

With fingers that trembled, he turned the key to start the car's engine. The street lamps went out as he drove away.

12

At five past six he was back in the rectory. He had been gone only an hour, yet it seemed a great deal longer. His bedroom had an unfamiliar, alien look about it—the way it did when he returned from summer vacations.

Having disposed of the raincoat, cap, scarf and gloves by dropping them in the clothing contribution bin outside the Salvation Army building on Brookline Avenue, and having meticulously cleaned up the few smudges of blood that he had discovered on the Volkswagen's seat covers and carpet, he now had little more to do. As he undressed to take a shower, he saw with satisfaction that his hands were perfectly steady.

The streaming hot water relaxed him marvelously, but when he tried to reconstruct in his mind the episode in the alley, he found that it was all muddled and vague. What had Cavanaugh said to him? What had he said to Cavanaugh? How many times had he struck him? Had it still been dark at the time? Or had the sun risen?

He was unable to answer these questions. He couldn't remember. Everything had transpired too fast, and he had been too excited to grasp details. It was as if his whole being had been totally occupied in the commission of the murder, and there had been no part of him left to make idle observations.

Returning to the bedroom, he inspected the clothes he had worn. The shirt was unmarked, but there were red flecks on the toes of the shoes and the legs of the dungarees. Painstakingly he cleaned and buffed the shoes. Then he recalled the dollar bills he had used as bait and dug them out of the trouser pocket. They were sticky with half-dried blood. Grimacing, he went into the bathroom, where he flushed them all down the toilet. After that he washed his hands thoroughly, donned fresh clothing and sat in his armchair by the window to read the morning *Globe* which he had bought at a stand in Kenmore Square.

At seven-thirty he heard Mrs. Keller arrive and start to prepare his breakfast. A short while later he went downstairs, carrying under his arm the dungarees rolled in a bundle. These he placed on the hall table near the front door, intending to discard them in a sidewalk trash basket the next time he left the house.

He ate his bacon and eggs with good appetite, and then, with his coffee, smoked a leisurely cigarette while wondering how soon the phone would ring to inform him of the tragedy.

Because of a case of vandalism the previous year, it was Lenox's custom to visit the church after breakfast, and, that day of all days, he wished to behave in his usual manner. Accordingly, he went out the kitchen door and made his way to the vestry via the flagged path in the garden. From there he wandered into the sanctuary and then down to the nave.

The small arched windows of the clerestory, alight with sunshine, resembled golden shields hanging high on the wall, yet despite their attempts at illumination, the building was as gloomy as ever. In the crooks and corners the shadows were so solid and dark that they might have been daubed there by some funereal cubist painter.

He sat in a pew. The church air was cool and a little dank, and in it a trace of incense—from the last burial service—lingered.

Up to this point Lenox's nerves had remained commendably steady, but now he began to feel uneasy. Perhaps it was foolhardy to undertake such a bold and risky venture, he thought. A dozen things might have gone wrong. What if the crime was witnessed—not by a harmless mantel clock, but by someone real? By someone who can identify me? The spot isn't all that secluded. A chance passer-by might have watched the entire episode from the mouth of the alley, for instance, and I would never have noticed him.

Or, if not that, I could have been seen lurking on Marlborough Street by some neurotic housewife who might have conscientiously made a note of my license-plate number. Christ! Wouldn't that be delightful?

And what of clues? Fingerprints? Footprints? Threads? Buttons? Telltale strands of hair? Did I leave any? I don't see how. I wore gloves, and there was no struggle or physical contact. As for footprints, the alley is paved and I was careful not to step in any puddles of blood.

No, I'm safe enough on that score, though there are plenty of other dangers. Suppose the old man hasn't kept silent about our secret agreement? Or suppose he's left references to it somewhere in his house? It wouldn't take much to blow the whole damn thing sky-high.

Then there is Professor Hofbauer to consider, too. Naturally he'll wonder about his client's swift and violent end. Yet, what can he do? He's certainly in no position to complain to the authorities. The only logical course for him would be to bide his time—to wait until I return from Switzerland with the money before making his move. And when it finally dawns on him that I'm not coming back, it'll be too late for the damn chiseler to do anything about it. The game will be over, and the swindler will have been swindled.

Lenox moved restlessly on the bench. His eyes wandered—to the choir stall, across to the dim altar with its ebony crucifix, up to the medallion window above it, down to the pipe organ and the limp American flag on its eagle-tipped standard, over to the empty pulpit and then to the numbers on the hymn board attached to the white wall. How quiet it was! Usually the ancient balks and planking of the place provided a certain amount of creaky noise, but now there wasn't a murmur.

The minister voiced a soft oath and continued with his speculations. What if Amos Cavanaugh isn't actually dead? What if he's merely injured? No, no—that can't be possible. The old bastard is as dead as a broiled beefsteak. All the same, I should have checked his pulse. That's what I should have done, instead of staring up at that window like an imbecile. But he must be dead—otherwise they would have come to arrest me by this time.

Once again Lenox glanced around the church. The scene appeared as lifeless as a picture in a book. He found that he was straining his ears to pick up the faintest sound, but there was nothing to be heard. It was as if he had suddenly become stone-deaf. He waited and waited, growing increasingly anxious. Why was there no noise at all? Why was it so still? There should be something—a rustle, a groan, a hum of vibration. The tranquillity was complete. It was almost unearthly.

Leaning forward in the pew, the minister glared at the altar. Then he called out in a loud, defiant voice, *"I have bruised him with a rod of iron, and broken him in pieces like a potter's vessel."*

The words crackled like pistol shots in a grotto. From floor, walls and ceiling they resounded sharply. Then the echoes died and the silence, like some not-to-be-denied elemental force, closed in once more.

Lenox grinned unevenly, got up, left the pew and walked toward the narthex. Throwing open the main doors, he stepped out into the light. Immediately his ears were dazzled by the noise of the awakening city. For a moment he looked back into the gloom of the church, then he slammed the doors and started up the hill to the rectory.

It was nearly eight-thirty. What was happening in the alley? he wondered. Surely they must have found him by now.

13

Before he could reach the house, however, he was hailed by a voice from the street, and on turning in that direction, he spied Jerry Gingerich standing behind a double-parked compact car. The florist was waving one hand while closing the car's trunk with the other. Then, smiling hesitantly, he came up on the sidewalk.

"I just this minute left an envelope on your desk," he said. "The receipts from our last sale, Reverend. We took in three hundred and eight dollars."

"Three hundred and eight? Marvelous, Jerry," said Lenox, arousing himself to a show of enthusiasm. "That will pay the way for a couple of kids at the Church Council camp this summer. You've done a wonderful job."

"Oh, thank you. We made a special effort, this being the last sale until the fall. Sold every stitch—coats, dresses, sweaters—all the shoes, too. I let a dealer from Cambridge have the leavings at a flat price."

"Terrific! Well, now you can take it easy for a while. Are you going on vacation this year?"

"Maybe for a week. I'm not sure. We might visit

relatives in Maine—if I can get away from the shop. It's hard. I've got a lot of bills . . . debts. I'll have to see."

"If anyone deserves a rest, it's you, Jerry. Make the trip, and don't worry about the shop. It will be there when you return. How have you been feeling lately?"

"Me? Great, Reverend . . . great." Gingerich replied, his round eyes expanding slightly as though the question had touched some sensitive optic nerve. "I did have a . . . a funny experience two or three weeks ago at a theater, but it didn't amount to much. A minor urge, it was . . . very minor." He produced a short, choppy laugh that was like the barking of a seal. "Yes . . . at the theater. A dignified elderly lady sat in front of us. She had purplish-gray hair, all in ringlets and waves. It looked sort of like a bunch of lilacs . . . or wisteria."

A motorcycle tore down the hill, creating a clamor. The florist paused and peered vacantly after it.

"Did anything awkward occur?" Lenox asked, striving to end the conversation quickly.

Gingerich brought his round eyes back to the minister's face. "Awkward? No . . . no," he said. "A crazy urge came over me, though. I felt a little bit violent. I wanted to grab the lady's hair in both my hands and . . . and give it a good yanking. I thought sure I'd do it, too—but after a while the impulse died down, thank God. Nothing happened. I was able to watch the rest of the movie without hardly thinking about the lady's purple hair. And that's the only trouble I've had recently. Makes me feel kind of hopeful. I think I'm getting back to normal, Reverend Lenox."

"Wonderful. I'm glad to hear it, Jerry. As I've said before, we all have fantasies and we all have mental quirks. Time cures them eventually, however."

: 83 :

"That's very true. Even the worst ordeals in a person's life get cured sooner or later, don't they? It's one of God's blessings." Gingerich smiled tentatively. "Well, I got to be going now. Have to get my car from the garage. This Toyota here is Vicki's, and she needs it for the shopping. My Ford is getting a tune-up. I'll see you Sunday, Reverend."

"Fine. Thanks for bringing the money, Jerry," Lenox said, watching him go back out into the street. "Give Vicki my regards—and the children, too."

Climbing the steps, the minister unlocked the rectory door and crossed the threshold into the vestibule. His glance went automatically to the hall table.

"Mrs. Keller!" he shouted.

The housekeeper appeared almost instantly in the arched entry to the dining room. "Yes?" she inquired mildly.

"I left a pair of trousers on that table. What's become of them?"

"He picked them up, Reverend—Mr. Gingerich did. I assumed they were left there for him. Weren't they?"

"Mr. Gingerich," Lenox repeated. Then, fully grasping the situation and realizing at the same time that it would be worse than useless to make a fuss about it, he quickly added, "Yes, of course. Good. I just wanted to be sure he got them, Mrs. Keller. Very good."

"Oh, he got them, all right—and three old aprons of mine, too," she declared. "He also put an envelope on your desk. Money he said it was."

Lenox nodded, turned and walked down the hall to his office. There he poured himself a large goblet of sherry and drank it off like water.

Bloodstains and all! he thought, glaring morosely at

the empty glass. Will that neurotic clod notice them? And if he does, will they mean anything to him? I wasn't gone fifteen minutes, and this had to happen. What a stupid accident! But he'll probably never imagine that the spots are blood. Why should he, after all?

The telephone rang. He hesitated for a moment, then lifted it from its cradle.

Clara Jenks, an infrequent attender of the church who resided on Beacon Street not far from Cavanaugh, was the caller. In a nasal voice and a disconnected manner, she told how she had gone out that morning for her newspaper and some fresh doughnuts, observed a cluster of people on Clarendon Street, moseyed over to investigate and arrived just as the body of old Amos Cavanaugh was being carried to an ambulance.

Lenox evinced the necessary astonishment before asking the question that was uppermost in his mind. "And he was dead, Mrs. Jenks? Are you quite sure?"

"Oh yes—the poor soul. He was killed," the lady answered eagerly. "He was murdered, Reverend. That's what the intern said. And to think I only saw him Monday in Eli's grocery on Dartmouth Street. Murdered—yes. Isn't it awful, the things that happen these days, Reverend? I couldn't see the poor soul's face—it was covered by a blanket—but they told me his head was bashed in horribly. All he was wearing was a bathrobe, they said. Murdered . . . and bashed in horribly. It must have been muggers. Isn't it awful? The poor soul!"

Once he was sure he had all the information Mrs. Jenks possessed, the minister wasted no time in concluding the conversation, but as soon as he hung up, the phone rang again. It was Geraldine Gargan. She proceeded to relate the identical tale he had just listened to—a circumstance that was not surprising, since she had learned it from the same source. A good five minutes elapsed before he managed to get free of Geraldine.

He then passed on the news to Mrs. Keller, dashed out of the house, hopped into the Volkswagen and retraced the route he had taken four hours—and half a lifetime—earlier.

14

He had expected to find considerable activity in the vicinity of the weather-beaten brownstone, but when he pulled up in front of it he saw none at all. He mounted the stairs and rang the doorbell. There was no response from within. The Palladian window to his left was now masked by drawn blue velvet drapes. As he raised his hand to press the button a second time, a voice behind him asked, "Can I help you, Parson?"

Turning, he saw a broad-headed, broad-bodied man in a pearly-hued raincoat standing at the bottom of the stoop.

"Hello," said Lenox. "Are you a policeman? I understand something has happened to my parishioner, Amos Cavanaugh."

"Yeah, I'm a detective. Quimby's the name," replied the man, none too graciously. He was in his middle forties, and had clam-shell gray hair and veined, pugnacious eyes. "Your parishioner is at the morgue. His head was smashed in. Somebody jumped him in the alley around the corner— brained him with a hunk of pipe."

Adopting an expression of pained bewilderment, Lenox descended the steps to the sidewalk. "How terrible!"

he murmured. "But who would want to kill Mr. Cava-naugh?"

"Usually I make a guess when I'm asked that kind of question," the policeman said. "This time I think I'll pass. There was nothing to steal, because the victim was wearing only a bathrobe, pajamas and slippers. Funny, huh? I never heard of a guy being mugged in his pajamas before—not out in the open. And the M.E. says it happened at about five A.M. Why would he be wandering in the alley at the crack of dawn? Maybe you can tell me."

Lenox didn't have to pretend surprise at this query. "I don't follow you," he said, genuinely startled. "How would I know that?"

"Well, he went to your church, didn't he? You're his minister, right? Was the guy eccentric? Was he a little soft? Senile? A nut case?"

The directness of the other's remarks caused Lenox to bridle. "I wouldn't say so," he answered stiffly. "Mr. Cavanaugh was an early riser, I believe. The elderly often are."

"Yeah, I know. He had his breakfast all laid out—even had a couple of bites of toast—and then he got up and went for a stroll in his pajamas."

"Might he have been killed indoors and . . ."

"No chance, Parson. He got whacked in the alley. The house is neat as a pin."

"I see. Perhaps he was taking out the garbage."

For a few seconds the detective looked at him without replying. At length he said, "Garbage. Funny you should think that, too. It's what popped into my head when I saw him laying in the gutter there. But it's no good. Why would he interrupt his breakfast to go dump the garbage? The sanitation men don't come that early. In fact, nobody is up at five in the morning—not muggers, not burglars, not rapists, not lunatics—nobody. It's a very weird time—too late for some crimes, and too early for others."

Quimby waggled his huge head from side to side, like a bored bear in a menagerie. "No, I think he was suckered out of his house some way—probably by a person he knew."

A thrill of fear sprinted down the minister's spine. Keeping his voice impassive, however, he said, "That doesn't seem to make sense. If the murderer was a friend of Mr. Cavanaugh's, why didn't he simply kill him inside? Wouldn't it have been much less risky? The old gentleman lived alone, Detective."

"Yeah, I know that. But maybe the killer was being cute, Reverend. The whole setup smells of cuteness. Maybe he was trying to outsmart us. Maybe he figured that if he whacked the man in his own living room, and the cops don't find any signs of breaking and entering, then they'd have to guess it was the work of an acquaintance. Ain't that how he'd look at it? So maybe he decided to frig around with it—to make it seem like something else. He gets the guy to come outside and gives it to him there, hoping we'll think it's a street crime. But I can't buy it. Cavanaugh, from what I hear, was too wise a bird to follow a stranger into a dark alley. Did you know he was a Shylock—a fancy, high-class loan shark?"

"I was aware of that—yes."

"We found a bunch of letters in his desk, and they show he's been leaning on the people who owed him money—leaning pretty heavy. It could be one of them got aggravated and paid him off with the iron pipe. We got his account book, too."

Lenox thought about the letters. No doubt Amos had been collecting every dollar he could, before his trip to the

Otherside. Just how much had he put on paper, though? Were there letters to Switzerland? He had promised to destroy anything connected with their arrangement, but had he? He glanced over the policeman's shoulder at the draped Palladian window. What else might they discover in there?

"I got a hunch we'll nail this character," Quimby said.

"Do you have any clues—besides the letters?" asked Lenox.

"Yeah, we got the pipe. Also, in the corpse's hand, the M.E. found a piece of a five-dollar bill—a ripped-off corner. The killer must have tore the money away from him."

Once again a tingle of fright scurried down the minister's backbone, but he frowned as if giving the matter thought and replied, "That is a curious circumstance. What can it possibly mean?"

"Who the hell knows? The hotshots over at Berkeley Street are working on it right now. It means something to somebody, Parson. As far as I'm concerned it's the key to the whole homicide. He wasn't paying the milkman—that's for sure. Those guys don't deliver before noon nowadays." Quimby scowled. "We'll have to interview all the neighbors, but it ain't going to be easy finding a citizen who was gaping out his window at five in the morning."

A taxicab drew up to the curb at that moment, and from it stepped old Edward Tilbury, a briefcase under his arm. Lenox introduced him to the detective. As Tilbury was not only Cavanaugh's financial and legal adviser but his lifelong friend as well, he was quite agitated.

For a while Lenox listened to the conversation between the two men. Hearing nothing of interest to him, however, he excused himself and went around the corner to the alley. There, guarding the entrance, was a lanky policeman drinking coffee from a paper cup. Around him a dozen people had formed a rough semicircle, some talking in subdued voices. Several yards beyond the patrolman, near where Cavanaugh had fallen, three men in civilian clothes were methodically sifting through a small pile of refuse. In the center of the alley, in a shallow depression in the asphalt, there was a partially coagulated puddle of blood. It looked like curdled red milk.

Lenox returned to Marlborough Street. Quimby and the banker were gone. He got into his Volkswagen and drove home.

15

"*The Lord is my light and my salvation; whom then shall I fear? The Lord is the strength of my life; of whom then shall I be afraid?*" Lenox chanted, in his gravest elegiac tone.

The church was remarkably crowded. He saw faces he hadn't seen in months. What brought them? They were certainly not close friends of Cavanaugh's. Perhaps they were enemies—come to verify, with gloating satisfaction, that the old buzzard was really dead at last. Perhaps some of them had even owed him money. Or perhaps they were mainly thrill seekers, attracted by the sensational nature of the man's demise.

Fervently Lenox wailed, "*Hearken unto my voice, O Lord, when I cry unto thee; have mercy upon me, and hear me.*"

In the aisle below, the coffin lay on its bier—a grim and forlorn object, despite the sprays of almost luminous flowers. It had been sealed at the undertaker's—a tacit acknowledgment that the deceased's shattered skull was beyond restoration. The minister was glad of it; he had no desire to view that wrinkled countenance again.

"Cavanaugh's niece, Lucia Pareto, was the only occupant of the first row of pews. She was a young woman, and rather pretty. Dressed in a long-sleeved, high-necked garment of charcoal-black, she sat very straight and very stiff—like a monument to mourning. She had only arrived the night before from California. What surprised everyone was that she appeared truly bereaved, and had actually wept when she kneeled at the casket.

"For a thousand years in thy sight are but as yesterday when it is past, and as a watch in the night," he rolled on, admiring the curve of the niece's cheekbone.

Selecting an appropriate theme for the eulogy presented some difficulties. Lenox solved them, however, by lauding the miser's great faith—particularly his steadfast belief in the Kingdom of Heaven, and in the treasures that there awaited the deserving.

When the ritual was at last over, six husky men from the funeral parlor hoisted the coffin onto their shoulders, bore it out into the sunshine and effortlessly slipped it in the gleaming hearse. The minister and the niece got into the hired limousine, and the cortege moved off to Mount Auburn Cemetery, in Cambridge.

Enjoying the fresh sweet-smelling air, Lenox recited a few more incantations, and then the box was slowly lowered into the grave. The mourners tossed their handfuls of moist earth, stood about uncertainly for a while and eventually straggled back to the automobiles.

Lucia Pareto sobbed softly into a ball of paper tissues. "He wasn't an evil man, my Uncle Amos," she said to Lenox. "People said he was stingy, but he used to bring groceries to my mother and me when we had very little. He gave me plastic toys, too." She dabbed her eyes. "You've been wonderful, Reverend. Thanks for everything—and God bless you."

The minister was touched. He patted the girl on the

shoulder. If the place had been less public, he would have put a comforting arm around her and given her a gentle squeeze.

16

Five days later Hofbauer phoned to tell him Cavanaugh had sent a note from the Otherside, and that in it he had asked for his money. Lenox, smiling to himself, explained patiently that because of church business, he could not leave for Europe earlier than the following Wednesday, though the truth was that he wished to put as much time as possible between the moneylender's murder and his own abrupt departure. Hofbauer was understanding. He would write to their friend and advise him not to worry. Since the anti-Englishman, Billings, was looking after Mr. Cavanaugh, there was no desperate urgency anyway, but of course, it wouldn't do to drag things out too long. The minister assured him that he would get in touch with him the minute he returned from abroad. On this cordial note the conversation ended.

At first Lenox thought it peculiar that the professor hadn't mentioned his client's violent death—surely it would have been natural—but then he realized it was not so strange, after all. The man was one of Cavanaugh's heirs, in a sense, and when legators die mysteriously, legatees grow shy. Hadn't Cain been reticent?

That week Lenox informed the church elders that he was taking three days off to visit an ailing college chum in New Jersey. Wednesday morning he left the rectory with all his possessions in a pair of flat suitcases and caught a flight to New York. In the washroom at Kennedy he got out of his dog collar and somber clothing, and donned a knitted sport shirt and a denim suit. He ate a sirloin-steak lunch and drank three Scotch and sodas. Then he bought a newspaper and ambled across to the Swissair jet that would carry him directly to Geneva.

He felt a glorious contentment. Had he been alone, he might well have burst into song. As the giant plane rose from the tarmac, he recollected Amos Cavanaugh's Biblical quotation: *A feast is made for laughter, and wine maketh merry: but money answereth all things.* Lenox grinned.

Yes, money—that was the answer. Money was the *sine qua non,* the very force that made the world turn—and now, at last, he was to have his proper share of the stuff. For a while at least, he could be a Croesus, a Dives, a Rothschild —or the mighty god Mammon himself. And he deserved it, too. Hadn't he taken the chances, done the deed with his own hands, staked his very existence on the strength of his nerves? Yes, yes—and he had won. The long shot had finally come in.

Staring out the window at the swiftly retreating ground, a myriad of little images began to flit about in his mind. He seemed to see his father, standing in the snow on the Common; he seemed to see his mother's wan face; he seemed to see Cavanaugh squirming on the pavement, and then Professor Hofbauer with an orange in his hand.

These eidolons and others bloomed and died swiftly, like slides flashed on a panel of his brain. He was overexcited, he realized. He was intoxicated by all that had happened. Closing his eyes tightly, he sought to make his mind a total blank, but again he saw the dignified figure of his father standing in the snow.

What would that saintly man say if he were alive and knew? Lenox wondered. What orotund malediction would he lay on his treacherous son? No matter, no matter—the crime was committed. Neither curses nor prayers would ever change that. And what right had his father to be outraged? Hadn't he insisted that his son be a minister? Yes—and by so doing, he had planted the seed of the murder many years ago. Why now should he complain of the bitter fruit? The sins of sons, say what you will, are all derived from foolish fathers.

He opened his eyes and looked at the earth far below. How smoothly it's gone so far! he thought. The newspapers, though clamorous at the start, had carried the story for only a few days, and then dropped it completely to make room for other atrocities. Two weeks elapsed, without any inquiries from the police. Except for the things he would need in Geneva, he burned all the papers Cavanaugh had given him, so that in the rectory there wasn't a particle of incriminating evidence. He was home free.

The sole task that remained now was to spend the money. He would draw it from the original account, deposit it in another account in a different Swiss bank, and with a fat checkbook and a pocketful of cash, head for Paris. There he would wallow to his heart's delight—drinking, gluttonizing, debauching. Ah, how pleasant to anticipate it! He would make the rake's progress look by comparison as innocent as a communion procession. He would immerse himself, body and soul, in the fragrant seas of hedonism.

Then, when he was sated, off to Dublin he would fly. No one would think to look for him there, should a hue and cry go up in Boston. He would be as well hidden at the Leopardstown race track, or Phoenix Park, as if he were in a monastery in Tibet—and be much better entertained.

The earth had vanished beneath a layer of clouds. He ordered a Scotch from the stewardess, lit a cigarette and read his newspaper.

17

They landed at Cointrin Airport early the next morning. Since he'd never been to Geneva before, he stared curiously out the taxicab window during the ride to the hotel. The terminal had been ablaze with tourist posters proclaiming a flower festival, and now he saw that the streets were decked with roses and green garlands. Remembering that this was Calvin's city, he was surprised and delighted to find it such a cheerful place.

His hotel room was spacious and overlooked the Rhône. Thoroughly exhausted by the night journey, he lay down on the bed and fell asleep. It was near noon when he awakened. He shaved, showered, donned his clerical habit, slipped some papers in his pocket and went to lunch.

At exactly two-thirty, well fed and in the best of spirits, he entered the beige marble lobby of the Banque Générale de Genève. He was carrying a large new briefcase. To the stolid receptionist he declared in English the nature of his business, and was requested in the same language to have a seat. A telephone call was made and a page in a blue serge uniform promptly appeared. After executing a little bow, the boy guided him to a gilded grilled elevator, brought him up to the third floor and then ushered him into the office of the man Cavanaugh had told him to see—a Monsieur Constant Picquet.

"Reverend Dr. Lenox?" the banker asked in an Oxford accent, rising from a massive swivel chair and extending his right hand across a broad mahogany desk. "I am most pleased to meet you, sir."

Lenox shook the hand vigorously and sat down, placing the briefcase on the floor. "Monsieur," he began, when they were both settled, "I have come here on a rather melancholy mission. I'm sorry to have to inform you that Mr. Amos Cavanaugh is dead. He was killed two weeks ago on a Boston street in the course of a robbery."

"Ah! I am desolated to hear of this," Picquet answered. "Murdered, did you say? How frightful!"

"Yes. There's an epidemic of violent crime in America these days," said the minister sadly, "and the aged are the principal victims. It's a shameful state of affairs."

Further remarks of commiseration were uttered by Picquet, though his face, which was pale and waxen, stayed as expressionless as the face of a haberdasher's dummy.

There ensued a few seconds' deferential pause, and then Lenox plunged directly into the more significant areas of the matter, declaring, "As you know, Mr. Cavanaugh gave me power of attorney over the money he has on deposit with the Banque Générale de Genève. It is my duty now to exercise that power. In order to carry out the deceased's various instructions, it is essential that I withdraw everything—and in cash—from his account." Lenox reached into his coat pocket. "I have all the necessary documents, I believe, including a photostat of the death certificate. And this is my passport."

Bowing his head an inch, the banker accepted the

papers, but he gave them only a perfunctory glance before handing them back. Suddenly Lenox felt uncomfortable. Picquet's features were too vacant, he thought—too dispassionate. It wasn't normal. Even an abacus-brained, iron-hearted Swiss financier was bound to display some measure of cordiality to his customers. Was the bastard suspicious?

Picquet remarked, "Ah yes. The poor gentleman died the eighth of June, it appears."

"That's correct," Lenox affirmed.

"Did you by chance encounter him during the week that anteceded the tragedy, sir?"

"Encounter him? Certainly. I saw him at the church service the previous Sunday."

"And he mentioned nothing to you?"

"Nothing of importance—no," replied Lenox, his confidence beginning to wither under the heat of these ominous inquiries. What the hell was the man up to? he wondered. It was all legal. Why was he stalling?

Though he longed to light a cigarette, the minister was now afraid to mar his holy image by revealing even so venial a vice as smoking. He licked his lips.

Picquet nodded moodily, and in a tone that held the barest trace of apology, said, "We have received from Mr. Cavanaugh a communication dated the first of June. Here is a copy." From a corner of the desk blotter he took a sheet of paper and passed it to his visitor. "You will perceive, Reverend Doctor, that this letter quite annuls and invalidates the original agreement. Consequentially, you are no longer—"

"Annuls?" Lenox whispered huskily. "Invalidates?"

The banker's clipped words had fallen on him like an avalanche. He blinked, and then looked at the paper in his hand—a paper whose bright white surface was filigreed by

Cavanaugh's distinctive, quavering script. Hardly breathing, he read what the moneylender had written.

GENTLEMEN:

Recently I sent you a signed form giving Rev. John M. Lenox power of attorney over my bank account. I have had second thoughts concerning this arrangement. Though the Rev. Lenox is a person of integrity, he has been poor all his life and, as a result, knows little about the management of large sums. Something might go wrong.

For the time being, then, I wish to retain complete legal control of my account. It is the whole of my fortune and I don't want to take chances with it. Please destroy the power-of-attorney authorization. If I decide to reinstate it or to delegate the power to someone else, I will let you know. I need a few weeks to think about it.

Yours truly,

AMOS CAVANAUGH

An enormous sensation of weakness came over Lenox —an irresistible lassitude that made it difficult for him to even remain upright in his chair. His muscles became flaccid, his mind disoriented. It was as if a great and greedy vampire had instantly siphoned off every drop of his strength, both physical and mental.

"I see . . . I see," he succeeded in mumbling, after a minute of awful silence. "And this . . . this was the last . . . the last letter he sent you?"

"Yes," said Picquet, observing him narrowly.

"But it's . . . incomprehensible! Why would he change his mind? Why? I . . . I don't understand."

The man behind the desk pursed his lips and shrugged.

Desperately, Lenox strove to get his brain working again. "And the money—what will happen to it now?" he asked.

"The account, sir, will be administered in exact accordance with Swiss law," answered the banker.

"Yes, but Mr. Cavanaugh hasn't appointed an executor . . . or an heir of any kind. The letter leaves the whole thing wide open. Under those circumstances, how can the law arrive at a just decision?"

"As it is a nonresident account, one would assume that the statutes relating to escheat and abandoned property would be most applicable. However, Reverend Dr. Lenox, I am really not at liberty to discuss this aspect with you. The unqualified cancellation of the power of attorney revokes your mandate, and therefore renders your legal standing in the proceedings null and void."

"Are you saying the entire fortune is irretrievably lost? That because of this little note—this memo scribbled in a nervous moment by a very elderly man—all the money must be forfeited?"

"The note is valid, sir. In the absence of a designated beneficiary, what other judgment can the courts make?"

"Surely it should at least go to the next of kin."

"But why? Has the client so specified? One must assume that if he wished to award his wealth to this next of kin, he would have made such a provision. The law cannot indulge in guesswork. It must be logical."

"And is that all there is to it?" Lenox asked faintly. "Can't you see it isn't fair? There must be a more reasonable means of . . . of resolving the problem."

"Ah! You can, if you so desire, engage a local solicitor, my dear sir, but he will merely confirm what I have already said. I am much experienced in these matters," Picquet

added severely, getting to his feet. "It is a great pity that
Mr. Cavanaugh did not consult you, or his lawyer, before
writing this unfortunate letter. However, there is nothing to
be done now. Nonetheless, sir, I am at your service if you
have any questions in the future." He put out his hand. "A
pleasure meeting you."

Lenox rose dazed, shook the hand and started for the
door, his legs rubbery. A sensation of hollowness was
spreading through his body like a virulent disease.

"You have forgotten your portfolio, sir," the Swiss
called after him.

Mechanically Lenox turned around. "Portfolio?" he
asked. "Oh yes . . . yes. Thank you."

He picked up the briefcase, and without another word,
hurried from the office. So anxious was he to flee the
building that he could not force himself to wait for the
gilded elevator. Instead he rushed down the flights of
marble stairs like a soldier escaping a military catastrophe.

Gaining the street at last, he dropped the briefcase in a
litter basket and scurried into the nearest café. There,
leaning heavily on the zinc bar, he gulped two quick
Scotches and ordered a third. The strength gradually
returned to his limbs. As he was about to lift the glass again
he noticed that the roly-poly bartender was glaring at him
with intense disapproval. Looking beyond the man to the
mirror on the wall, he immediately realized why. He was
swilling whiskey in his clergyman's uniform.

Hell and damnation! he thought. The Calvinist bastards are persecuting me. It isn't enough that they've
robbed me. It isn't enough that they've slammed the door in
the face of the one opportunity ever to come my way. Oh,
the mean sons-of-bitches! I must get out of here.

A taxi delivered him to the hotel, where he asked the

desk clerk to call the airport for him. While he was mournfully repacking his bags in his room, the clerk phoned to say there was a direct flight to Boston at five-forty that afternoon. He paid his bill and departed.

18

"The sauce'll bring you to wreck and ruin, kid. I seen it bring a lot of guys down. My old buddy, Lionel Naughton, was a boozer and he ended up bananas. Used to wear sneakers in the winter—and bet on hockey games."

"I only drink when I have troubles," Lenox replied thickly, adjusting the dark glasses on his nose.

"Yeah, sure," said Cheeks sarcastically. "And the more you drink, the more troubles you have. It's a vicious circus. Poor Lionel . . . he died two years ago of psychosis of the liver."

They stood in front of the cigar store on the corner of Boylston Street and Massachusetts Avenue. It was early evening, but still light. The sard disc of the sun loomed over distant Cambridge like a bullet wound in the sky. The city air was warm and dusty and smelled strongly of gasoline fumes. This was the day after Lenox's return home.

A swarthy man in a Hawaiian shirt approached them. "You seen Mashed-potatoes?" he asked.

"Not since yesterday," Cheeks answered, unwrapping a cigar.

"We're going to the harness races. You guys want to come?"

"Naw. You ought to know I hate them harmless races. In my opinion a trotter ain't no better than a dog. Hey, did you see the scrap out here last night?"

"What—George and Stanley? You call that a scrap? My broom fights better than that . . . and she's only ninety pounds in her high heels."

Cheeks nipped off the end of the cigar, thrust it in his mouth and lit it. "Yeah, it wasn't exactly championship caliber, was it?" he said between puffs. "More like a waltz. When Foley the cop came to break it up, I told him he was disturbing the peace. Did you hear me, Billy? It got a good laugh. I had a fight with George myself once . . . years ago, at the Rock."

"Who won?" Lenox asked, his voice mischievous.

"I did," said Cheeks modestly. "I let the bum do a lot of swinging and missing—then, when he was all wore out, I hit him a shot in the groin. That's what I always do in a fight—go right for the groin. I don't mess around. You hit a guy any place else, you're liable to bust your hand. Some people say you should kick your opponent in the groin, but me, I don't agree with them. A guy who would do that ain't no sportsman. Foreigners use their feet because they don't know no better, but an American guy should only box with his fists. When I was a kid I broke my mitt on a Swede's head, at a crap game in Southie. Caught him using bricks. The jerk could've got away with it, too, if he wasn't such a hog. He threw eight straight naturals, this guy. Didn't know when to stop. My hand was in a cast for a month, but I learned a good lesson. So, that day at Rockingham, I belted George in the groin—right in the old gentiles. You should've seen the look on his face! I lamblasted him to submarines. He figured he could push me around, on account of being bigger, you know? But size don't mean nothing. Once, in South Station, I seen a midget dump some clown who was six foot at least. How? By belting him in the nuts, that's how. One shot is all it ever takes. Pow! You don't even work up a sweat. The funny thing was, a cop ran up and arrested that midget. Yeah, he snaps cuffs on the little runt and drags him off to the slammer. Can you imagine? Books him for insult and battery."

"The midget should have belted him in the groin," said Lenox.

"Yeah," Billy agreed, laughing. "He could've blasted the cop to submarines."

A woman in blue stretch pants came across Boylston Street, and the three men paused in their conversation to watch the motion of her behind as she pranced by.

"That's where Mashed-potatoes is, I bet," the dark man said. "Up in his room, zigging some snake."

"I wouldn't be surprised," Cheeks said. "Me and him went to Provincetown on the boat once, and Benny did nothing but grab asses—the feeb. Every broad that went by got a free massage. Cheese and rice—it was embarrassing!"

Lenox grinned. "Sounds like good, healthy outdoor exercise to me," he said.

"Cheeks don't go in for that stuff," said Billy. "He'd rather spend his dough on horses than on women. Ain't that right, Cheeks?"

"Sure—why not? I ain't never got the clap from a horse."

"Maybe you just been lucky," Billy answered promptly, winking at Lenox.

"Hey, that's comical," Cheeks sneered. He puffed

angrily on the cigar, then added, "In my estimation, women are all long shots—sucker bets. You ever meet a guy who could handicap a woman? I never did."

"Yeah, I guess you're right," said Billy, laughing good-naturedly. "Anyhow, I'd better call that bastard before it gets too late. I don't want to miss the double."

He walked off in the direction of the phone booth.

"Who the hell is Mashed-potatoes?" Lenox inquired, frowning under the limp brim of his felt hat.

"Benny the Barber. His last name is Marziapato or something," the baby-faced horseplayer answered. "If you could unzipper his head, inside you'd see a glob of snapping ones. You want to play some poker over Monroe's place, Johnny?"

"Not tonight, Cheeks."

"Okay, kid. I'm going to drift. But remember what I told you about the sauce. Booze is bad news. See you."

Waving his cigar in a gesture of farewell, Cheeks strode to a cab at the curb, yanked open the door and got in.

For a few minutes after the taxi departed, Lenox stood uncertainly on the corner. Then he, too, left.

19

Sometime later in the evening Lenox, still wearing his maroon felt hat and his all-but-opaque sunglasses, sat crouched in a crimson leather booth in a bar room called Tiny's Heat Wave, drinking gin and ginger ale from a slender, tapered glass. Invisible strobes cast pulsing tongues of puce light upon the metallic blue walls of this otherwise dim lounge, and it was at these bogus flames that the minister's attention was steadfastly directed.

He was considering hell—considering whether or not the place could exist, and if so, what it would be like. Though this was a familiar field of speculation for him—he had often dwelt upon it as a child—recent events now gave the subject a much sharper relevance. Hell . . . hell. How real a region it sometimes seemed! Not the hell of the modern philosophers and literary acrobats—that homey setting in which clever characters argued interminably—but the hell of the medieval Christians, of Dante, of the German woodcuts and the Italian frescoes. In the flickering lights Lenox envisioned it clearly: the boundless and bottomless pit replete with writhing, smoldering, screaming naked men and women. He could smell the sulphur. And around this pitiful mass of tortured flesh, legions of hideous, horned, fanged and scaly demons danced, stabbing with their pikes and pitchforks and flailing with their scourges. Yes, that was the genuine hell.

Still, how much anguish could a human being absorb? Was there no limit? Was this devil, Satan, allowed to inflict an infinitely acute torment throughout the life of time? Evidently. Anything less might be construed as mercy, might it not? And where in hell could a man expect mercy?

The concept was staggering. Imagine suffering the greatest possible physical and psychic pain for a mere second—then, imagine enduring it for eternity!

Somnambulistically Lenox swallowed a mouthful of his iced drink, and a quotation, *Hell is a circle about the unbelieving,* drifted into his mind. A clever epigram, he decided, but too pat to be truly pithy. A good old-fashioned hell would make a believer out of the most obdurate skeptic, and what then would the circle encompass? Hell had to be a district of utter agony and utter fear—or it would be nothing at all.

From the adjoining room—a portion of Tiny's Heat Wave that was set aside for dancing—Dionysian sounds began to emanate. A doctored saxophone murmured and groaned, a double bass panted, a clarinet squealed lewdly, a trombone gave a satyric roar.

John Matthew Lenox continued studying the shimmering lights. There was no doubt in his mind that if there was a hell, he was certain to end up in it. The devil's cauldron for perpetuity. The inferno for eternity. It seemed a harsh sentence for braining a seventy-nine-year-old villain, however—especially since he hadn't profited from the crime, hadn't gained a nickel, hadn't received a moment's temporal joy to compensate him for all his onerous exertions. A bum rap, but there it was, like it or not. For murder, God threw the book at you. *Depart from me, ye cursed, into everlasting fire, prepared for the devil and his angels.*

No, he hadn't received a moment's temporal joy, and the blame for that belonged to Amos Cavanaugh. There was a fit candidate for hell, if ever there was one! Had the old wretch meant to be ironical when he stripped Lenox of the power of attorney on the grounds that he had "been poor all his life"? Perhaps . . . but there was more to it than that. What made him change his mind at the last minute? Probably some dormant instinct, some ancient and deep-seated Cavanaugh trait, had awakened in alarm and warned him of the folly of his scheme. But he, Lenox, was to blame, too. He should never have waited. He should have struck at once. Why hadn't he? Why? Why?

And so, neither temporal nor supernal joy would ever come his way. He could forgo the supernal joy easily enough—it being of dubious authenticity, anyway—but the other deprivation was a bitter dose. There would be no magnums of Taittinger to swig, no tournedos Rossini or quails in aspic to batten on. He wouldn't be smoking the finest Havanas over snifters of V.V.S.O.P. cognac at the best table of the Crazy Horse Saloon, nor would he ever get to spend a night in a Four Star Luxe hotel suite teeming with Four Star Luxe nymphs and houris.

No, for the Reverend Lenox there wasn't to be a posh life. It had been invalidated. His standing in such pro-ceedings was now null and void, as that fish-eyed Swiss thimblerigger had so aptly phrased it. Void. Empty. Nothing.

"I wish I could belt the world in the groin," the minister murmured in a viscous voice while his face remained turned to the dancing flames on the metallic wall. He drained his glass, then added, "It's a fruitless bramble—

the world. Belt it in the groin—right in the old gentiles."

His face was flushed, and his movements, when he lit a cigarette and signaled to a mini-skirted waitress for another gin and ginger ale, were excessively deliberate.

A tall black man in a satiny white cap, satiny blue shirt and flared linen trousers approached the booth. "How you keeping, Johnny?" he asked, sitting down.

"All right," Lenox answered. "And you?"

"Superfine, man. Ain't that group something? The trombone used to gig with Gillespie."

"Want a drink?"

"Me? No, thanks. Chugging screech ain't one of my habits." The black man began to drum on the table, using the tips of his fingers and the palms of his hands. His beat was perfectly synchronized with that of the music coming from the next room. After a moment he hunched forward and said conspiratorially, "I got a very young one—just turned seventeen. She's out of Albany, New York, and as fresh as a quart of milk. This is the only and original time her mammy ever let her go any place by herself. Naturally, I ain't going to throw a child like that in with a bunch of heavy dudes, 'cause then she's liable to retreat on me. You interested?"

"I don't think so."

"One bill—that's all it'll cost you. And you stay as long as you like."

"Not tonight, Hamilton."

"Hey, Johnny—don't you remember? I ain't Hamilton no more. I'm Hassan Abdul now."

"I thought you told me the Muslims wouldn't let you in?" Lenox asked as the waitress brought his drink.

"Yeah, they won't—not till I change my profession," said the black man ruefully. "But that don't mean I can't keep my new name. Hell, who's gonna stop me? Hassan Abdul—got a nice ring, don't it? You could play it on a tenor sax. But a brother told me to use my other name when I buy airplane tickets, unless I want the security guys to yank the lining out of my suitcase. This young chick, though—how about it? She's brand-new—not one of them floor models, either—and I'm giving you first go."

Lenox frowned, then scowled. "I think not," he said. "The last lady you sold me was dull and ineffectual."

"What are you talking about, man? Greta? How come?"

"She was too damn lethargic—that's how come."

"Greta was what?" asked Hassan Abdul indignantly.

"Lethargic. Half asleep. A wooden Indian," said Lenox.

"Oh. Hell . . . I thought you were trying to tell me she had something wrong with her."

"That's something wrong, isn't it? Who needs a zombie? If the girl wants to sleep, let her do it on her own time. She must have gulped a handful of tranx, for Christ's sake. I couldn't even get her to make conversation."

"Hey, man—now listen. Greta wouldn't take no tranx when she's working. She's a dedicated woman. My girls all got class, man, and that Greta—she's the star attraction. She's the best bounce in Boston. And she's pretty. I mean, the woman is an ebony goddess here on earth."

"When she was with me, she was more like a statue of an ebony goddess. I paid you a hundred and a quarter, and that dedicated woman of yours made me feel like an intruder."

"I can't figure it, Johnny. You must've got her on a bad, bad night. Usually Greta is an ocean of emotion, a real electric eel. Usually she just leaves the client dead in bed.

: 114 :

Honest, man—she has to help them get their clothes back on, they're usually so used up. Anyway, when I see her later I'll kick her ass for dogging it on you. She knows better than that." Hassan resumed drumming on the tabletop as the clarinetist in the adjoining room blew himself into a frenzy. "But this Adriana—you don't want to miss her. She's got a movement like high grass in the wind."

"Seventeen?" Lenox asked, eying his companion.

"Yeah, just turned. Couple of weeks ago, she was only sixteen. Ha, ha. Still got a little baby fat on her."

"And she's at the hotel?"

"Right—watching TV and feeling lonely."

The minister drank most of the gin and ginger ale, then inquired, "Will you take a check?"

"A check? Come on, man! Stop fooling with me," the black man replied. "When I walk in a bank the cameras start whirring, the guard goes for his zinger, and all the tellers slap their kicks on the alarm buttons. Why put everybody to so much trouble? Mine ain't a business that runs on checks. I ain't General Motors. What're you going to do—deduct it from your income tax? Hell, next you'll be charging it on a credit card. Ain't you got no cash?"

Lenox laughed. "Okay, Hassan Abdul, I was just making a joke," he said, drawing his wallet from his jacket pocket. "Here's the hundred—and it's the last in the exchequer. Tomorrow I'll have to rob a poor box. She better be worth it. 'High grass in the wind'—Jesus, you're getting poetic! What's the room number?"

"Forty-three. Like, four and three equals seven—right? A lucky number for you, man," said Hassan, slipping the bill into his shirt. "I'll call her and say you're on your way over. Wait'll you see how she moves."

Lenox finished his drink and left at once.

20

Lenox was appalled. Never had he seen the coffee hour so crowded. Half the people attending the service had wandered down to the basement, and judging from the manner in which they were munching and jabbering, they meant to stay awhile. Christ! Why can't the silly bastards eat at home? he asked himself fretfully. Tormented by a monstrous hangover, the minister wanted only to regain the quiet of his bedroom—there to tear off his stiff collar, swallow a few more aspirins and lay his aching head on a soft pillow.

But now that was impossible. Aside from everything else, he had stupidly allowed himself to be trapped between the wall and the refectory table by Mrs. Delorry, who was well launched into what augured to be an interminable attack on the mayor of Boston. The subject was one that agitated Mrs. Delorry exceedingly. She couldn't get her opinions out of her throat fast enough, with the result that she often showered her auditor with a glittering spray of saliva. She's like a goddamn Nereid in some goddamn Roman fountain, Lenox thought, restraining a desire to wipe his face. What was even worse, however, was the pitch of her voice. She was shrill—and shrillness was a vocal characteristic that he was abnormally sensitive to that morning. At each word his central nervous system flinched, cringed and winced. Yet, short of vaulting either the table or the lady, there was no escape. The wretched woman blocked his path as resolutely as had King Leonidas blocked the passage of the mighty Medes, or Horatius that of the Etruscans. He was stymied.

A few yards away Lucia Pareto, Cavanaugh's niece, stood talking to Vicki and Jerry Gingerich. In a long-skirted, tight-bodiced dark-green gown, the girl looked most attractive. The curve of her prominent breasts was positively entrancing, while her every gesture had an easy, natural grace. A dainty, toothsome morsel, he decided—a bonbon. If he had to remain in this cursed place, why couldn't it be with her, instead of with this great spitting dragon?

At that moment, though, Mr. Delorry arrived. Being a forceful type, he required less than a minute to stanch his wife's manic torrent. Then, by applying a firm hand on her fat wrist, he was able to lead her away to a waiting automobile. Lenox had to suppress an urge to applaud the performance. Hastily he got out from behind the long table and began to inch toward the exit himself.

But Geraldine Gargan suddenly appeared and brought him to a halt by remarking, "Pretty, isn't she?"

"Who? Mrs. Delorry?" he asked, wondering how a woman with a face like a mare's could be so described.

"No, no, no. Old Cavanaugh's heiress. You've been staring at her—first from the pulpit, and now here."

"Have I? Yes, she is pretty. A good, symmetrical face, and nice jetty tresses—like a Polynesian's."

"Or a gypsy's," said Geraldine, fingering her double

string of baroque pearls and frowning slightly. "I had a chat with her before the service and found her rather odd. But then, her mother, Martha, was also odd, as I recall."

"Odd?"

"Oh yes—distinctly odd."

"She doesn't look odd to me," Lenox said.

"No, I don't suppose she does," the woman replied meaningfully. "Still, she's a hippie. Did you know that?"

"Dear, dear!"

"You needn't be sardonic, young man. It's very well established that hippies are often emotionally askew, and this Lucia is a case in point. I'm sure she's more than a little distraught."

Vaguely the minister recalled old Cavanaugh making a similar remark, the day they'd signed the legal forms. "Are you hinting she's mad?" he asked.

"In Washington, in front of the White House, she once doused herself with gasoline and was only prevented from setting herself alight by the quick action of a couple of her friends. That's one of the stories she told me. It was to be an act of protest against the war in Asia. Do you consider that rational behavior, Reverend?"

"She was probably exaggerating—hoping to shock you, my dear."

Geraldine ceased playing with the pearls and let her hand drop to her side. "If that was her aim, she succeeded admirably," she said. "But the child is odd in other ways. Have you heard about the great mystery? Mr. Tilbury hasn't been able to locate the Cavanaugh fortune. It's vanished into thin air—and Lucia, the heiress, doesn't mind!"

Before answering, Lenox waited a moment. Then, cautiously, he said, "Vanished? How could it? Wasn't the money in real estate, stocks and bonds—that sort of thing?"

"Evidently not. Amos was secretive about financial matters, perhaps with good reason. Mr. Tilbury is all adither—and so are the police, I understand. They're convinced the murder and the disappearance of the money are somehow linked together. Only the girl is unperturbed."

The pains in his head began to multiply. Taking a cup of black coffee from a passing tray, he put it to his lips and drank almost the whole of it.

"Maybe he's buried it in his garden," he declared, attempting a grin. "Isn't that what misers usually do?"

"If he has," said Geraldine dryly, "it wouldn't surprise me. However, Cecily has quite a different theory. She's suggested that Amos has taken his wealth with him."

Lenox swallowed. "Very funny," he said.

"I thought so, but Mr. Tilbury didn't. He finds the entire affair distasteful, especially since he's being badgered by some rude Irish detective. But Lucia displays no interest whatever. Of course, she's received the house. That must be worth a good deal at today's prices—still, it's a bagatelle compared to the rest of the estate which, rumor has it, is valued at about a million dollars. Now, John—to ignore a million dollars just isn't normal, is it? Oh, oh! Don't look, but I think she's coming over."

Out of the corner of his eye he caught a glimpse of the green-gowned figure passing through a group of Sunday school children. An instant later, Lucia had joined them.

"Good morning!" she said pleasantly. "I must leave soon, but I couldn't go without telling you how impressed I was by your sermon, Reverend. It was fantastically inspiring. I even wrote some of the things down. I agree with you completely when you say that modern Christianity has lost its direction, that it has forgotten Christ's true mission. But how beautifully you phrased it! 'Jesus came to relieve mankind of a terrible illusion. He came to dispel the death fear.' That's the entire story—the whole New Testament in a few words. It's so simple, yet so important. Jesus Christ wanted to redeem people, to cleanse them of the awful belief in their own mortality. Death is resurrection. Even the whispering, murmuring sound of that word—resurrection—is beautiful. 'Flesh and blood may perish, bone may crumble to dust—but that which is the spirit can never die.' Fantastically inspirational! It was a deep experience, Reverend. Didn't you think so, Mrs. Gargan?"

"Oh yes," Geraldine answered, her patrician features inscrutable.

"I'm pleased you liked it," said Lenox, doing his best to remember the theme of the homily he had delivered only an hour earlier. "It's apparent that you're a person of strong beliefs, Miss Pareto. You must join us every Sunday."

"I shall—of course I shall. Your church has an atmosphere, Reverend, a very intense atmosphere. I can feel it, as I'm sure you can too. Is it an ancient church? Is it Colonial, by chance? The bricks look hundreds of years old."

"It was built in 1805. The architect was Asher Benjamin—one of Bulfinch's competitors. And it hasn't undergone any real modifications over the years. Indeed, histories of Boston often include pictures of our meeting house. The cupola is particularly interesting. If the idea appeals to you, I'll show it to you someday."

Lucia blinked her gray eyes twice. "That would be marvelous," she replied. "Oh, this has been such an exciting day for me—so full, so stimulating. In California, especially in Palo Alto, I used to have glorious days like this. Mr. and Mrs. Gingerich asked me to join them at the coffee hour, and I'm so glad they did. She's very nice, but he is absolutely intriguing—terrifically strange. He's aware of demons. Not many people here in the East are. Of course, he didn't come right out and admit he believes in demons— I guess he was embarrassed—but it was obvious from the way he answered my questions that he's very, very aware." The girl smiled and glanced up into Lenox's face for a moment. Then, in a tone of regret, she said, "I have to go now. It's too bad. I'd love to stay longer, only I'm meeting some Cuban refugees at West Newton Street and I'm late already. They've been having a hassle with their landlord, and because I can speak some Spanish—one summer I worked with a family of Chicanos—I've been trying to help them. Again, thank you for that fabulous sermon. Good-bye, Reverend. Good-bye, Mrs. Gargan. See you next Sunday."

Graceful as a dancer, Lucia turned and made her way through the crowd. For as long as he was able, Lenox watched her.

"Well? What do you think, John?" Geraldine asked.

The minister sighed. "I wouldn't call her mad," he said.

"No? What, then?"

"Well, I'd say she was a bit fervent—that's all. A lot of young people nowadays incline toward fervor."

"Pshaw! You're lenient. It's more like fever than fervor, if you ask me. Did you hear her rave on about demons? I can't recall the last time anyone introduced hobgoblins into a casual conversation, Reverend. Do you suppose Martha and her Italian lover were living in Salem when the child was born?"

Laughing politely, Lenox resumed his retreat to the exit.

21

Although he had been expecting Hofbauer to telephone, Lenox answered the call with a certain amount of anxiety when it actually came. Reason told him that a con man was most unlikely to raise a fuss over a capsized scheme (to whom, after all, could he appeal?), yet the mere fact that the German was privy to everything—that he knew all of Cavanaugh's plans and preparations—was enough to be disquieting.

"Reverend Doctor, I am surprised you have not before this communicated with me," Hofbauer began in his grating voice. "We have waited and waited, Mr. Cavanaugh and me. So! You have purchased the first quantity of gold?"

"No, I have not," Lenox answered bluntly, while reaching out with his foot to kick the door to his office closed. "I went to Switzerland, as I told you I would, but when I arrived the people at the bank showed me a letter from Amos Cavanaugh—a letter that completely canceled my power of attorney. Do you understand what that meant, Professor? It meant that I no longer had any legal position as far as they were concerned. It meant that they wouldn't give me the money. I was left with no course but to turn around and come home again—empty-handed."

"Canceled the power of attorney? What joke is this you are trying on me, Doctor?"

"It's no joke at all. Believe me, there's nothing amusing about an eight-thousand-mile wild-goose chase. Evidently the old man changed his mind at the last minute and made other arrangements. Frankly, Professor, I'm not too surprised that he did, since your proposition was a highly irregular one. There are some who might even question its legitimacy," Lenox added, injecting a threatening note into his words.

For half a minute the line was silent except for the soft, measured sound of the caller's breathing. When Hofbauer resumed speaking, his voice was heavy with sarcasm. "Yes, yes," he said. "And that was why you did not phone me up. You did not want to tell me such bad news, eh? And before that, three weeks ago, you did not even want to tell me the bad news that Mr. Cavanaugh was dead, did you? Only by luck did I read it myself in the newspapers. That is the way it is, eh?" The German paused, then snorted like a spirited horse. "Listen, you—I am a man of science. I have not time or patience for fairy tales, and what you are saying is a fairy tale. That is what it is. If it isn't, the bank must be lying—and why would a big famous bank tell lies about such a thing? If Mr. Cavanaugh made it impossible for you to get the money, why would he write me and ask when the gold is coming, eh? *Ach!* I am no cretin, Doctor. The money is not any more in Switzerland. No, you have it—and you want to keep it for yourself. But you are only being stupid, because you can not succeed with this . . . this robbery.

You must do what you promised poor Mr. Cavanaugh—
change it into gold and bring the gold here. If you do not,
sir, there will be bad troubles for you."

"Whether you're a cretin or not isn't for me to say,"
Lenox replied haughtily, "but you certainly seem to be
acting like one. I have told you the truth. However, if you
can't accept my word, then I suggest you write to the
Banque Générale de Genève directly. Their address—"

"Hah!" roared the professor. "Do not, please, talk to
me like I was a child. I know, and you know, that a Swiss
bank would never give out to a stranger information. And I
do not want letters, anyway. Letters, also, can be fairy tales.
What I want only is the money."

"You may want it as much as you like," snapped the
minister, "but it isn't going to do you any good."

"We will see. We will see. Maybe you are forgetting
there is such a thing as the police. How would it be if a man
like you—a pastor, a clerical man—was arrested like some
gangster for fraud, eh?"

"Fraud, Professor? I'll bet that's a subject you know
quite a lot about, isn't it?"

"I know that stealers go to jail."

"Yes, they do—and so do bunko artists."

"Stupid! Stupid! Do you not see, Reverend Doctor?
You will force me to make terrible trouble."

"The trouble won't be for me, though," replied Lenox,
determined to outbluff his opponent. "It will all be for you.
I may even save you the bother of calling the police, Herr
Professor. I may call them myself."

"Ah? Will you? Maybe they would like that. I have
read in the newspapers they are interested considerably in
talking to people about Mr. Cavanaugh, especially about
how he was killed by somebody in the street."

Hofbauer delivered this last remark with unmistakable malice.

Lenox's hand tightened on the telephone as a gust of fear swept over him. He hesitated for an instant, then recovered control of himself and said defiantly, "You're insane—a babbling maniac. What are you trying to say?"

But as soon as he had spoken he realized from the dull tone of his words that the line was dead. Hofbauer had hung up on him.

22

Only partially did the dimity fabric of the drawn curtains thwart the glaring sun. The air conditioner, which was on full blast and making its usual racket, helped a little, though not much. Lenox, however, seated in his armchair with his legs extended and his whole body nearly straight, was oblivious to the sultriness of the air around him. His mind was otherwise occupied.

"Groundless suspicion," he muttered moodily. "A shot in the dark. The son-of-a-bitch doesn't know a thing. How could he? He's guessing."

From some apartment across the alley, Dvorak's *New World Symphony* drifted on vibrant stereophonic waves into the bedroom. Absently Lenox glanced at the window. The normally maroon curtains were now, because of the intrusive sunlight, a flaming red. It was almost like the wall in Tiny's Heat Wave.

> *O hoofed and hornèd Lord,*
> *Thou sly and subtle liar;*
> *O scaly fright,*
> *O Prince of Night,*
> *Behind thy fence of fire.*

Where had he ever learned that? he wondered—and why must he keep thinking of hell? To hell with hell. Or, better still, to hell with Hofbauer! Let the bastard threaten all he liked; he could no more execute those threats than could Lenox fetch old Amos back from his moldy grave! Go to the police? He wouldn't dare. The fellow was a common crook, and it was axiomatic that crooks avoided the police as zealously as hens avoided weasels.

Nevertheless, the minister was worried. Suppose Hofbauer, in his anger, made an anonymous phone call? Or suppose he was arrested for some other flimflam? Wouldn't he divulge everything he knew about the murdered man, in order to gain leniency from his captors? Indeed he would!

There were other perilous possibilities, too. What if the German wasn't actually a con man after all? Good God! What if he was only some pitiful looney, a cuckoo, a crackpot living out a harmless Newton-Einstein fantasy? Then there wouldn't be a goddamn thing to prevent him from running to the authorities with his strange little story.

Lenox sighed and licked his lips. But no . . . no, he thought. The professor couldn't be a cuckoo—not him. Hadn't he taken Cavanaugh for a tour of M.I.T., and there introduced him to a couple of confederates? Surely a cuckoo wouldn't have collaborators! Nor would a cuckoo be capable of delivering such glib, plausible patter; nor would he show such an inflexible interest in money; nor would he possess the ingenuity needed to construct a tricky machine like the Charge Translator which caused rocks to vanish before your very eyes. Hofbauer was a con man, all right—and no mistake.

Picking up the Scotch bottle, Lenox drained the last remaining ounce from it into his glass, and then settled again in his supine attitude to continue his ponderings.

But why did he worry? he asked himself. He was safe enough. Even if the bastard went to the police, what would his story amount to? He didn't have any hard proof—not a shred. Let the police come with their questions. If they wanted to know why he hadn't told them of his dead parishioner's singular plans, of the Swiss bank account and the power of attorney, he could always say that Cavanaugh had sworn him to secrecy, which was pretty much the truth. Wasn't he a clergyman, and wasn't there something called "ecclesiastic privilege"? And should they press him further, he could easily form a second line of defense; he could pretend he kept quiet because he was scared of the Internal Revenue people—afraid they would arrest him for his part in the shady financial manipulations. Yes, that should do it nicely.

The cops might not believe a word of it—they'd be rather dense if they did—but so what? His explanation didn't have to be believable, only possible. It was up to them to produce tangible evidence that bound him to the murder itself, and there wasn't any. And without such evidence they were impotent.

Of course, minor problems might arise. The church elders would doubtlessly disapprove of his behavior, but would they actually have the guts to demand his resignation? He didn't think so. Still, the furor could very well kindle their suspicions—prompt them to examine the parish accounts and ask questions about his complicated book-keeping system. If that happened, he'd lose the benefice for sure . . . not that it mattered much. Let them fire him. As long as he could avoid being arrested for the old man's murder, he didn't give a damn about anything else. To hell with them, too!

Cheered by these conclusions, and also by the whiskey

he had consumed, Lenox drew in his legs, put down his glass and got to his feet. It was almost two o'clock and he was hungry. He decided not to eat at home, but instead to treat himself to a shrimp salad at the Neptune Bar.

Since Mrs. Keller had of late been taking an indecorous interest in his drinking habits, he wrapped the empty Scotch bottle in a paper bag and carried it out with him when he descended the stairs and left the rectory. On Charles Street he threw it in a litter basket and then started off in the direction of the restaurant, which was at Park Square.

Hot though the day was, there were many people abroad. The antique shops, clothing boutiques, art galleries and bookstores lining the avenue were crammed with browsers. In front of Gingerich's place of business the sidewalk was a jungle of rubber plants, snake plants, orange trees, philodendra, potted palms and other greenery, while a little farther on, the neighborhood's principal provisions market had its façade half concealed by great mounds of bright fruits and vegetables. Above the shops loomed the venerable red brick buildings, drenched in an aureate sunshine that highlighted their numerous structural eccentricities and coaxed forth their subtle variegated hues. It was almost full summer, and the atmosphere was aquiver with vitality.

None of this was wasted on Lenox. Benignly regarding the scene, he decided that life wasn't so terrible, after all—Swiss bankers and German swindlers notwithstanding. He'd survive, come what may. The good breaks and the bad invariably evened out. It would only be a matter of time before coy Dame Fortune relented and dealt him a winning hand. He was certain of it.

At that instant, however, his skein of thought was

abruptly severed by a rude event. He had reached Branch Street and was on the point of crossing when he received a fearful thump on the back. Instantly angered, he whirled around to see who had delivered the blow. It wasn't necessary to look far. Standing at his shoulder and grinning like a half-wit was the threadbare waitress who had wheedled money out of him that day at the rectory.

"Hello! Hello!" she cried lustily as the passers-by stopped and stared. "Four times I called you, Reverend, but you must have been wool-gathering—or else in a state of beatitude. Ha, ha, ha! You remember me, don't you? Mary—Mary Urquhart." Catching hold of his arm, she leaned on him familiarly. "You lent me ten dollars not so long ago."

"Twenty dollars," Lenox croaked, recovering slowly from the brutal whack she had given him.

"Twenty, was it? Oh yes—I guess it was. What a good-hearted man you are! Sorry I haven't paid you back yet, but I'm still unemployed. Isn't that shameful, dear? I'm sure you appreciate that ladies my age—albeit I'm a mere forty-one, and as game as ever—experience difficulties finding new positions, so to speak. And restaurateurs, when it comes to hiring waitresses, are a bunch of troglodytes—a baying, slavering pack of *Pithecanthropi erecti*. All they're looking for is mini-skirted, round-bottomed, round-heeled teen-agers—the ravishers. Shocking. The whole goddamn nation really is undergoing a moral decline, isn't it?"

Lenox tried to free his arm, but the woman had a grip like a Gila monster. "I'm rather short of money this week," he said quickly. "I haven't a—"

"Oh, you darling!" she interrupted him. "I'm not asking for a penny—not a sou—though I admit I'm faint with hunger. No, no. I wouldn't accept anything from you—not until I've paid back what I owe. One can't run counter to one's code, can one? Besides, it certainly won't hurt me to lose a little weight, especially around the bust."

Suddenly Mary halted her prattling, cocked her head and sniffed the air like a bird dog. "I smell whiskey," she announced. "Yes, that's what it is. But is it your breath or mine? Ah well, I'll give you the benefit of the doubt, Padre, though I don't believe I've had any whiskey today. A couple of jiggers of Puerto Rican rum, a little chianti and a can of beer—but no whiskey. Never mind. We all have our peccadilloes. The point is, dear, I'm not after your money— as the lady on the subway said when she was caught with her hand in a gentleman's pocket. I only accosted you because I remembered what a cultivated—more, an eru- dite—person you are, and I was hoping you'd come over to my flat, which isn't a stone's throw from here, and give me an opinion on something. Would you?"

"What kind of a something?" Lenox inquired warily.

"Oh, nothing like that!" Mary protested, winking salaciously and jabbing him in the ribs with a surprisingly stiff forefinger. "No, this something is a knickknack, a geegaw, an *objet d'art*. I found it in a parking lot on Dartmouth Street—jettisoned there by some fleeing bur- glar, I suppose. A solid-silver bowl it is, and hoary with age. I'm sure it's one of Paul's."

"Paul's?"

"Paul's."

"Who the devil is Paul?" asked the minister in exasperation.

"Paul Revere, you silly!" she replied. "And if Paul made it, you can bet your booties it will be worth thousands. Come and see it. Right now. It won't take long."

"Sorry. I can't. I'm in a hurry," he retorted, making another attempt to liberate his arm, though without success.

"Don't be obstinate. Aren't ministers supposed to be helpful?" Mary said, pulling him along beside her. "For all you know, it might be of enormous historical value. Paul Revere—think of it. As a reverend, you should revere Revere. Ha, ha! Watch the curb, love."

Though Lenox was strongly disinclined to accompany the shabby woman, he was even less inclined to create a fuss in front of so many patently curious bystanders. Confident he could escape at the next intersection, anyway, he allowed himself to be steered into Branch Street without a struggle.

But escape proved an idle dream. Before they had traveled very far, he was suddenly hustled down a narrow side passageway and then summarily propelled into a miniature courtyard that was ringed by ramshackle, peaked-roofed houses of uncertain age and vague architectural pedigree.

"This is it, dear—Mary's nest," she proudly proclaimed, opening the basement door of one of these structures and nudging him forward. "Careful! Don't you trample Ogadai."

The minister stepped into a hot, murky living room. While his eyes were slowly adjusting to the dismal light, he heard a noise that sounded like the toot-toot-tooting of a toy trumpet. Staring down, he discovered its source—a small animal that was leaping up and down at his feet. As the creature appeared to be some kind of rodent, he was on the point of giving it a vigorous kick when his vision improved somewhat and he realized the thing was only a tiny dog. Lenox regarded it curiously. Frail and furry, it might have been a hairy Mexican hairless, he decided—if there was such a breed. He glared at the little brute, which immediately turned tail and slithered under a humpbacked couch, though still tooting defiantly.

"Don't frighten him, Reverend," Mary said, banging the door shut so hard that the building shuddered. "He's sensitive. Ogadai is a Chinese foo dog, and foo dogs are incredibly high-strung—as you probably know. Sit in the tub chair there." She indicated a rickety armchair. "All my best furniture is in storage in Cambridge. I'll bring you a mug of Chianti."

"No, thanks," he answered hastily. "I don't care for any. Where's the bowl you wanted to show me?"

"Oh yes—it's in the kitchen. I'll get it at once. But do sit. I can't stand men who hover."

She walked across the creaky floor, her step none too steady, and disappeared through a portiered doorway. Lenox lowered himself cautiously into the armchair and glanced around. On one wall a dusty chromolithograph of a lady strumming a mandolin hung crookedly; on another there was a cheap reproduction of a Degas ballerina. The furniture, while abundant and varied, looked as if it had all been salvaged from a town dump. It was chipped, scratched, splintered, and generally decrepit. As for the curtains, the portiere, the rugs and the upholstery—these were, without exception, ragged and rent. Even the scarf on the mantel and the antimacassars on the couch were hopelessly threadbare.

"Tatterdemalion," Lenox muttered under his breath.

Alongside his chair there stood a gate-leg table—badly warped—and on it, an old-fashioned typewriter. A sheet of paper was in the machine. He bent forward and began to read what was typed on it.

DEAR SIR,

You can't know how *agonizing* it is for me to have to write a letter such as this. Only the most *forlorn* and *desperate* circumstances, be assured, would force me to bare my heart *so shamelessly* to a stranger.

I am, sir, a lady of genteel birth and good education (Radcliffe '49), but through a series of *unimaginably ghastly* occurrences—occurrences over which I had *no control whatever*—I find myself today in a state of *total abject misery*.

I am ill with chronic cholecystitis. I am literally penniless. *And I am alone.*

My home, a small basement room, though it is without sunlight and has no amenities, is *very, very* precious to me. It is my *last* refuge, my little citadel, my island in a sea of *sorrow*—yet, unless I can obtain some money in the next seven days, to pay *at least* a part of what I owe in rent, I will be *evicted*. I will be hurled into the streets, there to subsist as best I can. Dear sir, I know what that is like. Once before I was reduced to such an extremity—sleeping in doorways, eating cold foods from cans, sitting for hours in the Public Garden on benches as hard as stone—and it is something *I dread worse than death.*

This, then, is why I write you. Having seen the story of your good fortune in a newspaper at the library, I indulged in a daydream. I thought that possibly, *just possibly*, a fellow human being, upon whom God has smiled more generously than He has on me—might be willing to come to my aid. You see, my plight is such that I have swallowed *all* pride. If you could *please, please, please* put a ten-dollar bill in an envelope and send it to the address below, I would

"Why, Reverend! You're peeking at my little epistle!" said Mary, reappearing in front of the portiere. "Aren't you a curious man! I mean to say, one filled with curiosity. I don't mind. Finish reading it if you like."

"No, no. I . . . I didn't want to read it," Lenox stammered guiltily, his cheeks beginning to glow. "I was simply glancing—"

"You needn't apologize, love. There's no harm done. It's not a billet-doux, after all—only a begging-letter. I write them now and then, when my resources are depressed. Do you like that particular style? It's one of many—the well-bred, fallen-on-evil-times scenario—and fairly successful, too. But the deserted-mother-of-five is even better. Neither of them, however, is as lucrative as the blind consumptive or the arthritic, palsied old lady who keeps reproaching herself for making typing errors. Heart wringers they are. Sometimes, of course, I eschew the typewriter and turn the stuff out by hand. That has certain advantages because you can convey moods with script. Frantic scrawls, trembly squiggles, blots, scratch-outs—there are all sorts of gimmicks. In both methods, water drops are highly effective."

"Water drops?"

"Yes. Tears, silly. I suppose you think I'm unprincipled, yet it's either that or become a public charge. Here's the bowl. Fabulous, isn't it?"

From behind her back she brought out a kind of compote, and set it down on a wattled bamboo table. Lenox looked at it without getting up. Even to his inexperienced eye it was clear that the bowl was a cheap, mass-produced, silver-plated piece of trash. Patches of brown copper showed through the thin argentine coating, especially along the outlines of the numerous dents that dimpled its surface.

"Revere never made anything like that," he growled, unable to conceal his disgust. "It isn't solid silver—it's just electroplated junk. Can't you see the copper underneath?"

"Is that copper? Are you sure? I thought it was tarnish," said Mary, picking up the article again to inspect it. "Jesus, you're right! Copper. How about that!"

Then, abruptly abandoning her interest in the treasure, she tossed it back on the table, where, after landing on its side, it rolled unsteadily over the edge and fell with a thud to the floor. Under the couch, Ogadai gave a toot of alarm.

"Well, what about sherry, eh?" the woman asked brightly. "I have some grand sherry—Vallejo Bristol Cream. Been saving it for the proper occasion, and what could be properer than sharing one's sherry with a minister of God?"

"I must go," said Lenox gruffly.

"Go? What are you talking about? You only just arrived. Don't act ill-bred, Reverend. You don't think a glass of wine is sinful—do you, love?" Mary smiled angelically. "Even our Savior took a jolt now and then. They say he made the stuff out of water, the sly dog. Isn't it a pity the New Testament doesn't give the recipe?"

Skipping over to a closet, she reached inside and brought out a bottle and two aluminum tumblers. "Here we are," she declared, putting everything on the gate-leg table. "You'll adore this, because it's as gentle as ewe's milk—an appropriate drink for a baby lamb like yourself. The bartender at the Mountjoy Manor gave it to me. Bernard Stringfellow his name is, and he's a former merchant mariner. Knows eight languages, including Portuguese—which, according to him, is the toughest of the lot. He claims Portuguese is so difficult that even the natives speak it with an accent. Swedish gives him trouble, too. Bernard says that the problem with Swedish is that it suffers from loose vowels. Yes, he's a cunning linguist, all right. Ha, ha! A tongue twister, that. Say when, Reverend."

"When," Lenox said immediately.

His hostess paid him no heed, however, and kept pouring until the wine slopped over onto the table. She handed the dripping glass to him, and then poured one for herself.

"Well, here's looking up your old address," she murmured.

The tumbler rose to her lips and descended a moment later completely empty. After a sigh and a hiccup she wiped her mouth on her sleeve.

Lenox hesitated. The wine smelled like vinegar. He tried to read the label on the bottle, but all he could see of it was a garish picture of a one-eyed pirate with a cutlass between his teeth.

"Drink, for God's sake!" Mary said, refilling her glass. "Where are your manners?"

Reluctantly he took two swallows of the sherry. They went down his throat like two swallows of molten lead. Hot tears came to his eyes, and he gasped softly.

The waitress seemed indifferent to his reaction, however. She dropped into a chair—the one that was nearest the bottle—and resumed talking. "It's an old and honorable profession. Goes back to classical times," she said blithely. "And in the nineteenth century, half the literate population of England engaged in some form of it. Wrote begging-letters, I mean. Ha, ha! You might try it yourself someday if you're strapped. More than once it's enabled me to make both ends meet—though, not being a greedy girl, I'm content enough if I can make one end meet."

Lenox could hear his stomach rumbling. He glowered at the woman and said maliciously, "Isn't it against federal law to use the mail to obtain money under false pretenses?"

"Oh blather! My pretenses aren't so false," she replied, slurring her sibilants. "I may color things a trifle, but that's just literary license. You must realize my epistles are almost minor works of art—they honestly are. Yes, minor works of art. Here, listen to this one."

Snatching a sheet from a pile on the table, she began to read it aloud in melodramatic fashion.

"DEAR MRS. ROTHWELL,

It said in the paper that you are a very rich lady and live in a fancy rich showplace in Brookline. I don't like bothering you, but I am a very poor lady that lives on Branch Street in one room in a basement. I read at the library where your dog won first prize at the dog show in Madison Square Garden in New York and I thought maybe you might help me because I got a dog, too. Of course, he is only a mutt and wouldn't win no shows or anything. But I love him. Anyhow, he's sick. Something is wrong with his insides and he don't eat no more—not even hardly water. I want to bring him to the vet, only it would cost 30 or 40 dollars and I do not have money to pay bills like that because I'm on social security. Could you lend me 30 or 40 dollars, Mrs. Rothwell? If you did I would never forget you for it and would mention your name in my prayers every Sunday at church. I love him like he was my baby. If he dies I will be broken-hearted until I die, too. His name is Skippy.

Yours truly,

MARY URQUHART."

"But it's all lies," said Lenox. "The postal inspectors

would send you to jail for ten years if that woman filed a complaint."

As she was busy finishing her second tumbler of Vallejo Bristol Cream, Mary didn't immediately answer. Even after the final drop had been imbibed she waited awhile, savoring the tang of the sherry, before saying indignantly, "Poppycock, Reverend—poppycock! What I wrote was the truth. I used to call Ogadai 'Skippy,' and he did have a tummy ache at the time."

"Did Mrs. Rothwell send you the money?"

"Only twenty dollars, actually. I was a bit let down. She owns the Great-Buy supermarket chain, you know. So I didn't exactly victimize her—did I, you handsome devil?"

Mary winked at him, then appeared to have difficulty getting her eye back open again.

"I have to be going," the minister said once more.

"Sit still, darling," she said. "I like your lips. They're lovely—like rose petals. My first lover had that kind of mouth, but unfortunately it was always full of deceits and falsehoods. What a plausible rascal he was, though. Could talk me out of anything, which is how he became my first lover, you see. Dennis Tweedsmuir was his name, and he hailed from York, Pennsylvania. He had a magnificent figure, equipped with all the essential charms, but he didn't have any scruples. A conscienceless con man—that's what he was, Reverend. When I got wise I used to call him 'The Prince of Condom.' Dennis was too dense to get the joke, however. We met on a summer's day in the Harvard Yard. I was reading *The Arabian Nights* and he, being a prominent member of the gymnastic team, was doing handsprings and cartwheels on the grass. Dennis was the first of many prominent members I was to encounter in life. Ha, ha! God, was he ever beautiful! One roguish glance from his azure eyes and I was reduced to a mindless, servile, slobbering wretch. I was so innocent in those days. Do you realize, Padre, that I honestly didn't know where babies came from? I'd heard a few rumors, but they all sounded ridiculous. And I was in college, for the love of Jesus—a Radcliffe girl! I remember being at a dorm party once, and a knowledgeable sophomore mentioned fellatio. I thought she was talking about stamp collecting. For all my purity, though, I had a passionate nature. I wasn't sure what I wanted, but I wanted it pretty badly. That's why I succumbed to young Tweedsmuir. It was a case of a lass and a lack. Ha, ha! Not that it was a long romance, because it only lasted a couple of months. To tell the truth, I was very glad when it ended, too. Gymnasts can be awfully demanding. He was double-jointed—so to speak. While most of my friends went to gynecologists, I went to a chiropractor. Reverend—what are you doing? Are you leaving so soon? What the hell's the hurry, dear? You just arrived a minute ago."

During the course of the lady's monologue, the hungry Lenox had slipped out of his tub chair, and pretending an interest in the framed mandolin player on the wall, had surreptitiously sidled across the room. He now took a ten-dollar bill from his pocket, laid it on the bamboo table, smiled and said, "Thanks for the drink, Mary, but I have to run. Must go up to Irving Street and call on a poor old fellow who's dying of dropsy."

Before she could utter another word, he opened the door and escaped into the courtyard. After the darkness of the basement, the sunshine was painfully bright.

Can any of her stories be true? he asked himself, still smiling. The woman really should be on the stage.

From inside the house, Ogadai toot-tooted furiously.

23

Just as he was going out the back door, on his way to the church, he was intercepted by Mrs. Keller. "A Professor Somebody on the phone, Reverend," she said.

"I can't talk to him now. I have a baptism to perform," Lenox replied. "Get his number, and I'll call him later."

"He said it was important." The housekeeper's plump face exhibited disapproval.

"I'll call him later," the minister repeated, dashing from the house.

However, when he got back from the church other things occupied his attention. Mrs. Osler and her daughter, Phoebe, dropped in to discuss the girl's impending wedding, and after they left, a boisterous delegation of teen-agers arrived with elaborate plans for a Fourth of July picnic in the Blue Hills.

There were moments when he might have telephoned Hofbauer, it was true, but he kept putting it off. Then, during the course of a dull lunch with three ladies from the Beacon Liturgical Music Society, he resolved finally not to return the call at all. What was there to say to the man, anyway?

Late that afternoon, while he was sitting in his room listening to the racing results on his transistor radio, Mrs. Keller banged on the door. "A lady is waiting to see you in the office," she announced.

Muttering oaths, he got into his jacket, turned off the radio and went downstairs. When he recognized the visitor as Lucia Pareto, however, he brightened considerably.

"Hello," he said.

"Hi," she responded, smiling uncertainly. "Sorry to bother you, Reverend. I tried to get in touch with Mr. Tilbury, but he's away for the weekend—up in Vermont. It's about my uncle's money. Nobody seems to be able to find it, so there's a big commotion. They wanted to dig holes in the backyard, to see if that's where it was hidden, but I wouldn't let them. Have you ever heard such an imbecilic thing? I adore that backyard, too. If it isn't raining, I usually sleep out there nights. The whole place is wild with weeds and creepers, like 'the forest primeval' in Longfellow's poem 'Evangeline.' Then, just a week ago, a fat detective whose name is Quimby said he was going to bring in some carpenters to sound the walls and pull up the floorboards, but I told him he'd have to shoot me dead first. That was that. Even though a lot of policemen are real fiends, they don't scare me. I've had too much experience with them, at sit-ins and demonstrations and things."

Lenox said, "I see," though his aspect was puzzled.

"Mr. Tilbury thinks there's a heap of money some-place, maybe as much as a million dollars," the girl went on. "It's a fantastic, fabulous idea, but I don't believe it myself. I mean, you only had to look at Uncle Amos once to know he wasn't a millionaire. He didn't even own a car!"

"True—still, you never can be sure about these matters, Lucia," he answered tentatively.

"I suppose not. He asked me to sort of search the house, Mr. Tilbury did, though he's already taken the stuff from the big desk. He says he's looking for a clue. The trouble is my uncle left boxes all over the place—boxes full of papers. They're in the cellar, the attic, the closets—everywhere—and some of the junk is fifty or sixty years old. I've been poking around but it's an awful job. Anyhow, I did find these this morning, up in his bedroom."

The girl dipped her hand into a woven-leather bag she was carrying, and pulled out an envelope. When she passed it to Lenox he accepted it uneasily, drew from it two sheets of coarse paper and read the words that Cavanaugh had scrawled on them. The first was a list of Swiss banks, with addresses and phone numbers. Though there were nearly twenty in all, the Banque Générale de Genève was not one of them. He almost smiled. The second page was also a list, but it contained only three names:

John Lenox
Walter Minton
Edward Tilbury

Beneath these was written: *Men you can trust.*

Lenox glanced at Lucia. "Do you believe the money is in a foreign bank?" he asked.

"Isn't it a possibility? Uncle Amos once told Mr. Tilbury that the banks in Switzerland were the best in the world." She wrinkled her forehead. "If he did send his wealth there, then this list ought to make it easy for them to find it. Did he ever mention banks—or anything like that—to you, Reverend?"

Pretending to search his memory, Lenox studied the girl's comely features. Was she suspicious? he wondered. At last he said, "I'm afraid he didn't confide in me on financial or business matters."

"Oh. I was hoping he did, since you were one of the few people he trusted. Funny. I had a strong intuitive feeling that you'd be able to tell me something. Just wishful thinking, I suppose. Could my uncle have put money in all those banks, Reverend?"

"Perhaps, but it hardly seems likely."

"It's almost as if he was deliberately trying to confuse everybody. This Walter Minton—do you know him?"

"Minton was an old friend of Mr. Cavanaugh's. He can't help you, though. He died last winter of diabetes."

"That lets him out, then, I guess," she said, shrugging her shoulders. "I'll give the bank list to Mr. Tilbury. Maybe he can do something with it. To tell you the truth, I'm really not anxious to inherit anything else because I wouldn't know what to do with a huge amount of money, except to give it to a charity maybe. I'm very satisfied just to own that wonderful old house. It's the best thing that ever happened to me in my whole life. And yet a lot of the neighbors think I'm crazy for living there all alone—because of the murder, you understand. Actually I'm extremely comfortable . . . and contented. I'm not frightened. That would be silly. I know God is looking after me."

"Yes. All the same, it might be wise to take ordinary precautions," said Lenox paternally. "Don't go in that alley after dark, for one thing."

"But I'm not afraid, Reverend—honestly. Morning, noon and night, I can feel God near me, and while He's by my side, how can any of them touch me?"

"Any of them? Any of whom?"

"Any demons. Demons like the monster who killed poor Uncle Amos," she answered forthrightly, her eyes fathomless pearly-gray pools. "Probably a godly man like you wouldn't be too aware of demons, but I've met so many. The Lord has always protected me, though."

There was a gap in the conversation then, the minister not knowing quite what to say. Perhaps Geraldine is right, he thought. The girl's intelligence does appear to be a bit flaccid. "Do you mean you've actually encountered demons, Lucia?" he asked at length.

"Yes, I have. Of course, I'm not talking about little imps with pointed tails. The demons I've met were wicked people—men and women who have spent their lives being selfish and cruel. You've met them, too, I'm sure. Just as some human beings become saints and angels through generous actions, other human beings are transformed into monstrous brutes through their crimes. Angels are hard to find, but the demons are everywhere. That's why there's such a tremendous need for kindness, honesty, love, humility—all those virtues Jesus Christ represents."

Adopting a seraphic expression, Lenox murmured, "Yes. I couldn't agree with you more." From beneath hooded lids his eyes made a quick, covert survey of her splendid figure. Her brain may be feeble, he thought, but there's nothing wrong with her body. He cleared his throat. "I'm delighted to hear you're happy in your new home. That's the most important thing. I imagine you're kept busy with housework. It's a big place. Those boxes of papers—are there many more of them to go through?"

"Oh yes! Six or seven, not counting the small ones. And it's such a boring, time-consuming job. The only reason I stick to it is because I feel it's my duty."

"Perhaps I could come over and help you."

"Do you mean it, Reverend? That would be great."

"For that matter, I could go back with you right now,"

said Lenox. "I have nothing on my schedule for the rest of today. How would that be?"

Lucia Pareto nodded eagerly. "It would be fantastic," she said, smiling and showing some very white, even teeth.

He told Mrs. Keller he was leaving, and they went out to the Volkswagen.

24

As he parked the car it occurred to him that this would be his first sight of the brownstone since the day of the murder. Involuntarily he glanced down Marlborough Street at the Palladian window. The blue velvet drapes were open wide, and the small table at which Cavanaugh had once enjoyed his morning meals was clearly discernible. For an instant he wished that the old miser were seated there now, bundled in his woolly robe and munching his slice of toast.

They mounted the stoop, entered the house and climbed the steep staircase to the master bedroom. There on the floor were three dusty cardboard cartons, seemingly afloat in a sea of age-yellowed papers. Without ceremony they sat down on the rug and began to sift and sort this chaotic mass of documents. There were rent receipts, tax notices, check stubs, packs of canceled checks, bank statements, bills of sale and reams of business letters—all of it mixed together in a jumble. Most of the material was dated prior to 1960, but occasionally more recent items would appear—and it was the recent items that Lenox was after. His inquisitive eyes scoured everything, for if any of those papers had his name on it, he was determined to discover it first and take it with him.

Yet for all his concentration on this task, he was keenly conscious of the girl close beside him. In the car on the way over, he had noticed she was wearing perfume—musk, patchouli or some other heavy, exotic scent. Now his nostrils seemed incapable of smelling anything else. The room was as full of fragrance as a sultan's seraglio. From time to time he would look at her—at the blackness of her hair, at her neck, her shoulders, her breasts, at the voluptuous curve of her thigh under her cotton dress, at her strangely pretty fingers and her narrow, sandaled feet—and a thrill of desire would gambol in his heart. With an effort he would drag his attention back to the scraps of paper and resume the search.

They worked thus for an hour, finding nothing of interest. Lucia got up then, stretched gracefully and went down to the kitchen to make tea. The minister took advantage of her absence to thumb feverishly through as much of the stuff as he could, and his diligence was rewarded. In with a bunch of vouchers he came upon a receipt for thirty-eight thousand dollars from the Banque Générale de Genève. He folded it hurriedly and slipped it into his pocket. What satisfaction he derived from intercepting this potential threat, however, was much diluted by the disquieting realization that there were probably others. He cursed Cavanaugh under his breath. Why hadn't the old scoundrel destroyed all references to the Swiss firm, as he had sworn he would?

The girl returned, carrying a tray. "Find anything?" she asked.

"Not yet. It's discouraging," he answered. "We're almost finished with this batch, though. Where are the rest of the boxes?"

"In the attic, in one of the upstairs bedrooms and down in the cellar. We can't possibly check them all today."

He didn't reply.

After pouring the tea, she took chocolate cookies from a package and arranged them symmetrically on a plate. "It sounds idiotic," she said, "but I'm a little afraid of finding the money."

"Why?"

"Well, I guess because I'm happy with things as they are. A fortune like that—it's bound to bring problems. When I was a child I had a bad experience connected with getting a lot of money. My father won twelve hundred dollars in a dice game."

Lenox's eyss brightened with interest. "Really? Where was this?"

"At a club in Revere. His friends escorted him home because they were afraid he'd get held up. He had loads of friends, my father did—mostly Italians, like himself. He was tremendously handsome, and at parties and things he could be very lively and amusing. At home, though, he was different—irritable, bitter and sometimes brutal. My poor mother told me once that he was like a stone on a beach: you see it lying on the sand, washed by the waves, and it's as brilliant as a jewel, but if you take it home and put it on a shelf it soons dries, and then it's nothing but a drab, gray pebble. I believe he married her, thinking she was rich. If so, he miscalculated. After the two of them eloped, my grandfather wouldn't give her a penny.

"When he won that money we were living in Swampscott, in a tumble-down house near the highway. He made a big fan of the bills and laid them on the table. I could hardly believe my eyes. I really thought it was a dream, because at that time I was having a lot of fantasies. The next day he took us into town and bought my mother a blouse and me a pair of loafers. Three days later he walked out of the house and never came back. He deserted us. He used the money to return to Italy, we found out eventually."

Lenox sighed. "How old were you?" he asked.

"Twelve. He never even sent us a letter—nothing. It was like he died, only worse. My mother was so shattered that she began to look like an old woman. As for me, Reverend—well, I couldn't stop thinking about him. Day and night, that was all I had on my mind. I started doing crazy things—cutting my hair very short, wearing shoes that didn't match, breaking car windows with rocks, stealing junk from the local stores. Then one afternoon I went into the bathroom and tried to hang myself. The only reason I didn't die was because the pipe I tied the rope to split open, and water came gushing out. My mother heard it dripping from the landing and ran up the stairs. There I was, hanging by the neck, but she was able to get me down and revive me. Right after that we moved to Beverly, although I made dozens of trips back to the old neighborhood, always hoping I'd see him. Even today, if I catch a glimpse of someone who looks vaguely like my father, I become very agitated. And it's so silly, really, because I wouldn't have a word to say to him, anyhow. What can you say to a person who is that evil? All you can do is pray for them."

The girl's story genuinely affected Lenox. He shook his head in dismay. "Well . . . I'm glad that pipe broke," he said gently. "The whole ordeal must have been awful, Lucia."

"It was awful, yes—and yet I think it made me appreciate life more. Afterwards, everything was more vivid. I have to admit, however, that I was sorry I didn't die—at the time. Do you consider suicide a sin, Reverend?"

"I'm not sure," he answered honestly, "but I would certainly say that suicide is a mad and morbid business. A healthy mind would never attempt it."

"I disagree," she replied firmly. "What about Socrates and Cicero and Cleopatra, and all the ancients who killed themselves after they had calmly decided that death was preferable to the life they were living? And the martyrdom of the early Christians—wasn't that a kind of suicide? Even Jesus' crucifixion was an act of self-destruction, wasn't it? He allowed it to happen—for the salvation of mankind, of course, but it was still suicide. The Church's view of suicide is one tenet I can't accept. Death, I think, is better than a life that has become unbearable."

Lenox opened his mouth to contradict her, then changed his mind and simply said, "You may be right, Lucia. Who's to decide such a grim question?"

They lapsed into silence and drank their tea.

After a time the clock that had tolled the hours the night he dined with Cavanaugh broke the stillness with five tinny peals.

"Should I tackle the boxes in the attic while you finish what's left here?" he asked, quite sure now that there was nothing incriminating in the remainder of the papers.

"Okay, Reverend, if you want to. I think you'll find it hot, though. The sun's been beating on that roof all day."

"I don't mind heat," he said, standing.

The attic, he found when he reached it, was cluttered with odds and ends of furniture. As there was no electricity, and the only illumination entered through a dirty skylight, he had trouble locating the cartons. However, when at last he did, he was pleased to see that there were only three of them, and none especially large. Moreover, two of the boxes were so thick with dust that it was obvious they hadn't been touched in years. He cut the twine on the third one, tore it open and dumped the contents on the floor.

A half-hour later, having discovered nothing significant, he came back down. Lucia was in a top-floor bedroom, examining a stack of water-stained, clothbound ledgers.

"You're not finished already, are you?" she asked.

"Yes. It wasn't as bad as I thought it would be," he answered, wiping his forehead with a handkerchief.

"Great! We're almost done then. Find anything?"

"No. Did you?"

"Nothing at all. Frankly, I don't expect to. Not now. I'm convinced Uncle Amos gave his fortune away on the sly, to avoid paying gift taxes." The girl threw the ledgers back into a box and dusted off her hands. "I'm done with this mess, too. That only leaves the stuff in the basement. Look, I was wondering if you'd like to stay for dinner. It wouldn't be anything grand—just some cold ham and cheese and potato salad—although I do have a bottle of French wine. Can you—or do you have other plans?"

"No, I'm completely free . . . and it sounds lovely."

"Terrific. If you don't mind a few ants, Reverend, we can dine alfresco—as my father used to say. We can eat out in the garden. It's very pleasant, and it doesn't get dark until late."

"All right. Why don't you go to the kitchen while I go down to the cellar to continue the treasure hunt?"

Lucia agreed to this, and he helped her to her feet. As they turned to leave, however, the chandelier hanging from the ceiling caught his eye. It appeared somehow familiar. Glancing around, he saw on the mantelpiece a bulky, black keyhole-shaped clock, and next to it an elaborate candelabrum. Instantly he remembered that this was the room he had peered up into—the room in which he had imagined glimpsing a human face—the morning he had battered the old man to death. Automatically he looked toward the window. There below, looking incredibly close, was the alley with its lines of garbage cans.

"Is something wrong?" the girl asked, a puzzled expression in her eyes.

"Wrong? No, no," he said quickly. "I was just . . . just daydreaming. Let's go."

25

Except for a couple of mature trees—one was an immense oak with boughs like gorged pythons—the backyard garden was a mad tangle of tough saplings and dense shrubs, wild flowers and weeds, high grass and vagrant ivy. She guided him through this woodland to a small clearing over which an army poncho had been suspended in such a way as to make a crude, slanted canopy. On the ground there was a sleeping bag, a hibachi stove, a mound of paperback books, a camp chair and sundry other amenities. They ate their dinner sitting on the sleeping bag.

And Lenox thoroughly enjoyed the meal, too. The potato salad—garnished with pimentos, green peppers, oregano and sprigs of fresh parsley—was delicious, while the wine, though only a cheap Burgundy, tasted as good as champagne. He finished the bottle before the girl finished her glass.

Above them, beyond the edge of the poncho, the green foliage and the sapphirine sky formed an intricate fretwork through which the last rays of the sun filtered down in a shower of gold. In the direction of the alley he could just see the lofty brick wall with its scintillating glass-fanged coping, and its stout iron door. *A bed of roses, and a thousand fragrant posies,* he quoted to himself. *Paradise enow.*

The search in the basement had yielded nothing. Lenox was very pleased. He felt safer now than he had the day before.

"Did you say you sleep out here?" he asked as they were concluding the picnic with cups of aromatic Italian coffee.

"Most of the time—yes," Lucia replied. "I love the naturalness . . . the wildness of the place. Do you see the ship's lantern there? I use that to read by. Sometimes, though, I just sit in the dark and stare up at the moon and stars. When I do that I get a gigantic feeling, as if my soul were as big as the universe itself. Do you know what I mean?"

"Yes," Lenox said. "I used to get the same sensation in Paris, gazing out my garret window late at night. It's intoxicating, isn't it? Almost rapturous."

"Paris? What were you doing there? Did you like it? They say it's fabulous. I've never been out of the country—except for an afternoon in Tijuana once."

"Paris is marvelous, and not just because of the famous landmarks, either. It's the way of life. The French seem to enjoy everything. They have so many different foods, drinks, entertainments. I was living in a chilly little room on the sixth floor of an old building that had no elevator. I wrote short stories and some poetry. It was . . . idyllic. Then my father died. I came home for the funeral, thinking I'd be able to return afterwards. There wasn't any money, though. My father had been the minister of the church for forty-four years, and he died penniless. I couldn't even raise the fare. Did you know my father had the church before me? He did, yes. I grew up in the rectory. Nevertheless, I was surprised when the elders offered me the benefice. I had the qualifications, of course, but I hadn't ever put them to use. Well, I accepted—assuming I could always leave when the chance arose. I'm still waiting."

The girl made a wry face. "You'd never desert the Church," she said. "I can't believe that. You have such a strong vocation. It shows so clearly when you're at the altar or in the pulpit. How could you dream of leaving, Reverend?"

"Dream? It's more than a dream, Lucia," he answered curtly. "Until I went abroad, I had never breathed anything but an ecclesiastical atmosphere—seven days a week, fifty-two weeks a year. I was like a prisoner."

"Kids always feel that way. I suppose your father was truly dedicated, and you found his dedication hard to live with. But now that you're older . . ."

"The man was too holy. It wasn't natural. Everything he owned he gave to God and the church. It was a form of sacrifice. I can remember him buying lilies for the altar when my mother didn't have money for a decent meal or a new dress. His flock took precedence over his family. At Christmas he would . . . But you don't want to hear about my childhood tribulations. The point is, even religion should have its limits."

"Probably your father was meant to be a monk—an anchorite. Was your mother pretty, Reverend?"

"Yes, until she became sick. She had gray eyes, like you." Lenox grinned wistfully. "However, the past is gone . . . and it won't return. Why don't you go to Paris someday?"

Lucia rested her dark head on the seat of the camp chair. "That would be fantastic. Héloïse and Abélard lived in Paris," she said, smiling.

"Who? Oh yes. What made you think of them? Abélard taught at the University of Paris. I attended some classes there myself—though, after a time, I lost interest."

"Recently I read an article about them in a magazine. Their lives were awfully tragic . . . and they were like saints."

"You're attracted to such things, Lucia—aren't you?"

"Yes, but I wasn't always so aware. It wasn't until I had a couple of religious experiences that I began to understand. I guess the most important one happened outside a doughnut shop in Lynn. That changed me completely. What happened was I opened the trunk of my car to get a pack of cigarettes, and inside the spare tire I saw the head of Jesus."

"In the spare tire?"

"Exactly. It was in the middle . . . hanging there . . . floating. The tire was like a picture frame for it."

Again the minister recollected the Gargan woman's comments. However, he maintained a grave countenance and said, "You must have been quite startled."

"I sure was. I don't think I've been the same since," the girl answered earnestly. "I mean, this was a true, genuine revelation. He was wearing his crown of thorns, and there were beads of blood on his forehead. I could see the scratches very clearly. Although He didn't say a word, just looking at his face and into his eyes—especially his eyes, Reverend—was enough to throw me into a tailspin. It happened in broad daylight, too—and I wasn't high or anything. Alfonso, the boy I was with, heard me cry out, but by the time he got there, Jesus was gone. Then I fainted."

"Amazing, Lucia."

"It only lasted a few seconds—the whole thing—and

yet it seemed much, much longer. It was an inconceivable experience . . . a tremendous jolt. Afterwards I changed my way of life. I bought a Bible that same day."

"Visions aren't as rare as we think," he declared. "Besides the Bible, what else do you read?"

"Everything," she replied. "Everything concerned with sin and virtue, good and evil."

She leaned past him to snatch some paperbacks from the nearby pile. As she did, her breasts brushed against his arm, and the short cotton dress she was wearing rode rapidly up one sleek alabaster thigh. To Lenox, this was a true, genuine revelation, but he managed to keep a grip on his impulses.

Sitting back once more, she handed him the books. The first was entitled *Excerpts from St. Augustine*; the second, *An Insight into the Sermon on the Mount*; the third, *A Handbook of Fiends and Werefolk*. The fourth and last was a dog-eared copy of *The Imitation of Christ*.

He turned a couple of pages of the volume on fiends, and then looked into the one on St. Augustine. "Aren't you rather young to be a mystic?" he asked.

"What has age to do with it?"

"It's usually the elderly who, being closer to death, take up the search for . . . other possibilities."

"Sometimes I feel close to death—though I feel close to life, too. Have you ever been ascetic? I mean, have you ever done any extreme fasting? That's like death, because it's a suspension of desire. At Stanford, where I took some courses last summer, I lived for three weeks on water and Uneeda biscuits. I didn't even take vitamin tablets. My roommate, Jilly Kravitz, was afraid I was going to die and kept begging me to eat something solid. She used to leave hamburgers and slices of pizza all over the place, but I wouldn't touch them. It was a fascinating experiment. I got awfully skinny, and I found out that when your mind is completely free of ordinary physical demands, incredibly strange thoughts come to you. At the end of the third week I could close my eyes and in a few minutes I'd see my father. The funniest part was that seeing him again actually made me feel good—made me feel warm and joyous. It was very beautiful. I could almost forgive him . . . almost love him. Asceticism is a great discipline. It gives you loads of objectivity and perspective."

Lenox gave the books back to her. "You're an unusual girl," he said.

"Do you think so? I'm glad," she said. "Everybody should be as individual as they can, I believe."

It was growing dark. The sky-leaf fretwork, so bright and colorful a short while ago, was now a dull pattern in black and gray. Outside the brick wall, a car engine muttered to itself as it moved down the alley.

Lucia leaned around him again to replace the books on the pile. Her shoulder pressed against his chest. Her hand grazed his leg. The oriental perfume, mingling with the natural fragrance of her long raven-black hair, was a pungent narcotic to his senses.

Having arranged the paperbacks to her satisfaction, she began to straighten up, but in doing so, she brought her face quite close to his and lingered in this position for what seemed an unnecessarily long time. That was too much for Lenox. He bent his head and kissed her on the mouth. She made a soft, soughing noise. He kissed her again, and felt her arm go around his neck. Together, they fell back on the sleeping bag. Whatever restraining notions had been in his mind before, whatever concepts of propriety had governed his actions up to that point, they now vanished in an instant. His hand groped over her body like a small creature with a will of its own. The front of the cotton dress was swiftly opened, and her breast emerged from it like a plump jack-in-the-box.

She made no resistance, uttered no protests. In seconds, they both succumbed to a wanton delirium.

26

Rupert Hofbauer phoned the next morning and demanded that he come immediately to the house on Blagden Street—"to consult about this Cavanaugh business," as he put it. Lenox, in a cheery mood and feeling confident he could convince the German that the money was lost forever, agreed to go and see him.

As he drove the Volkswagen to Copley Square, his mind played happily with the events of the previous night. How beautiful Lucia had been—and how ardent! The entire episode had unfolded like some sweet, ecstatic dream. She'd been flustered when it was over, of course, but there hadn't been any tears of remorse or counterfeit cries of indignation.

"I don't even know your first name," she had remarked.

"It's John," he told her.

"John," she repeated. "That's a name I've always been terribly fond of—since I was a little girl. Well, John, I never meant to start a thing like this. It happened awfully fast, didn't it?"

"I can't understand what came over me," he said, doing his best to look penitent.

"Oh, don't worry about it. These . . . emotional storms sometimes catch us by surprise, and maybe it's better that way. Anyhow, there's nothing sinful involved. Love can't be a sin, because it just isn't wicked. Love is blessedness. Love is the warm and comforting light of the soul."

Hearing this, Lenox, who had been standing up getting dressed, joined her again on the sleeping bag.

By the time he returned home and crawled into bed, he was quite groggy from it all. He slept soundly, however, and felt very fit when he awoke in the morning.

"It was like a dream," he whispered as he sped down Beacon Street, "like a page of poetry."

On Huntington Avenue he found a parking space, left the car in it and walked around the corner to the house. From an open front window the wail of a violin came, but it ceased when he rang the buzzer. Hofbauer, his expression saturnine, let him in. They went into the parlor. The violin and its bow were resting upright in one of the Queen Anne chairs, and there was sheet music on the wrought-iron music stand.

Lenox sat down, crossed his right leg over his left, and said, "I'm sorry if I was rude to you, Professor, that day on the telephone. I was upset by the way things had turned out. To waste so much time and effort on a fool's errand is enough to make anyone irritable. Have you been in touch with the Banque Générale de Genève?"

Hofbauer's thin nose trembled infinitesimally. He shook his head.

The minister shrugged. "It's not for me to tell you what to do," he declared, his voice conciliatory, "but I'm almost certain a properly worded letter to those people would bring a reply that would clear up the whole matter."

"You are saying still that the money is in Europe, Reverend Doctor?" the professor asked.

"Of course," said Lenox.

"It is a funny story."

"It's a true story."

"I don't think it is true."

"Write to the bank, then—or phone them. They'll inform you that Cavanaugh actually did revoke my power of attorney. They'll verify every word I've said. The old man changed his mind, wrote them a letter, and that's all there is to it."

"He did not write such a letter," Hofbauer replied firmly.

"Oh, come on, Professor! How can you say that?"

"I can say it because he told me he did not write such a letter."

"Has he been sending you more messages from the Otherside?" asked Lenox, sneering.

"Yes, yes. He wants his gold. He is very furious."

The two men, each regarding the other with hostile glances, fell silent. Neither seemed willing to attempt a fresh verbal thrust. On an upper floor of the house someone turned on a shower and the faint noise was like the patter of distant rain.

At last Lenox smiled affably. "You aren't being reasonable," he observed. "A man of science ought to recognize what's perfectly obvious. You think I stole the money, but if that were so, why would I be sitting here talking to you? If they gave me the million dollars in Switzerland and I decided to keep it for myself, why would I return to Boston? I have no wife, no children—no ties at all. Why should I come back and run the risk of being asked awkward questions by, among other people, yourself? Why?"

"Bah!" said the German. "If you went away unexpectedly, the police officials would at once be suspicious, and they would look for you. No, your scheme is to escape when everything is quiet, to run out of town when the complete affair is forgotten. That is your tactic—but it doesn't fool me."

"You're wrong. Had I remained abroad, believe me, no one would have thought it especially peculiar. And even if anyone had, what difference would it have made? If the power of attorney was still valid, then the money was legally mine. You and I had no written contract. Under the law, Professor, I wouldn't have been obliged to give you a penny."

"But other dangers existed for you—worse dangers."

"Really? Such as?"

Hofbauer, who had been standing near the fireplace with his hands in his coat pockets, now walked to the far end of the room and sat down on a straight-backed chair. Behind him, on a sideboard, a half-dozen bronze or spelter busts were arrayed. Flanked by Dante and Beatrice on one side and Benjamin Franklin on the other, his own head was almost lost in the crowd.

"Let us suppose I tell the criminal authorities this funny story," he said. "What, Reverend Doctor, would be their immediate behavior?"

"They'd write to the Swiss bank—that's what their immediate behavior would be. And they'd find out Amos Cavanaugh canceled my power over his account."

"*Ach!* You are not amusing, sir. With my information the police would take you to their office, and there they would propose many questions—difficult questions—for you to answer. The thing that would interest them most extremely would be the coincidence, of course—the coincidence of the poor gentleman's murder coming so soon after he gave you control of his money." Hofbauer smirked. "Such a coincidence is very mysterious. It is against the mathematical laws of probability. Perhaps they would not consider it a coincidence at all, eh? Perhaps they would conclude it was cause and effect."

"Are you serious?" Lenox asked, feigning astonishment. "Are you actually accusing me of killing Mr. Cavanaugh? You must be insane."

"They will not think I am insane, the police. They are not stupid. So, if I tell them where to investigate, their scientists will discover quick the evidences they require. A hair, a speckle of dust, a little blood on a shoe, a fingerprint, a thread of clothing—that is plenty of proof for detectives. Yes, and plenty for a jury and a judge, also."

"No doubt—only I didn't murder the man."

Hofbauer lengthened his smirk into a sly grin. "But you did," he said softly.

The three words, uttered as they were with absolute conviction, fell like three drops of burning poison on Lenox's ears. A numbness swept over him. He tried a scornful smile, and found that his lips weren't working properly. He fidgeted, coughed and rubbed his hands together as if they were cold.

At last he managed to say, "You . . . you're a raving maniac."

"I know positively you killed him," declared Hofbauer, manifestly enjoying himself.

The minister glared at him. "You do, do you? How?" he asked in a tone barbed with sarcasm.

"Because the deceased victim told me—that is how."

Again the professor's reply had a ring of certainty, and again his hearer was rattled by it.

"You must take me for a . . . for a simpleton," Lenox retorted. Then, recovering some of his poise, he went on more steadily, "Listen, Hofbauer, listen to me. It's time to stop spouting nonsense, to stop pretending you're a genius with a magic machine, and that there's life after death and a place called the Otherside. What you really are is a damn swindler. Your game was to hustle a senile old man out of his fortune. Yes—and who the devil knows how many other elderly people you've robbed with the same trick. Did you believe for an instant that I was taken in by your absurd contraption? Did you actually imagine that your blathering about anti-matter, cosmic rays and electromagnetism would hoodwink someone of normal intelligence, someone whose brain wasn't addled by age and illness? If you did, you're a jackass. I've known you for a confidence man since the night Cavanaugh showed me the advertisement in his newspaper."

Hofbauer's black eyes narrowed, his face flushed slightly and his wild mustache quivered. Yet when he answered, his raucous voice was free of rancor. "Why, then, did you not inform the officials, eh?" he inquired. "Was it not your duty to unmask this frightful, nasty swindler?"

"Well . . . I meant to, originally. I didn't, though, because I could see it made the poor fellow happy to think that his money would follow him into the next world. Telling him the truth would have shattered his dream."

"How noble and commendable! Only, now he is dead, and you still do not go to the police. Why is that?"

"Because I don't like getting involved in sordid affairs

of this kind. I wasn't anxious to send a man to jail. Besides, no crime had been committed."

"But—excuse me—would it not be your duty to protect other people, other victims? Your conscience—wouldn't it push you to the police station? An honest man like you couldn't permit a humbugger like me to continue onward—cheating sick old folks out of their money with a crazy machine. Isn't that so?"

Uncrossing his legs, Lenox wriggled deeper into his chair. "I hadn't any proof," he muttered. "None at all."

The German made a derisive noise. "Proof you would not need. Just a word to a policeman would be completely sufficient. No, the true reason you did not go to them is that you, not me, are the swindler. And worse even than that, you are a murderer also. Such a person would not desire conversations with policemen. Such a person would stay very far away from them—as you have done. Am I not correct?"

"Don't talk rubbish, Professor. What about you? If you're so sure I'm a murderer, why haven't you called the police? Aren't you an honest man?"

"I might yet do it," Hofbauer replied stolidly, "though not for morality reasons. Remember, I am not a minister. I am a scientist only. To me, ethics are variable factors. They differ in one country from another. Previously I have told you, Reverend Doctor, that my work is everything to me, and that the commission Mr. Cavanaugh was paying for this service was for my future projects and experiments desperately vital. I cannot stop to worry about morality. What are human laws compared to the laws of the universe?" He sighed heroically and folded his hands over his round stomach. "But we have chattered enough, eh?

Tell me now when you will bring the gold—or the cash, if you prefer. I myself can change it into metal."

Upstairs the shower was abruptly turned off. The parlor became very quiet. Lenox, his optimism gone, morosely contemplated the ebony grand piano. He had argued valiantly, yet he had gotten nowhere. His antagonist was as slippery as an eel. And it was all so ridiculous—messages from a dead man! There had to be a way of tripping him up, of demonstrating the silliness of his contentions. The machine—that was the weak point in the whole elaborate fantasy. What a shame he knew so little about physics and chemistry!

"It would for myself be most convenient if you brought the money this morning," said his host. "I can arrange every detail—and after, when word comes from the old gentleman on the Otherside, I can commence the translations. But first I will subtract my twenty-thousand-dollar fee." He chuckled. "I have truly earned it, have I not?"

Lenox glanced up. Something goaded his memory—some vague association. Mechanically his mind began replaying Hofbauer's last remarks: ". . . *and after, when word comes from the old gentleman on the Otherside, I can commence the translations.*" He shook his head and whispered, as though thinking aloud, "The Otherside. There just isn't such a place."

"Ha! For a pastor of the Christian church," said Hofbauer amiably, "you hold unorthodox opinions. No heaven, Reverend? You talk like an atheist—a skeptic."

But Lenox was no longer listening. In a nook of his brain he suddenly discovered the thread he had been hunting for. What had pricked his laggard memory was the phrase *"when word comes from the old gentleman."* Word, word. That was it, of course! Why hadn't he thought of it sooner?

The word! The "insurance policy" Cavanaugh had devised. During the turmoil of the past few weeks he had forgotten all about it!

Concealing his elation behind a somber countenance, however, he recrossed his legs and said, "Professor, you keep insisting you've heard from Mr. Cavanaugh since his death. Naturally, that's difficult for me to swallow. It's fantastic— absurd! Still, there happens to be a way you could convince me—convince me beyond a doubt—that you're speaking the truth."

"Excellent, sir! Excellent! To do so would be my sincerest pleasure. Tell me, please—how?"

The minister, clearing his throat and fixing his eyes on his companion, replied, "As you probably know, your client didn't entirely trust you, which was why he brought the stone for you to send the day we came here. He had qualms. He dreaded being tricked out of his wealth—an understandable attitude, I think, given the peculiar circumstances. Therefore, to protect himself, he contrived a clever stratagem. He furnished me with a secret password—one that only he and I would know. His intention was to tell you the password, too, but not until he was dead and had reached the Otherside. Do you see the point? When the time came for me to bring the gold, I was to ask you first what that password was—and if you were unable to provide it, I was instructed not to give you anything at all. Because, Professor, if you didn't know the password, that would mean you weren't in touch with Mr. Cavanaugh, and that there really wasn't an Otherside—that, in short, the whole deal was phony from beginning to end. Now, what is the password? Can you tell me?"

The satisfied look on Hofbauer's face had, as he listened to Lenox's brief exposition, gradually faded away.

It was replaced by an expression of almost animal wariness. "I have heard nothing of this," he said defiantly. "Is it some stupid idea you have made up?"

"It could be, couldn't it? But on the other hand, it could be the truth, too," answered Lenox, permitting himself a smile. "Suppose we make a bargain, a pact, a gentlemen's agreement? You get the password from the dead man, and I'll deliver his money to you."

The professor scowled. "This is more funny business. I am sure of it. You are attempting a deception—something dishonest or . . . treacherous."

"If that's what you believe, why don't we go down to the Charge Translator, press a few buttons and ask Mr. Cavanaugh for the password right now?"

"But maybe he is not available. Do you think, over there in the anti-universe, he waits all day by the machine?"

Lenox laughed and got to his feet. "No, I don't," he replied, "but you can have one of those anti-people scout around and find him, can't you? Come on, let's give it a try. Don't you want the twenty thousand dollars, Professor?"

Standing up quickly, Hofbauer put his hand in his pocket. "You play a game, I think," he said in his raspy voice. "This I do not like. We will see, though. Very well. Very well. Go then to the cellar, Reverend, and I will follow. Do you know the way? It is to the right."

The minister shrugged his shoulders and sauntered past the frowning Parian head of Richard Wagner on its marble column. Hofbauer trailed along behind, muttering to himself. They went to the basement door, descended the wooden stairs, passed through the room filled with packing cases and at last reached the carpeted and whitewashed cubicle that was their destination. The bulky electrical appliance sat against the opposite wall like a squat automated octopus awaiting its next victim.

Going up to it, the German began fiddling with dials and switches. The dentist-drill hum broke the stillness. "To warm, it requires some few minutes. But do not have big hopes, because it is strongly improbable that we will catch him in their laboratory. He might be miles and miles far away."

Groping inside his jacket, he brought out a small loose-leaf notebook and a ball-point pen. He wrote a hasty message on a page of the book, removed it by opening the rings and showed it to his guest.

Lenox, who had been leaning complacently against the frame of the slate blackboard, took the page from him and read what was on it.

FOR MR. CAVANAUGH, PLEASE.

THE REV. DR. LENOX IS HERE, AND HE SAYS THERE IS A PASSWORD I MUST KNOW ABOUT. YOU DID NOT TELL ME THAT. WILL YOU SEND AT ONCE THE PASSWORD, PLEASE?

HOFBAUER

"This should do splendidly," the minister remarked, his eyes alight with amusement. "I hope we won't have any short circuits or burned-out fuses now, Professor. If that happened, it would be a pity."

Ignoring the gibe, Hofbauer unbolted the oblong hatch and placed the letter inside the machine. He shut the door tightly, tapped and studied a crescent-shaped gauge, turned a ruby-colored knob, threw a green switch and stepped back.

Both men were silent, each peering intently at the

piece of paper. After a short while the cloud of yellow light flashed abruptly behind the gray-tinted window. It endured a fraction of a second, and then was gone—taking with it the loose-leaf page. The chamber was empty again.

In spite of himself, Lenox gaped. The Charge Translator's performance was no less impressive this time than it had been previously. He decided that, for all his faults, Rupert Hofbauer was a first-rate illusionist. Not even Harry Houdini could have managed the thing better.

"We will wait," said the professor, "a half-hour, an hour—I do not know how long."

"Okay," Lenox said, still gazing in wonder at the vacant compartment.

"It is unfortunate there is all this foolishness. In my own life, sir, I try to accomplish tasks simply and efficiently, without wasted energy and crazy mix-ups. When he first came to visit me—Mr. Cavanaugh—I told him I would do what he desired, but the arrangement must be confidential and . . . not complicated. He agreed totally. After, though, he wanted to bring here lawyers and other people. We had an emotional discussion, very loud, and at the end I capitulated a little and allowed him to bring you. Now, what has occurred? We have a big mishmash. Passwords! This story you tell me—if it is true—is a children's game. But I would not be surprised. He never trusted me one inch, that man—and I am respected by the scientific fraternity on every continent in the world." Mustache trembling, Hofbauer heaved a piteous sigh. "He thought always I was a crook . . . just like you do."

"Human beings are suspicious creatures," Lenox said urbanely, offering him a cigarette. "We can only hope they will be more cordial on the Otherside."

"*Ach!*" snorted the German, refusing the cigarette. "I

do not want to talk about over there, but I think also they have suspicion and misery."

"Misery?" Lenox looked sly. "Wouldn't it have to be anti-misery, Professor—and wouldn't anti-misery be happiness?"

A hint of a smile appeared briefly on Hofbauer's lips. "Quite so—only you are forgetting there would exist anti-happiness, too. Therefore, you could not escape sadness that way, eh? Everybody desires heaven. They want a nice place to go when they die. It is silly—this heaven business. What, Reverend, would be the value of angels, of dead people in nightgowns playing harps and flying around with wings that make ridiculous the laws of aerodynamics? And who would be happy floating for eternity on fluffy clouds? Religion—bah! That is why, when you speak morals to me, I don't get excited. No. Virtue . . . justice—they are intellectual toys. For myself, what is good for science is a virtue, and what is bad for science is an evil. But when I write my treatise—my grand book—I will include all these things so the world will stop dreaming stupid dreams finally."

Lenox listened tolerantly to this spate of opinions, assuming that the professor, behind the smoke screen of words, was busy trying to work out a solution to the dilemma that faced him. Yet there was no adequate solution. Sooner or later the fellow would have to murmur a lame excuse, and then the whole ludicrous frolic would be at an end. Lenox felt a bit sorry for him. The poor bastard had expended a great deal of effort on his scheme. To have it collapse just when it looked like it was going to pay off would surely be demoralizing for him. He recollected his own bitter experience at the Swiss bank. Ah well, those were the breaks of the game. A gambler must be prepared to lose.

Taking a drag on his cigarette, he glanced at his wristwatch. There didn't seem to be much point in hanging around in a cellar waiting for a message that couldn't possibly come, so he said, "I have some errands to do, Professor. It might be better if you call me this evening and let me know how you made out."

Hofbauer frowned. "If it is what you wish—but I wanted badly to settle every detail today."

"You said yourself that he might be miles away. Call me about six o'clock, why don't you?"

"All right . . . all right. I hope, sir, this business is not a crooked trick. You understand, there is still the police I can go to. If you are lying—"

A burst of light in the Charge Translator's chamber interrupted Hofbauer's comments.

"Ah! An answer!" he exclaimed. "Very good. Excellent."

Together, the two men hurried forward and stared in the window. There, on the ceramic tile of the little compartment, lay a slip of blue deckle-edged paper. Hofbauer quickly opened the door and took it out, but before he could read it, the minister snatched it from his hands.

A single glance was enough to send Lenox's heart plummeting to the pit of his stomach. The message was in script, and the script—frail and jerky—was undeniably the dead old man's. It said:

Tell that damn butcher hell is waiting for him. He killed me—coaxed me out into the alley with a trail of dollar bills, and then beat me to death. He did, he did—and I trusted him. Tell that murderer the password is "Rupert Hofbauer." I want my money. I need it. I must have it, at once.

A. Cavanaugh

27

Crossing Arlington Street, he almost hit a girl on a bicycle. She yelled at him, but he took no notice. He drove the Volkswagen as if in a trance. Scraps of unpleasant dialogue echoed softly in his ears. On the windshield he could see a faint, spidery writing—ominous words, sinister phrases.

What happened? he wondered.

Hadn't he, with his own hands, hammered the miser down and smashed his skull to shards? With his own eyes, hadn't he watched them bury him in the earth at Mount Auburn Cemetery? How could the man now testify against him?

Lenox clutched the steering wheel so tightly that his knuckles blanched. Once more, through a viscous mental haze, he saw Hofbauer smiling—heard him say, "That is a smart idea, to make my name the password. Ha! It is amusing. Never would I guess it—never." Once more he felt despair chill his bowels and paralyze his tongue. Once more he listened to the German demand the money, bluster angrily, threaten to phone the police.

What happened? What happened?

Cavanaugh was dead—as dead as Caesar or Charlemagne or Raphael or Isaac Newton or Abraham Lincoln. How could this broken-headed corpse write a letter? It was impossible. And yet, who but Cavanaugh knew the password? Who but Cavanaugh knew about the ground bait of dollar bills? No one—no one on this planet. There wasn't any way Hofbauer could have obtained such information—unless he could read his, Lenox's, mind. No, it must all be true. It had to be. The professor was genuine. He really had made some scientific breakthrough in the field of anti-particles, with his weird little Charge Translator. And there actually was an anti-universe, and a region in it called the Otherside.

"What a terrifying notion!" the minister mumbled. "It means that anything is possible . . . anything at all."

He shot a quick look at the milky-blue sky over Beacon Hill, as though hoping to fathom with the naked eye the billions of light-years of space that lay in that direction.

"There might even be a God," he said tremulously.

28

Somehow, after the initial shock, he had been able to gather his wits together and convince Hofbauer that the money couldn't be produced immediately. Remembering that it was Saturday, he had sworn that the million dollars was stowed in a safe-deposit box—and thus unavailable until Monday.

The professor had ranted and grumbled, but ultimately he was compelled to consent to the delay. He warned, however, that if the money—all of it—wasn't in his possession by noon, Monday, then Lenox would wake up Tuesday morning "in the penitentiary."

A second message had been sent to Cavanaugh explaining the situation. That was the last macabre act of the ghastly episode. Vaguely the minister recollected going back up the stairs, being shown to the door, finding his automobile and driving off. It had been a nightmare.

Slumped now in a chair in the rectory office, a large glass of sherry in his unsteady hand, he realized there was only one cannonball left in his locker. He must pack his bags and flee. As soon as the bank opened, Monday, he must clean out the accounts, head for Logan Airport and grab the first jet for England. Later he could make his way to Dublin and lay low there until he was able to formulate some kind of long-range plan. The church accounts still contained more than three thousand dollars. That should be enough for a few months at least.

Lenox drained his glass and set it on the desk. The telephone rang. The jangling noise caused him to jactitate sharply. With his heart pounding, he picked up the receiver. The caller proved to be Geraldine Gargan, gay and effusive as ever, inviting him to lunch. His thoughts were so disordered that he could think of no excuse for refusing, and therefore agreed to see her in half an hour. Wearily he got up from his chair. How glad I'll be when it's over, he reflected.

Since Geraldine lived on nearby Lime Street, there was no need for him to take the car. He left the house and walked down Pinckney Street, his mind churning. He'd have to phone the terminal and find out the flight schedules. The Volkswagen—should he try to sell it? It wouldn't bring much; still, every little bit helped. And then there was Cheeks, the horseplayer, who owed him sixty or seventy dollars. Perhaps, tonight or tomorrow, he could collect a part of that. Would the police be waiting for him at the London airport? No, no. Hofbauer wouldn't go to them that quickly. He would hesitate, sit around hoping, until late in the day. Should he peddle the rectory television set? He had bought the damn thing out of his own money. What else was there? In his letter Cavanaugh had threatened him with hell. Was he only chattering, or did he know for a fact that the place existed? Those two paintings in the dining room, the primitive landscapes that had been hanging there for a hundred years—an antique dealer might pay a high price for them. And there was the cut glass in the china closet. But how would he have the time to do all this? Suppose the police didn't believe the German's story? What then?

Turning into Charles Street at the bottom of the hill, he spied Jerry Gingerich standing in front of the pet shop midway down the block. The man was staring in the window at something, his form as motionless as a form of stone. Imprinted on his face was a hard smile—an icy, rigid, lifeless sort of smile.

When he drew near, Lenox said, "Hello, Jerry."

The florist turned slowly. His smile lingered for a moment, then faded away. "Reverend! How are you?" he said. "I was just looking at the aquarium here. I often do. It's become a regular habit with me."

In the pet-shop window, a large glass tank full of bubbling green water sat amid a hodgepodge of rubber bones, packaged birdseed, dog collars and similar wares. Undulating goldfish, dozens of them, moved languidly about in the tank's murky depths.

"Oh? I didn't know you were interested in fish," Lenox replied. "Do you have any at home?"

"No. I used to, when I was a boy down in Maine. I kept shubunkins and fantails. I wouldn't mind getting an aquarium for Joseph and Jerome, but I guess they're too young to take care of a thing like that—and I can't do it myself. I have no time. You have to take good care of them, you know—otherwise they die. Lately I don't have time for anything. I noticed this morning that my fingernails were very long—like a woman's, almost—because I hadn't cut them in weeks. I just forgot—forgot I had fingernails."

"Have you been feeling okay, Jerry?"

"Pretty good. I love to watch them swimming around and around in there. It's very restful. I wish I could jump in myself."

The minister was anxious to be on his way, but he was struck by his parishioner's appearance. There were livid half-moons beneath Gingerich's eyes, and his cheeks didn't have much color. His speech, too, was peculiar—the pace slow and deliberate, as though he were examining each word before uttering it.

"How are Vicki and the boys?" Lenox asked.

"Fine, fine. Couldn't be better," Gingerich answered. He turned to regard the goldfish once more, and in so doing, gave off a fragrant whiff of flowers that was almost as strong as perfume. "She's been after me to go to Dr. Lifkin for a talk. He's a nice fellow—Lifkin. But, like I've said, he can't help me. My problems aren't exactly in his field. I keep telling Vicki that."

"Well, he's a psychiatrist. What sort of doctor do you think you need?"

"I'm not sure, Reverend."

"Have you been getting more of these impulses?"

"A few. I get angry, sometimes . . . feelings of rage. I want to hit people—to beat them with my fists or with a stick or something. All at once, for funny reasons, I become furious. I want to knock people down and kick them. It's crazy, but the odd thing is, it never seems crazy when it's happening. It seems perfectly reasonable. The other day I actually got into a fight with a man in Woolworth's—a man I didn't know from Adam." The florist shook his head in perplexity. "I found him . . . offensive."

"Offensive? In what way?"

"I don't know, to tell you the truth. It's so stupid. I couldn't stand him, though. I couldn't bear to be near him.

Then, when I moved to another part of the store, he seemed to follow me. It was his ears, I think. They were hairy and large . . . and their shape was strange. They didn't look human—I mean, like human ears. They looked like monkey ears to me. But that's all right. It wasn't too bad. We just pushed each other a couple of times. It wasn't really violent. I wonder if I'll ever do something really violent."

"I can't believe you would, Jerry. You're not by nature a violent person. However, you're obviously having difficulties—perhaps it's an attack of some type of mania—so I would strongly advise you to go back to Dr. Lifkin, as Vicki says."

"Mania? Mania? You used to tell me it was only nerves, Reverend. Mania is a psychosis. Manic people are schizophrenic. The word 'maniac' comes from 'mania.' "

Lenox saw the florist's face reflected in the window. He suddenly realized that Gingerich wasn't watching the goldfish. Instead, he was using the glass as a mirror to watch him.

"By 'mania' I simply meant agitated behavior—a tendency to get excited," said the minister. "Nerves can cause that, just as they can cause depression or hypochondria or any illness. You're not a madman, Jerry. If you were, how could you operate your shop . . . or run those clothing sales?"

"But madmen can act normal, and normal men can act mad," Gingerich replied, his speech still measured and slow. "You often read terrible, cruel stories in the newspapers. Look what happened to poor Mr. Cavanaugh—murdered on his doorstep. And it wasn't robbery, either. He was killed for nothing—slaughtered. A lunatic must have done that. Maybe he's walking around like you and me, and doesn't even remember it."

"I doubt that that's the case," said Lenox shortly.

"You do? Why? The human brain is a funny instrument. It's full of circuits and gadgets, and the nervous system shoots out of it like wires. They say it's a computer, and computers can break down, can't they? I've had times when my brain seems to stop working, which is a strange experience. It becomes empty. You don't have any more thoughts. Has it ever happened to you, Reverend Lenox?"

"No. According to scientists, it isn't possible to stop thinking. Even when you sleep, you think."

"Scientists don't know everything. It's possible, all right—and it's also very scary. The brain becomes a void. All activity shuts off. You feel dead . . . completely dead. You're destroyed. Not only that, you feel as if your soul is dead, too. Obliterated. And the worse part is that you're somehow conscious of what's happened. 'I think, therefore I am.' You know that quotation, don't you?"

"Yes," answered Lenox, perceiving that the blue vein in Gingerich's temple had begun to squirm fitfully. "Descartes was the author of it. *Cogito, ergo sum* in Latin."

"I didn't study Latin but I've heard the quotation, and believe me, what the man says is true. If you think, then you are. And if you stop thinking, only for a hundredth of a second, then you aren't. You don't exist. You're gone. You're annihilated, at least until your brain starts working again, which you can't be sure it will do. I wish I could describe what it's like. I can't, though. Words are . . . just words. They're ideas, words—not feelings. You can have the word 'fear' in your mind, but that doesn't mean you're afraid, does it? Terror, panic—they don't come close to the reality. True terror is huge. It's a gigantic world—one that very few people know about. Most human beings are like those fish. They believe the world is the size of an aquarium. They don't know what's outside their own little fishbowl . . . but I know. Maybe it's just as well that I can't give a good description, Reverend, because if I could—if I could paint a clear picture of nonexistence for you—well, for the rest of your life you might keep thinking about it. You might not think of anything else."

These odd statements were delivered with such earnestness by the florist, that they made Lenox apprehensive. Where did he get these wild notions? What was he suffering from—some sort of depersonalization? Why the hell didn't he go back to his psychiatrist?

"I don't know what advice to give you," the minister murmured weakly. "It must be hard to bear up under such severe emotional attacks. The only thing you can do when you feel this way is to hang on."

"It's strange that you should say that. Vicki keeps telling me the same thing. She thinks if I hang on long enough, pretty soon I'll be all right—and it's true, as a matter of fact, but I have to hang on longer and longer. I drink too much coffee, especially in the evening. I just can't seem to cut down. And it's getting so I hate to go to bed at night. The pills don't help any more. I wake up very easily, and then I lie there . . . listening."

"Listening? Listening to what?"

Gingerich didn't respond immediately. When finally he did, he made a small deprecatory gesture with his right hand. "To my brain," he said, glancing furtively over his shoulder at Lenox. "We all listen to our brains, don't we? My brain is especially powerful, I guess, because it . . . it . . ." Unable to find the appropriate words, or unwilling to voice what he was thinking, he left the sentence incomplete. "But . . . but, those times I wake up, I really hang on," he resumed after a moment. "I hang on with all my strength. We have antique brass beds, Vicki and me, that we bought one summer in Madawaska, near the Canadian border. I lie there, holding on to the bars above my head. I don't want to get up, you see. I'm afraid that if I let go, I'll get out of bed, put on my slippers and robe and walk out to the kitchen. So I hold on to those brass bars like a drowning man. My muscles begin to ache, but I won't let go. Pretty soon I'm shivering and my breath becomes . . . I have trouble breathing." His eyes returned to the fish tank. "Look at that fat fantail in there. Look how he swims, Reverend Lenox. Not a care in the world. Animals are happier than men, I think. Ignorance is bliss. Don't you agree?"

"In a sense, perhaps," said Lenox. "But why are you so afraid of going to the kitchen?"

"I don't really know. I'm not afraid of the room in the daytime—only at night. There's something in there I'm scared of—something awful. It's like . . . like the worst thing in the whole world," Gingerich said, talking more rapidly and with greater emphasis. "I can't figure out what it is, though. In my mind I try to see it, but it's fuzzy . . . indistinct. It seems to be lying in a dark corner, waiting for me. Whatever it is, it's terrifying—and yet, when I wake up, I'm overwhelmed by this desire to go out to the kitchen and face the thing, once and for all. It's as if I want to get it over with." The florist again peeked around at Lenox, but this time there was a large pendent tear on the curve of his cheek. His round eyes glistened like spheres of quicksilver, and the blue vein in his temple throbbed and throbbed. "Funny, isn't it? Some nights my body shakes so much that the bed rattles. It's lucky my wife is a heavy sleeper."

With the ball of his thumb Gingerich wiped away the tear. "I believe in God," he said, "but belief is an emotional thing. You don't believe in God with your brain, do you? It's emotional . . . a feeling. That's why the Bible says, 'God is love.' "

Lenox placed his hand on the man's shoulder. "Listen, Jerry," he said, in a no-nonsense tone of voice. "Make an appointment with Dr. Lifkin. Call him Monday morning. Don't put it off. There's no reason for you to suffer like this."

"Lifkin can't help me, though. He can't, Reverend. To tell you the truth, I can't even talk to him openly any more. You—you're about the only person I can confide in now, outside of Vicki."

"But you've got to do something."

"Yes, I know . . . and I will. I will. There's a clinic in Newton I've heard about. Maybe I'll pay them a visit—take some treatments," said Gingerich, attempting a smile. "But don't you worry. It'll be all right. I don't feel upset or . . . or gloomy every minute of the day, Reverend Lenox—just once in a while." He took a last look at the goldfish and then turned. "Well, I'd better get back to the shop. I have to make two big wreaths this afternoon for Judge Winton. He died yesterday at St. Elizabeth's. So long, Reverend."

"So long, Jerry."

The florist nodded a couple of times, waved vaguely and walked off at a quick pace.

When Lenox arrived at Geraldine Gargan's apartment, he discovered that he wasn't the only guest. Cecily Harper-Jones was there with her gentleman friend, a crotchety old wool broker named Gibby. The minister made an effort to be sociable. This wasn't an easy matter, however, as his mind was preoccupied with a myriad of disquieting considerations.

29

After he had eaten his dinner that night, he phoned the airline and was told there would be a flight to Heathrow at ten forty-six Monday morning. If he was to sell the car he must find a dealer who opened early, and then conclude the transaction quickly. As for selling anything else, there just wouldn't be sufficient time.

He had hardly replaced the phone in its cradle when Angela Bosquet called and asked him to come over for the evening and play some bridge. Pleading a previous engagement, he turned down the invitation. He'd had enough social contacts for the day.

During the next couple of hours he sat in the living room, sipping whiskey and glumly pondering his plight. Hofbauer and his damn machine . . . Cavanaugh's message . . . life after death—what other enigmas did the world hold? What other disagreeable surprises did it have in store? The whole wretched affair was too mystifying, he decided—too hard and protean to come to grips with. For instance, why did the old man pretend the power of attorney was still in force? He knew perfectly well he had canceled it, and that therefore it would be impossible for

Lenox to produce the money. It made no sense . . . unless the bastard was being crafty. Perhaps this was his way of inflicting a punishment, of getting back at him, of wreaking his revenge. Yes, of course! He was egging Hofbauer on, knowing that the German would run to the police when Lenox failed to bring the money. How shrewd and diabolical Amos Cavanaugh was!

But the plan wasn't going to work, because the minister had no intention of waiting for the police to come knocking on his door. He was leaving. He was going away to make a new life. Hofbauer and the miser were in for a shock.

At ten o'clock he made an effort to rouse himself, thinking that if he went to the Boylston Street restaurant he might catch Cheeks there and be able to collect his sixty dollars. Attractive as the idea was, however, he lacked the energy to put it into execution. The events of the day had evidently drained him of his strength. Surrendering to this lassitude, he drank a final whiskey and went up to bed.

30

He delivered the sermon—a lesson on the need to worship God—with great skill. Having slept well the night before, and conscious that this would be his last appearance in the pulpit, he felt almost buoyant. And his father had provided him with an excellent script, too—one composed in 1938 that was full of multisyllabic words, alliterative phrases, pithy quotes from The Book, and catchy snatches of verse by Donne, Milton, Blake and other lyric divines. The material lent itself to eloquence. Lenox preached it like a man inspired.

Afterwards, at the coffee hour, he was roundly complimented by everyone—including Lucia Pareto, whose pretty face positively gleamed with admiration.

"What was the little poem at the very beginning, Reverend?" she asked, as formally as if they had never writhed together on a sleeping bag. "It ended with the line 'Ever faithful, ever sure.' "

The minister contracted his brow. "Oh yes," he said. "That's a paraphrase of a psalm. Milton wrote it when he was fifteen years old.

Heart of Gold

"Let us with a gladsom mind
Praise the Lord, for he is kind,
For his mercies ay endure,
Ever faithful, ever sure.

"It was a favorite of my father's, because of the purity and simplicity of the sentiment."

"Really? Isn't that odd! That's exactly how it struck me," the girl replied. She then proceeded to laud at length all things childlike and innocent.

Pretending to listen to her gush of platitudes, Lenox let his thoughts wander. What a pity she's such a rattlebrain! he lamented. If she had just a bit more sense, I might carry her off with me. Even so, she's not unpleasant to have around. Of all these people here—most of whom I've known for eons—she's probably the only one I have a tender feeling for. The poor creature is as mindless as a maggot, but she has a generous nature—and a fantastic torso. There are worse combinations than that in the world.

When she finally paused for a breath of air, he asked if he could come to see her at three o'clock that afternoon. Obviously delighted by his request, she gave a quick, half-shy nod which, like all her movements, was quite charming. A moment later, however, she was chirping away—telling him how lucky he was to have had such a sensitive and devout father.

Mr. Spears and Miss Drake joined them then, and shortly thereafter the minister drifted off to chat with some of his other parishioners.

It was nearly one o'clock by the time he got back to the rectory. The collection bag awaited him in his office. Dumping its contents on the desk blotter, he rapidly tallied the jumble of bills and coins. It came to a little more than two hundred dollars, which was less than he had hoped.

"They're away for weekends and vacations," he muttered resentfully.

Replacing the money in the bag, he carried it to his bedroom and put it in a dresser drawer, where it would be ready to hand for his early departure next morning. He had his lunch alone, and ate with a good appetite.

Promptly at three, Lenox arrived at the Cavanaugh brownstone. No sooner was he in the door than Lucia threw her arms around him and gave him an ardent kiss.

"Oh, John—you were terrific, magnificent!" she said. "Do you know, I could almost imagine I was listening to Jesus on the mount."

"Ah well, I didn't think I was as good as that," he answered with a laugh, breathing in the sweet oriental fragrance she wore and running his fingers along her buttocks.

"Maybe it sounds crazy, but you looked just like a saint to me up there. Your voice was so strong, so sure, so full of faith. I think you were exalted . . . I really do."

"I was—by your presence," he said, kissing her again.

"That's not true," the girl replied, slipping out of his grasp. "You were moved by something from above—something celestial. The whole church was alive with spiritual electricity. It was like listening to a prophet . . . or even an angel."

She took his hand and led him down the hall and into the living room. Lenox eyed her avidly. The dress she had on was little more than a light, flowery T-shirt.

"I've been reading this," she said, pointing to an open book on the seat of the armchair that Cavanaugh had occupied the night he revealed his plan. "I came across it yesterday when I was at the Copley Square library with a

Cuban friend of mine. *Héloïse and Abélard*, by George Moore. Have you read it, John?"

"No. Any good?"

"Oh yes. It's powerful. I had trouble getting into it, but once I got used to the style I was captivated. It was two in the morning before I could put it down, and then I stayed awake thinking about it. I'm almost finished. The story is so beautiful . . . and so sad. Poor Héloïse! How was she ever able to bear up under all those misfortunes?"

"It wasn't too easy for Abélard, either," Lenox remarked dryly.

"No, of course not—but for her it was very complicated emotionally, because of her father and the baby. I cried a couple of times, and I haven't done that over a book since I read *The Sorrows of Young Werther* last year. I'll lend it to you when I'm through. You'll love it. It's an experience."

"It might be too grim for my tastes. Don't you find it depressing?"

"I don't know if it depresses me. It's certainly sad in parts. But the idea of a brilliant, holy woman and a brilliant, holy man being passionately in love is genuinely fascinating. A love like that would be perfect, wouldn't it?"

She gazed artlessly into his face.

"What about the unhappiness they suffered, though?" he asked, smiling. "If they hadn't fallen in love, Lucia, they would have been better off."

"I can't believe that. Their misery wasn't caused by their love. It was the work of her wicked father, the canon. He was an evil demon, if ever there was one—and the horriblest kind, because he pretended to be a man of God. I just don't know how Héloïse stood all the grief he inflicted on her."

Having little interest in the problems of a couple of people who had been dead for eight hundred years, and even less interest in another disquisition on demons, Lenox took up the book and tossed it on a table, then sat in the chair and pulled her down on his lap.

"You've lost my place, John," she complained mildly.

31

He departed shortly after eight o'clock, somewhat subdued by the realization that he would never see her again.

In the car he shed his coat, collar and dickey, and donned a madras sport shirt, a blue gabardine jacket and his gold-framed dark glasses. He contemplated the façade of the weathered old brownstone for a minute or two, then shrugged his shoulders, engaged the clutch and drove away.

On Massachusetts Avenue he found a parking space almost directly across from the cafeteria. As he was about to open the door he spied Cheeks standing on the sidewalk in the company of a slightly built, sandy-haired man who appeared vaguely familiar. But before Lenox could place him, a rush of traffic intervened and blocked his view. Once the cars had passed, however, he had no trouble at all distinguishing who it was. He promptly crouched down in his seat. The slightly built man was Rupert Hofbauer!

Heart thumping and eyes blinking, he raised his head and looked again. It was no illusion. There they were—Cheeks and the German, deep in conversation.

What was going on? he wondered. How was it possible

that they knew each other? Was it a bizarre coincidence, or something more sinister? What the hell did it mean?

He fumbled in the canvas bag beside him, got out his floppy felt hat, put it on, yanked the brim over his brow, and for the third time, stared across the busy street. At that very moment Hofbauer grinned at Cheeks, patted him on the back, turned and then sauntered off toward Boylston Street, his bandy legs moving in a crablike manner. Cheeks pulled a newspaper from his hip pocket and went into the restaurant.

During the next five minutes the minister remained in the Volkswagen, deliberating whether he should leave and abandon his sixty dollars, or go over and ask Cheeks a few questions. In the end, his qualms were conquered by curiosity. He got out of the car.

The baby-faced horseplayer was seated alone at his usual table in the alcove, the newspaper spread before him and a half-smoked cigar wedged tightly between his lips.

"Cheese and rice—look who's here!" he exclaimed when Lenox sat down. "I ain't seen you all week. I figured you eloped with one of them hookers or something. What's happening?"

"Not much. I was here Tuesday," said Lenox. "You weren't around."

"Tuesday? Oh yeah! I went to my nephew's, in Clinton. He's got a nice little house there, out in the woods. We had a big dinner—porterhouse steak, baked potatoes, custard pie. I would've been back earlier, but I fell asleep on the lawn for a couple of hours. When I woke up, all the stars were in the sky, winkling and twinkling. Very enjoyable it was, Johnny. I like commuting with nature once in a while. The only trouble was that my nephew gave me a horse to play, Ritz Royal—and like a feeb I hung ten on his nose. What I got from Ritz Royal was a royal screwing. I seen horses on a merry-go-round run faster than that zebra. So I didn't get the steak for nothing."

Lenox looked at his companion closely, wondering if there was more to the little man than met the eye. "I drove by here a few minutes ago, Cheeks, and saw you out on the sidewalk. Was that your nephew you were talking to?"

"What? Who? The guy with the funny mustache? Naw! He ain't my nephew. Are you kidding? For him to be my nephew, I'd have to be as old as Macushla. He's a joker I know from when we worked together at the Bavarian Chalet on Stuart Street, more than twenty years ago. His name is Gus . . . Gus Vogel. A slick operator."

Lenox inhaled deeply. He had a presentiment that everything was going to be all right. "Slick?" he asked.

"Yeah. When he seen he wasn't making no dough scratching a fiddle, Gus got a hold of this big blonde from Melrose and put together a stage act—mind reading and magic stuff. But they didn't do too good. That was around 1950. Vaudeville was dead as a doorknob and the night clubs only wanted stand-up comics or greasy crooners in tuxedos. Pretty soon they were both starving from malnutrition. So he started being a grifter. He started promoting the quick dollar—hustling dumbskulls out of their life savings. Gus always was a strong talker. Even with his heiniekaplotz accent, he could make you believe the floor was the ceiling. I guess he did okay at first, but then he clipped some old broad in Brighton who knew somebody at City Hall. Judge Dunahue gave him three-to-five in Walpole. After he came out, I seen him at Suffolk and the big blonde was still with him. She was a foreigner, too—a refugee from Hungaria. She had dimples. A nice piece of gash."

Lenox sighed audibly. He felt light-headed—like a

man who has suddenly been told it was all a joke after he has mounted a scaffold and has a rope placed around his neck. He wanted to lean across the table and embrace the horseplayer. What a break it was that he had driven up just at the right time! He would never have known otherwise. He would have gone through life believing that the Otherside actually existed. Jesus! But now he knew—knew conclusively. Hofbauer wasn't a scientist. He was only a cheap crook. Yet . . . how did the son-of-a-bitch obtain the password . . . and the details of the murder?

The minister said casually, "I can't understand why people let themselves get swindled. There must be an awful lot of chumps in the world."

Cheeks grunted and removed the unlit cigar from his mouth. "There are," he agreed. "Didn't Barnum say a sucker was burnt every minute? And real promoters can find a sucker blindfolded. Zing! It's like they got radar. Let me tell you a little story—an antidote that hardly anybody knows. Gus Vogel actually conned a guy out of twenty-five thousand dollars. No crap, Johnny! Twenty-five G's. He rigged up this phony machine—a bunko box, all wires and light bulbs—that he said could send money to your relatives who had died. Now, you'd think no person in his right mind would fall for a pitch like that, but a character named Harvey Glassman who had a fancy office on Washington Street, in the Jeweler's Building, swallowed it—hook, line and sinker. Gus convinced the boob that his mother, who was dead fifteen years already, needed some cash up in heaven. Can you imagine? It didn't even make sense. I mean, if you got to pay for things in heaven, you might as well go to hell, right? But Glassman figured it was all legit because Vogel kept telling him information—inside stuff— that only his mother knew about. It was a gimmick, though—a dodge. Why? Because at the time, Harvey Glassman had a girl friend, and he was always blabbing to her about how tough his life was when he was a kid in Dorchester, and what a wonderful, hard-working woman his poor mother was, and so on. Yeah—and who was this girl friend? She was the big blonde—the refugee from Hungaria! Whatever the chump told her, she just passed it along to Gus. Slick as vaseline—the two of them.

"Anyhow, the yo-yo would bring his money in an envelope, the envelope would get stuck in Vogel's contraption, the bulbs would start blinking, and right in front of his eyes the thing would disappear. Vinnie Goukas, who knows a lot about fast shuffles, said Gus did it with mirrors—that when you thought you were looking at the envelope, all you were really seeing was a deflection. Then, the minute the lights flashed, the mirror would flip up and you wouldn't see nothing any more. The whole trick was the way he slipped the envelope in the machine at the beginning. Get it, John? Of course, Glassman believed the dough was going straight to heaven—the feeb. He didn't snap to it until six months later, when somebody finally wised him up. But he never got a dime of his twenty-five grand back, and he couldn't even holler for the cops, neither, because it happened the money came from a couple of cute deals he made on the side—deals he didn't ever pay any income tax on. So he was scared to open his mouth. Another reason for keeping quiet he had, too, was he didn't want all the people in the Jeweler's Building to find out what a big jerk he was. Ain't it funny, kid, the way things can work out against you? You wouldn't think a guy could get hurt just because he loved his mother. It don't pay to have a maternity instinct, I guess."

Lenox scarcely heard the last part of the gambler's

narrative. Having lit a cigarette, he was now staring blankly at a flyspecked placard on the wall that said LINK SAUSAGE AND EGGS—FULL ORDER $1.45 while his mind busily assimilated the details of Harvey Glassman's misadventure. Bit by bit, the plot was unraveling. The blonde— she was the key, the missing piece in the jigsaw puzzle. Hadn't Cavanaugh smugly boasted of having a lady friend? He'd met her at an auction, he said. And wasn't she the one who pointed out Hofbauer's advertisement in the newspaper to him? Yes . . . yes. They had set the old man up beautifully. Then, after he went to the house on Blagden Street, Vogel-Hofbauer took over from there—putting on his reluctant act, bringing the victim to M.I.T. to meet a bunch of henchmen, snowing him under with a pseudo-scientific spiel, and finally, revealing to his astonished eyes that glittering marvel, the Charge Translator.

But what about the rest? What about the password? Cavanaugh had first mentioned it the day they signed the power-of-attorney forms. He'd said it was his "insurance policy" and . . . and that his friend had "put him on to it." Yes, his lady friend—the night she came to give him a rubdown. As to the password itself, obviously they dreamed that up together, and later she told it to the German. How clear it became, once you possessed the thread! When Lenox went to see him, Hofbauer was probably just sitting there waiting for him to remember to ask for the password, and meanwhile the goddamn letter, neatly forged in Cavanaugh's shaky writing, was already in the machine with the answer on it! What an actor the bastard was!

Cheeks returned the cigar to his mouth and said, "I'm going to Lincoln tomorrow, Johnny, if you want to come. Emil Green is giving me a ride. You know Emil? His uncle was Fritz Green, the numbers taker who ended up in the

Fens with his head full of bullets six or seven years ago. They say he held out on a customer—one that didn't have much patience. Fritz was queer, anyway—half man, half lady. A hybird. Maybe I'll bet that Gray Apache. For a mile and a sixteenth he can go like the wind, but if he has to travel more than that, he can't sustain."

While his companion orally handicapped the next day's races, the minister continued with his ratiocination. There was still one mystery that remained to be solved. How had Hofbauer, in the fake message, been able to describe the murder so accurately? Where the hell had he gotten his information? Quimby, the detective, had spoken of a piece of the five-dollar bill being found in the dead man's hand. If any of the newspapers had reported this, and the German had seen it, then conceivably he might have worked out the money-decoy notion all by himself. That seemed rather far-fetched, however. It would only have been a wild guess, and if he was wrong, the whole illusion would have been irrevocably shattered. And why should Hofbauer take such an all-or-nothing chance? It wasn't necessary; the password alone was fully convincing. Yet, if the scoundrel hadn't been taking a chance—hadn't been guessing—then he must have really found out how the murder was accomplished. But that was utterly ridiculous. To know, he would have had to be there; he would have had to witness the bloody deed.

Lenox drew hard on his cigarette and shot a silver stream of vapor toward the sausage-and-eggs sign, where it burst into a diaphanous cloud—and as the curls of smoke dissipated, he suddenly remembered the face in the window.

God! he thought. Could that be the explanation? The grim face in the top-floor window. He'd been sure he imagined it, but suppose he hadn't? Suppose someone was actually there—someone who, seeing him stare up, had quickly ducked out of sight? Lenox, then, might well have doubted his eyes, and too readily assumed it was merely the dial of the mantel clock that had frightened him. Due to his agitation, his vision would not have been sharp, nor his brain discriminating.

That had to be the answer. And anyone at the window could have watched Cavanaugh gathering up the dollar bills, could easily have distinguished the features of the man lurking in the alley doorway, and could have had a ringside seat for the murder itself. He could have observed everything. He . . . but why *he?* It wasn't Hofbauer. It wasn't he—it was she. Of course! It was the blonde again. Cavanaugh must have had her sleep over—the lewd old hypocrite! Or perhaps it wasn't entirely his idea. Perhaps she was sticking close to him, to keep him from changing his mind. Perhaps the two connivers could see that their pigeon was growing suspicious about the deal. Yes—hadn't he canceled the power of attorney? And though they didn't know about that, they must have noticed a wariness of some kind in the miser's attitude.

Clearer and clearer. She saw the murder. It probably scared the life out of the woman. And after he drove away, she must have left the brownstone as fast as she could. But Hofbauer hadn't been scared, evidently. Murder or no murder, he wouldn't abandon his scheme. It was the size of the bank account that made him persevere, no doubt. For such a sum, he was prepared to take risks. He was prepared to tackle a man with blood on his hands. So he had phoned the minister and continued the deception as though nothing had happened.

And that was all there was to the great mystery. The rest—the talk of scientific breakthroughs, of the instant production of anti-matter, of the Otherside, of life after death, and of heaven and hell and God and the devil—was simply hokum. Amos Cavanaugh might still exist, but only as a corrupting corpse in a plot of earth in Cambridge. Death was final. When you died, you were dead forever.

". . . came back from Raynham," Cheeks was saying, his baby face more colicky than usual. "But he didn't win no perfecta. He's full of crap. Tully's the kind of guy, if he won a perfecta he'd take off for Old Orchard Beach for a week with some bimbo. I told Lou Ardoise, 'He didn't win no perfecta down Raynham. It's just a frigment of his imagination—a lot of hooey.' Hey—where you going, kid?"

"Have to see somebody," said Lenox, standing and snuffing out his cigarette in the ashtray. "I was supposed to see him tomorrow, but I think I'll drop in on him now. Take it easy, Cheeks."

He turned and strode jauntily from the restaurant, thinking, It was just a frigment of my imagination—that's all it was.

32

If he was surprised, Hofbauer concealed it well. "I did not at first recognize you, Reverend Doctor," he said blandly. "You are wearing your unprofessional clothing."

"I'd like to talk to you," said Lenox.

"So? What is there to discuss? I can see you do not have with you the money."

"That's what I want to talk about, and I think it would be wiser to talk inside than here on the doorstep."

The German looked doubtful. Then, shrugging, he stepped aside to permit his unexpected visitor to enter the house.

In the parlor Lenox took a Queen Anne chair, and without prelude said, "I'm not bringing you any money— not tomorrow or ever. I've had a private detective investigate you, Professor. Your real name is Gus Vogel. You're a petty thief, an ex-convict. You served a sentence in Walpole Prison for stealing an old woman's savings."

Hofbauer regarded him impassively. "Bah! You talk nonsense," he said. Wandering to the other end of the room, he gazed for a few seconds at the alabaster head of Caesar on the side table, opened the table drawer, put something in it or took something out, grunted as though annoyed, and added, "A private detective? Somebody is telling lies."

"Oh? There's a man named Harvey Glassman who wouldn't feel that way. He was taken for twenty-five thousand dollars by you and a confederate. Or is that also a lie?"

"But of course! Why do you come here and talk silly? On the radio at ten," said Hofbauer, pointing at his cuckoo clock, "they are playing Anton Bruckner. That is fifteen minutes away, and I want much to listen. Tomorrow come back, Reverend, before noon. And do not forget the package, eh?"

Resenting his host's nonchalance, Lenox said acridly, "You just don't know when you're defeated, do you?"

"It is not me, sir, who is defeated. *Ach!* What a foolish person you are! Why do you want to make for yourself a bunch of bad troubles? The police will not listen to fairy tales about old ladies. No, the murder of Mr. Cavanaugh is only what they will be interested in. They will interrogate you over and over, until you surrender and give your confession."

"Your Charge Translator is nothing but a magician's prop, Hofbauer—a trick box equipped with sliding panels, pivoting mirrors and trap doors. There's no anti-matter universe, nor did any of those things really disappear."

"Stupid lies. More stupid lies."

"The whole rigmarole was a conjurer's act—a little sleight of hand and a lot of slick patter. Cavanaugh's so-called message, for example, was composed by you and planted in the machine before I ever got here that day; and the information the message contained was provided by your blond Hungarian girl friend, who had been very cozy with the old man for weeks prior to his death. She picked him up at a furniture auction, discovered he was wealthy and told you about it. And in the deception that followed, she played a principal role. It was she who showed him your notice in the paper, she who suggested the password, she who helped convince the old fool that your absurd proposition was on the up and up, and she who was staying in his house at the time of the murder."

"I do not understand what you are saying," Hofbauer retorted contemptuously, slipping his right hand into his coat pocket. "You are raving like a madman. Bah! I am very, very tired of this business. My patience is all worn out. The money I will earn is not equal to the many bothers I have suffered. It has been unpleasant for me. I do not like dealing with an assassin, a killer—a nasty, dangerous type. I do not like doing negotiations with such a cruel, unhuman animal as you are. Bring here the money tomorrow, sir, and no more funny games, eh? If it is not in my custody by one second after twelve, I will call up the police straightaway. I am disgusted with your stories. Now get out, please."

Stung by these harsh words, the minister jumped to his feet. Immediately Hofbauer drew his hand from his pocket. In it was a gun—a black Luger. Lenox, confronted by this menacing weapon, hastily retreated a step, and in so doing, tripped over the cabriole leg of his chair and started to fall. He grabbed for the wrought-iron music stand nearby, but it was just out of reach. Down he tumbled, landing heavily on his rump.

That, however, was only the beginning, for as he fell, his outstretched arm banged the tripod base of the stand and a moment later it toppled also. While sheet music from the lectern fluttered up toward the ceiling like a flock of frightened doves, the lectern itself smashed against the green marble column, on whose entablature Richard Wagner's pale Parian head rested. The column teetered. With a cry of alarm Hofbauer dashed forward to save the imperiled composer, but before he could accomplish this, the pedestal lost the last of its balance and went over. Wagner flew through the air like one of his Valkyries. Hofbauer made a desperate dive for him, and missed. Simultaneously, both Germans crashed to the floor—the less sturdy of the two disintegrating into a swarm of scintillating splinters.

With that, the clamorous concatenation finally ended. Since Lenox had been the first to fall, he was the first to recover. He surveyed the scene and spotted the black automatic lying on a piece of music in the middle of the rug. Almost casually he crawled across the intervening space, picked up the Luger and pointed it at his adversary. Then he rose to his feet.

The room was now eerily quiet. Hofbauer broke the silence with a long sigh. He stood up slowly and looked at the china fragments that surrounded him. "I brought all the way from Bavaria, from München, this exquisite representation," he murmured, evidently more disturbed by the destruction of the bust than by the loss of the gun.

As Lenox bleakly appraised his captive, he began to see the struggle between them in a new and lurid light. He realized with chagrin that no easy resolution of their differences was possible. Nothing he could ever say would convince Hofbauer he didn't have the million dollars. Nothing he could ever say would dissuade Hofbauer from going to the police. Hofbauer was too confirmed a liar to have any faith in the veracity of others. Even after Lenox had made it crystal-clear that he was acquainted with all the details of the plot, Hofbauer still refused to capitulate— refused to admit anything. What was there left to do?

The German met his gaze steadily for a while; then a

flicker of fear arced in his black-olive eyes, and he frowned. "Reverend Doctor," he said raucously, "maybe after this upset we should sit and have a glass of kümmel, eh?"

"Stand still and keep your mouth shut," the minister replied in a voice as cold and sharp as an arctic wind.

Hofbauer shrugged his shoulders resignedly and appeared to relax—but the very next instant he leaped over the fallen marble column and, bowed legs jackhammering, sprinted for the door.

Aiming the automatic carefully, Lenox squeezed the trigger twice. However, instead of the double explosion he had expected, he heard only two dull, hollow clicks—rather like the snapping of fingers. Something was wrong. The gun, moreover, felt unnaturally light and flimsy in his hand. Gaping at it, he saw at once that although it resembled a Luger in every detail, it was made of hard plastic—the whole thing, including the barrel. It wasn't actually a firearm; it was only a well-designed copy of one.

"Even your goddamn gun is phony!" he yelled, flinging the bogus weapon at the fleeing German, just as the latter attained the hall and headed for the rear of the house.

An instant later Lenox himself traveled the same course, in hot pursuit. Having reached the cellar entry, his surprisingly agile quarry ducked in and slammed the door behind him. The sound of a bolt being shot into place fell on the minister's ears like the crack of doom. Furious, he rammed his shoulder against the panel that barred his way, more out of frustration than because he expected to achieve anything. But to his great delight the door groaned and opened inward almost an inch. He repeated the maneuver, this time putting all his strength into it. There was a loud shrieking as screws were wrenched from timber, and then the door swung aside. With a cry of triumph he raced down the stairs. A swift inspection of the first cubicle showed him that his man wasn't hiding behind the packing cases, and so he ran to the second room.

Illuminated only by the hall light that entered through the doorway above, the place was fringed by leaden shadows. He searched the gloom and spied Hofbauer standing with his back to the wall, a yard or two from the shiny machine. Though his haystack mustache was quivering and he was a little out of breath, the German appeared quite calm and collected.

He smiled, and in a tone that was conciliatory but not contrite, said, "I am sure, Reverend, we can settle forever this matter of your skepticism. It is not unusual for people to think I am a crook. Not everybody are scientists, eh? And the performance of the instrument is for them difficult to believe. Permit me, please, to give you another demonstration."

Lenox approached him slowly, returning his smile. "No more demonstrations, Professor," he answered.

Hofbauer maintained his cool demeanor, but he began to move laterally along the wall. "You are extremely upset, and it is my fault," he remarked, his voice solicitous. "To make believe that I was going to phone up the police was not considerate of me. I give you my apology, sir. I did not really expect that an intelligent man like you would take so serious such a silly statement, though. I call the police? Ha! I hate those people. I have always hated them."

Since he was not looking where he was going, he bumped into a small aluminum storage bin—the one from which he had procured the orange that very first day. The bin pitched forward onto the spinach-green carpet, spewing an assortment of objects: a reel of insulated wire, a paperback book, a fluorescent-light tube, some tools, an oil can and several glass fuses. There was also a string bag containing four oranges, and when this tumbled out, it cleared the way for a last item that immediately attracted Lenox's attention. Almost as if it were motivated by a supernatural will, this article came to rest at his feet. He stooped and picked it up. It was a large stone, oval and streaked with gray—the sort of stone a cave man might have bound to a stick to make a tomahawk.

"Ah, Professor! What have we here?" he asked, his smile warping into an ugly smirk. "This is the rock Mr. Cavanaugh brought, is it not? Yes, of course. It's quite distinctive. But how can that possibly be if, as you claim, you sent Mr. Cavanaugh's rock to the Otherside? You did translate it, didn't you?"

Hofbauer hesitated a fraction of a second, and then, seeming to realize he was hesitating, blurted out an answer: "I did . . . yes—only they sent it back to me. Mr. Billings and I—we did a test . . . to check on the electromagnetic circuits. *Ach!* I hope you are not making a wrong conclusion, Reverend Doctor. It is an innocent circumstance—a thing of no signification. Why do you get excited?"

A pink flush tinged the minister's face. His eyes and nostrils dilated, and his lips drew back from his teeth to such an extent that his grin became a wolfish grimace. "You lying little bastard," he said. "Even when your life depends upon it, you can't speak the truth!"

In a desperate effort to escape, Hofbauer lunged sideways, but the Charge Translator blocked his path and he fell on top of it. Immediately the dentist-drill hum commenced, its single tedious note like a tocsin.

"Nein!" Hofbauer cried out, his features suddenly going limp with fright.

Very deliberately Lenox seized him by his necktie and

struck him on the crown of the head with the oval stone. The German's eyes crossed and his eyelids fluttered. From deep in his chest there came a feeble whimper. A second blow landed in front of his left ear, and a third on the ear itself. Blood began to surge from one of these wounds, rising and ebbing like a dancing flame. Hofbauer shivered, floundered, jerked. His legs gave way under him, and he would have slid to the floor were it not for the firm hand on his necktie. Lenox growled and hit him twice more—two terrible thumps that cracked his skull against the rigid metal surface of the machine. The battered man lost his look of fear. Brains and serous fluid seeped from a depressed triangular hole in the center of his forehead. Down his thin nose this gray sludge dribbled, and onto his bristly mustache.

The minister released him and he crumpled in a heap on the carpet, his legs awkwardly twisted beneath his body.

"What . . . what have you got to say now, Professor?" Lenox whispered, his breath coming in gasps. "Haven't you any . . . any new proposals to offer? Speak! Can it really be possible that you're at a loss for words? *Ach!* At least answer one little question, sir . . . if you would be so kind. Tell me . . . what's it like on the Otherside, eh?"

Chuckling softly at his grim joke, he prodded the dead man with the toe of his shoe. Hofbauer, however, took no umbrage at this indignity, though his mutilated head rolled languidly over onto its cheek.

Then, becoming aware of the nagging electrical drone that still filled the air, Lenox muttered an oath and conferred a savage kick on the Charge Translator. To his surprise and satisfaction the racket ceased, and the room was at once plunged into an almost palpable silence. His eyes darted around—at the whitewashed walls, at the slate blackboard with its mathematical runes, at the bag of oranges, at the bloodstained carpet and the graceless corpse.

"What else could I do?" he asked the silence sullenly. "The man wouldn't listen to me—wouldn't admit the truth."

Intending to put the stone on the machine, he stepped forward, but before he could accomplish this action, the sound of a door opening reached his ears. It came from the floor above. He looked up at the ceiling, his brow furrowed. Quite distinctly, he heard the door close.

Lenox, moving with stealth, crossed into the adjoining cubicle, hurried through the stacked shipping crates, mounted the wooden stairs and cautiously peeked around the doorjamb.

A tall blond woman stood at the front end of the hall, staring into the parlor. She wore a blouse, slacks and high-heeled shoes, and carried a white paper bag in her hand. Realizing that she was preoccupied by the topsy-turvy scene in the room, Lenox emerged from the basement entry, and making good use of the wall, furtively crept toward her. Not until he had got to within two yards of where she was standing did she at last sense danger and spin around. Her stalker leaped forward, swinging his arm in a broad crescent.

Though the woman ducked, the stone caught her above the eye and sent her reeling into the parlor. There she tripped over the music stand, caromed off the ebony piano and fell by chance into a wing chair. Groggy from the solid knock she had received, she nevertheless made a determined effort to get up and flee, but the chair was soft and deep, and before she could extricate herself, Lenox was upon her. Screaming something unintelligible, she tried to push him away with her feet. He side-stepped, lifted his arm again and drove the stone at her bobbing head. The blow missed the target by several inches. Enraged, he launched a ferocious attack, hammering blindly at the now thrashing figure in the wing chair. The woman covered her skull with her hands and sought to burrow into the thick upholstery, but it was a futile defense. Time after time the stone found its mark.

Finally the minister perceived that his victim was no longer struggling—that, indeed, she was no longer moving at all. Her bruised face was flaccid. Her eyes were shut, though her mouth hung open—as slack as the mouth of a ventriloquist's dummy. Her hands, with their broken fingers, had fallen into her lap.

Panting, Lenox retreated a step. "Finished," he said. "She's . . . she's finished."

Then, hearing a whirring noise, he turned around quickly, but it was only the old cuckoo clock on the wall, getting ready to strike. "Cuckoo, cuckoo, cuckoo," the device called out mindlessly while its little wooden bird nodded and spread its beak on the tiny projecting platform. When the tenth cuckoo had sounded, the bird slipped back into its house, the doors closed, and the room was again tranquil.

"Hofbauer . . . has missed his radio program," said Lenox wryly.

Then, catching a glimpse of himself in the mirror above the mantel, he saw that he was completely spattered with blood. His hair was a mottled carmine, and his face and neck were both hideously freckled, as though he were wearing war paint. The madras shirt and the blue gabardine jacket that he had donned after leaving Lucia were literally drenched with gore. He could feel the tepid dampness against his skin.

What a mess! he thought. Cavanaugh wasn't this bad. I must wash. Cavanaugh had been very chary with his blood.

Throughout his exertions, the minister's brain had functioned remarkably well. From the instant Hofbauer had pulled the fake gun he seemed to know, almost by instinct, exactly what he should do. Even when the blond woman had entered the house, even when he was frenziedly beating her, there hadn't been any uncertainty or confusion in the busy corridors of his mind.

Now, continuing to maintain this logical self-posses-sion, he left the parlor and went up the stairs to the second floor, where he found a green-tiled bathroom and in it cleaned his hands, face and hair. Since the blood was fresh, it came off easily—yet a residue must have stayed in his pores because when he was done his cheeks were uncharac-teristically rosy. He then washed the stone and put it on the toilet tank. Next, he thoroughly wiped the basin and the faucets with a towel and went back downstairs.

In ten minutes he succeeded in cleaning all the surfaces that he might have touched in the parlor, the hall and the basement. That accomplished, he got a plaid raincoat from a closet under the stairs, wriggled into it and buttoned every button. It was an extremely tight fit, but he was sure it would serve him adequately. His car was only a short distance away.

At the front door he took a last look around. For the first time he noticed on the floor of the hall the white paper bag the woman had been carrying. It was an insulated ice cream bag. From its partially opened mouth a sickly, milky stream was flowing lethargically.

"In the midst of life," he whispered, *"we are in death."*

Then he rubbed the doorknobs with his handkerchief and slipped out into the street.

33

No sooner had he stepped over the rectory threshold than the telephone commenced to ring. Locking the door behind him, he hurried into the office.

"Is that you, Reverend Lenox?" a high-pitched voice inquired when he raised the phone to his ear.

"Yes," he answered. "Who's this?"

"It's me. I've been trying to get a hold of you all night. I think I called a hundred times. But . . . but you're home now, thank God. I didn't know what I was going to do. There isn't much time left. I'll be at the rectory in a few minutes—okay? I'm at the bus depot . . . on Stuart Street."

"I'm afraid you can't come tonight," said the minister. "Who is this? I still don't recognize your voice."

On the other end of the line there was a garbled noise, as though the speaker had turned his head away from the mouthpiece. This was followed by a brief fit of coughing.

Exasperated, Lenox considered hanging up. He wondered if his bloody clothes were dripping on the office broadloom.

Then the caller said, "Yes, it's me—Jerry. I guess you thought it was some stranger. Been trying all night to get

: 213 :

you. I had to keep at it because I was afraid to go home until everything was settled. Soon as I found out about it, I . . . well, I decided to have a talk with you."

"Jerry Gingerich?"

"Yes, that's right, Reverend. It's me. And as I was saying, I made this discovery. I found out what they're doing to my brain. I found out . . . I found out how it works—the brain, I mean. They've been cutting my strings, you see . . . which is why I've been having so much trouble."

"Cutting your strings? I don't understand what you're saying. Have you been getting more of those impulses, Jerry?"

"The human brain is a hub, Reverend," Gingerich exclaimed, increasing the tempo of his speech. "It's a hub in a wheel. The rim of the wheel is the body, and the hub and the rim are connected by these little strings—like spokes. Before tonight I never understood how it worked. I only suspected things . . . but the image I had was mixed up . . . confused. Do you follow what I'm saying, Reverend? Do you see? The strings run from brain terminals straight out to the parts of your body—to your hands, and so on. All your feelings and dreams travel along those strings, just the way electricity flows through wires. Isn't it amazing? But they've been snipping my strings . . . one by one. There's hardly any left now. I'm sure you'll know how to help me, though. In five minutes I'll be over . . . maybe less."

Lenox realized that the florist was very ill, that he had finally lost his grip altogether; yet under the circumstances he couldn't possibly let him come to the rectory. There was too much to be done.

"Wait," the minister said sharply. "You can't see me tonight. It's out of the question, I'm afraid."

"Can't see you? Can't see you, Reverend? Why?"

"Because I won't be here, Jerry. I have to go back out again—right away."

"I can be there in five minutes. That's all it will take . . . five minutes."

"Tonight is impossible. I'm terribly sorry. I have to visit a woman who's had a seizure, and I'm late already. Listen to me—come in the morning, at ten-thirty. Do you understand? Now go home, take some sleeping pills and get to bed. Everything is going to be all right."

"But they're cutting my strings," said Gingerich, sounding bewildered. "They'll snip them—every single one."

"Who are 'they,' Jerry?"

"They? They? The string cutters? I don't know. I don't know, Reverend Lenox. I don't. If I did, I could do something . . . maybe. I've never seen them, though. I've only felt them working in there. Why did they decide to attack me? That man I had the fight with in Woolworth's— the one with the hairy ears—is part of the gang, I'm almost positive. But, Reverend, if you don't help me, how can I get rid of them? How can I? They keep cutting . . . and there's not much time left."

Lenox frowned, closed his eyes tight and tried to think. At last he said, "Perhaps the best thing for you to do would be to call Dr. Lifkin. You have his number, don't you, Jerry? Phone the doctor and tell him you require immediate treatment. He can help you far more than I can. Will you do that, Jerry?"

For a few seconds the rasp of Gingerich's breathing could be heard. Then there was a click and the line went dead.

Lenox replaced the telephone in its cradle and muttered a curse. When he switched on the lamp, he noticed that his fingers were trembling, and this annoyed him. "Jerry Gingerich," he said, scowling. "Jesus Christ!"

A rapid examination of the floor showed there was no trace of blood on the carpet. The minister left the office, went upstairs to the bathroom and began to undress. So sticky was the clothing that he had to peel off his shirt and trousers as though they were pieces of adhesive bandage. He was in the shower scrubbing himself when through the roar of the water he heard the doorbell ring.

The crazy son-of-a-bitch! he thought angrily. He can press that button all he wants, but he's not getting in. Him and his goddamn fantasies! Him and his goddamn strings!

The bell rang intermittently for at least fifteen minutes, its peals grating on Lenox's nervous system. But finally it stopped, and he sighed with relief.

He finished his shower, got dressed in clean casual garments and went downstairs. From the cupboard and pantry in the kitchen he got three plastic garbage bags, four large cans of baked beans and two of sliced peaches, a ball of heavy twine and a pair of scissors. Using one bag as a carrier, he toted these articles back up to the bathroom and arrayed them on the floor.

He chose Hofbauer's raincoat to work on first. With the scissors he removed the labels and tossed them in the toilet bowl. Next, after he had carefully wiped off two cans of beans, he tucked them in the middle of the coat, rolled coat and cans into a compact cylinder and stuffed the cylinder into a garbage bag. However, the resulting parcel contained a great deal of air, so he was obliged to do a lot of squeezing and flattening to get rid of it. Satisfied at last, he tied the mouth of the sack with a length of twine.

A second bundle was made of his own trousers, socks and shoes in the same fashion, and then a third, duly weighted with the cans of peaches, was put together from the remaining bloody apparel—his shirt, gabardine jacket and underwear.

This task completed, he flushed the labels down the toilet and gave the tile floor a vigorous washing, then hauled his parcels out to the Volkswagen. A half-hour later he dropped them all off the Harvard Bridge into the Charles River, hoping fervently that they would never rise up to testify against him.

It was just midnight when he returned to the garage, but his chores weren't finished yet. Diligently he vacuumed the inside of the car; scrubbed the upholstery, mats and foot pedals; and swabbed the steering wheel, the knobs on the dashboard, the side windows, the door handles, and the doors themselves.

Then he locked the garage and went upstairs again.

There he smoked a cigarette, drank a tall glass of neat Scotch whiskey and climbed into bed.

Several times during the night Lenox thought he heard the doorbell, but when he sat up in bed and listened, the sound was never repeated.

In the morning, at the usual hour, Mrs. Keller knocked on his door. Though still fatigued, he was glad to hear her cheery voice and see the daylight coming through the window.

Have the bodies been discovered? he asked himself as he got dressed. Are the police there already? Probably. I forgot to turn off the lights in the house. Someone is sure to have noticed them burning.

He ate his breakfast; then, at a quarter to ten, he went out to inspect the church. Everything was in order.

Returning to his office, he sat for a while at his desk, occupied with apprehensive reveries.

When the doorbell rang at ten-thirty he assumed it was Gingerich and answered it himself, but it was only the postman with a box of maple-sugar candy from Mrs. Delorry, who was vacationing in the Green Mountains.

He went back to his office and looked at his desk calendar. The only urgent duty listed there was an evening memorial service for August Sander's father.

Lenox downed two shots of whiskey, left the rectory, got into the Volkswagen and drove to Marlborough Street.

34

"It would be that grayish-green color that artists never seem to get right when they paint seascapes," said Lucia, peering at him over her naked shoulder. "The wind would howl and the water would roar. I'd be chilled to the bone—my clothes all wet, my face all chapped, my nose and eyes all itchy from the rough salt spray. Sometimes I really believed the surf would swallow me, that I'd lose consciousness and not wake up again until I was at the bottom of the ocean. But I wasn't frightened, John—not even a tiny bit.

"I used to cut classes in high school to go there and sit on that cold stone sea wall. The other kids thought I was crazy. People always do, don't they? What nasty, spiteful things they said about me! A couple of those girls were completely evil—cunning, devilish types. I didn't care, though. I just ignored them. As long as I could go and sit by the ocean, none of their remarks mattered."

Lenox and the girl were lying nude on the counterpane of Amos Cavanaugh's spacious old sleigh bed—she on her stomach, he on his back with his hands clasped across his chest. They had been there for half the afternoon. Perspiration glistened on their bodies.

Lucia continued talking dreamily. "Far, far out in the distance you could see the surf being born," she said. "You could fix your eyes on a single wave and watch it grow—watch it get taller and stronger, watch it swell until it was gigantic. Then suddenly the foam would sprout from its curling head, and it would start to fall. Down it would tumble, exploding in a million billion fragments and covering the shore with a million billion little bubbles—all blinking like babies' eyes. Fantastically stimulating. The slow gentle beginning, the tremendous mound of green water, the swift surge, the crash, and the inevitable annihilation. It was like watching a great cosmic tragedy unfold. I can really sympathize with people who throw themselves into the ocean—can't you?"

Lenox, though he was paying scant attention to his companion's monologue, nodded. From the middle of the sallow ceiling a multifaceted globe hung on a gilded chain, and around it two buzzing flies circled incessantly. The minister, his expression speculative, studied them. There were probably flies at Hofbauer's house, he mused—a good many, too, if the bodies hadn't been removed yet. Surely, by now, however, the crime had been discovered. Surely, by now, the police were in that cluttered parlor—searching, measuring, photographing, poring over the woodwork and doorknobs that he, Lenox, had so energetically wiped the night before. Surely, by now, his victims were lying in the city morgue, their rigid faces hidden beneath cool bleached sheets.

How strange it all was! That he had committed one murder was marvel enough—but three? When they want to, events go forward at a snappy gallop. Three murders . . . yet, after such a spree of slaughter, he felt no different from the way he had felt before. If he owned a conscience, it was sound asleep. No dreadful burdens of remorse weighed on him; no pangs of penitence oppressed his heart.

"Sometimes I'd see them flying deep inside the valleys of the waves," Lucia was saying. "The huge frothy cliffs would hang right over them, and I'd be positive that when the crash came, the sea gulls would be caught by the sea—but it never happened. Fast as the surf moved, the birds always managed to keep ahead of it."

Yes, thought Lenox—not to be caught. That was all that really mattered. And as long as there was nothing at the German's house to give him away—no fingerprints, no slips of paper with his name or phone number on—he wouldn't be caught, either. The next day or two would be the critical period. If the police didn't come for him by Wednesday, he calculated, they wouldn't come for him ever.

"One day you and I should go there, John, up to the sea wall. You'd like it, I'm sure. It isn't far—just past Beverly. We'll go in the fall, on some day when there's a good strong wind—all right? We can sit on a blanket so we won't get too cold, and imagine we're sailing to France or Italy aboard some fabulous ocean liner. I'd love to see the Vatican and meet the pope—wouldn't you? Maybe I'd have a vision in St. Peter's. I bet I would. The influences there must be overpowering."

Lenox, not having heard her, made no answer. He gazed at the circling flies.

35

"A gruesome double murder was discovered this morning by Back Bay police in a small house on Blagden Street, not far from Copley Square. Patrolman William Nugent, who had been summoned by a suspicious neighbor, climbed through a ground-floor window and found the savagely beaten bodies of a middle-aged couple, Mr. and Mrs. Rupert Hofbauer. Both were said to be musicians. Detectives of the Homicide Division theorized that the brutal crime was the work of a burglar who gained entrance into the Hofbauer home by means of a basement door.

"Turning to national news, a threatened strike by West Coast dockers has—"

The minister switched off the radio and gazed thoughtfully through the windshield. "Detectives theorized," he murmured.

Behind him a horn honked, to let him know the traffic light had changed. He shifted gears and drove down Charles Street.

"A burglar?" he asked himself incredulously. "How the hell can they believe that? There wasn't anything stolen. But I suppose they have to make a statement of some kind."

Approaching the rectory, he was surprised to see

Geraldine Gargan and Cecily Harper-Jones standing in his driveway. As he pulled up, they stepped aside.

"We've been waiting for you ever so long, Reverend," Cecily said. "Where have you been?"

She was a youthful-looking old lady, carefully made up with powder and rouge, and very modishly dressed. Her eyelids batted tremulously, signaling that she was agitated.

"Have you heard of the murders?" Geraldine inquired.

Momentarily stupefied, Lenox could only stare at her. Were his ears playing tricks on him? he wondered. Averting his face, he yanked the key from the ignition and opened the car door. "What are you talking about?" he asked, feigning mild exasperation.

"It's perfectly ghastly—a massacre," Cecily said.

"The Gingerich murders—that's what we're talking about," Geraldine proclaimed in a hollow, funereal tone.

"Gingerich? Gingerich?" he echoed.

"Yes, Jerry Gingerich. He's killed his wife and children," Cecily blurted out, frantically waving a beringed hand. "He cut their throats with a breadknife, Reverend— murdered them in their sleep! Mr. Davis, his assistant at the flower shop, was the one who found the bodies. He went there when he couldn't get them on the telephone this morning."

"Gingerich," Lenox said for the third time.

"The poor man went completely mad, it would seem," said Mrs. Gargan. "He left a note on a brown paper bag—however, it was nothing but gibberish, according to Mr. Davis. Something to the effect that he had killed them for their own good because a mysterious enemy had captured their minds. Paranoia, I expect. It happened in the middle of the night."

"My God! And Jerry himself? Did he commit suicide?"

"No, Reverend, not as far as anyone knows. He's fled—taken his car and vanished."

"Isn't it utterly terrifying?" Cecily asked breathlessly. "He came to my house often—collecting my old clothes."

Dazed, Lenox got out of the Volkswagen and shut the door. "If only . . ." he began to say. Then he stopped.

"If only the man had called his psychiatrist? Yes, I quite agree," said Geraldine. "It was common knowledge he was undergoing treatment, yet none of us ever dreamed he was as sick as this. Who would have thought he'd run amok? He seemed a rather drab, ordinary fellow."

"Their throats were slashed open, Mr. Davis told us, and there was blood everywhere," said Cecily, shuddering.

"Poor Vicki—and those two little boys," the minister declared. "Good God! I had no idea . . . I always believed he was suffering from a kind of hypertension. I should have realized there was more to it than that."

"Oh, now! You mustn't blame yourself, John," Geraldine said severely. "If his psychiatrist couldn't foresee his breakdown, how could you? Mr. Gingerich just went suddenly insane. It could happen to any of us, I suppose."

"So true!" chirped Cecily. "I had a great-uncle who went berserk one day and smashed every single window in his house, even the attic skylights. Brain fever, the doctors called it. He lived in Albany, New York. And afterwards he was never the same, really. Sat around the kitchen all day, drooling and mumbling curse words to himself."

"Should I go over there, Geraldine?" Lenox asked.

"I don't know. Do you want to?"

"No . . . not at all."

"Well, don't go, then. What use could you be there,

anyway? Mr. Davis said the police had already phoned Vicki's sister in Auburndale, and I'm sure the bodies are gone by now. There'd be nothing for you to do." She patted him on the arm. "Besides, if I may say so, you look a bit shaken. I think you should go upstairs and have a glass of port, Reverend. If I hear any news, I'll call you after dinner. Now, Cecily, I suggest we trot along."

But Cecily appeared loath to depart. "Will they be buried from our church?" she inquired, her eyes still blinking rapidly.

"Yes," Lenox replied. "Yes, Cecily, of course."

"How sad it will be! How dismal! Imagine, a young woman like that, and two small children. What an awful, awful business! I'll be so depressed."

"Come along," said Geraldine impatiently. "We were due at Angela's an hour ago. Good-bye, John—and for heaven's sake, don't get all broody about this, will you?"

36

The Gingerich murders had a curious effect on the minister. He was more upset by the destruction of the small family than by the murders he himself had committed with his own hands. Why had everything happened at once? If he could have spoken to Jerry that night, the tragedy would never have occurred. Yet how could he—covered, as he was, in blood? Why did the florist have to go crazy at that particular time?

All in all, the week that followed was an extremely trying one for Lenox. Each morning when he awoke he wondered if the police investigating the crime at Blagden Street had discovered any clues in Hofbauer's house. Before the day was out, would they come around to visit him? And if they did, what story could he possibly tell them? Some of his confidence had leaked away, and though he remained outwardly calm, he was inwardly anxious. No longer was he certain that he could withstand a rigorous police interrogation. He had the jitters. The ringing of the phone or doorbell was sufficient to make his heart contract like a clenched fist.

Yet the days passed and nothing happened. The

newspaper stories of the crime grew shorter with each edition, until by Thursday there was no mention of it at all. Lenox allowed himself the luxury of hoping the whole wretched episode would soon fade away like the memory of a bad dream.

Friday morning he conducted the funeral service for Vicki Gingerich and her two sons. Cecily Harper-Jones had been right—it was an awful, awful business. Throughout the ceremony the muffled sound of sobbing filled the little church. Almost two thirds of the pews were occupied. Never before had Lenox looked out upon so lugubrious a gathering.

At the cemetery, things became even worse. Cecily, Angela Bosquet, Alice Drake, old Mrs. Collier and many others wept openly, and the dead woman's sister and mother went completely to pieces. Lucia, too, was there, and cried copiously, though she hardly knew the unlucky victims. Badly shaken by this gale of hysteria, the minister had difficulty finishing his task. Eventually the end was reached, however, and the mournful crowd dispersed.

Riding back with one of the relatives in a limousine, Lenox wiped tears from his own eyes. What a raw deal life is! How cruel and idiotic! he reflected bitterly. *O that I had wings like a dove—for then I would flee away, and be at rest.* Life is a senseless misery.

37

Three days later, on Monday, Detective Quimby came to the rectory. When Mrs. Keller told him, Lenox received the information stolidly—though he feared the worst.

"Hiya, Parson," the burly policeman greeted him. He was sitting in the easy chair with his legs crossed and made no attempt whatever to get to his feet. "Remember me? We met over there on Marlborough Street, the morning old Cavanaugh got clubbed to death."

"Yes, of course, I remember you," said Lenox. "How have you been, Detective?"

"Not bad. I'm here to talk to you about that case, in fact."

"Oh?"

"Yeah. I decided you were the man to see, since you knew the both of them."

Lenox settled into the chair behind his desk. "Both of them? Both of whom?" he asked, keeping his face impassive.

Quimby grinned so broadly that his huge head resembled a jack-o'-lantern. "Cavanaugh and the guy who whacked him—that's whom," he said with relish.

"Then . . . then you've found the murderer?"

"Not exactly. But I know who the murderer is, Parson—which is almost as good. And I had to dope it out all by myself, too. Cavanaugh was slain by a guy named Jerome Gingerich."

The minister leaned forward in his chair. "Who?" he asked loudly.

"Jerome Gingerich. Comes as a surprise, huh? Don't feel bad, though. It surprised those smart-ass clowns on Berkeley Street, too—and they're supposed to be cops. But you can't tell a killer just by looking at him, can you? You got to use your brains once in a while. Not that this job needed a genius, because it was mostly simple arithmetic. One and one makes two—Jerome Gingerich. Some of those hotshots at Division Headquarters ain't used to using their brains, though. They depend on the lab for everything. I'm surprised they catch anybody. This case is a good example. The tip-off hits you right in the eye. But you don't see it, Reverend, do you? Look—if you got one man who is murdered, and then you get another man who is a murderer, and they both go to the same church—isn't that a little suspicious? Doesn't that tell you something? Or maybe you figure it's only a coincidence. A coincidence! That's exactly what the captain at Berkeley Street called it, but he's so thick he thinks one-and-one-makes-two is a coincidence. This Gingerich wiped out his whole family, right? After a performance like that, you got to say the guy has homicidal tendencies . . . don't you?"

Although his features still registered perplexity, Lenox nodded slowly. While he turned the detective's remarks over in his mind, he wondered if Quimby was trying to trick him somehow. At last he said, "Surely you would require more evidence than this . . . this flimsy link, however."

The policeman sneered. "Flimsy, hell! I've got the

bastard's hide nailed to the barn door. Once I knew which direction to go, the rest was strictly a matter of routine. I took another gander at Cavanaugh's books and there it was, big as life and twice as pretty: 'Jerome Gingerich owes $3,500 plus usual interest. Payment due June 30th.' Thirty-five hundred bucks! Many a Shylock's been put on ice for a lot less than that, Parson—believe me."

"Do you mean Jerry borrowed money from Mr. Cavanaugh?"

"Yeah, that's what I mean. And he paid him back with a broken head. Gingerich was in the barrel—he didn't have any dough. He was strapped. On the eighth of June, the day the old man got brained, Gingerich only had two hundred and ninety dollars in his checking account. I talked to his bookkeeper and he said the guy worked like a dog, but his store rent was too high, and the payments on his house and cars were bleeding him white. He was messed up, which ain't especially remarkable these days. We all got problems—only Gingerich, being a nut case, solved his by murdering people."

Quimby shifted his weight in the easy chair and folded his hands in his lap. "So, when I saw how things were developing, I went over to the suspect's house and began searching. The uniformed man on duty thought I was losing my mind, I guess. And after I dug around for a couple of hours without finding nothing, I was almost ready to agree with him. Then I went out into the garage and struck lucky. There was a Jap compact there—a Toyota. Gingerich took his own car when he split, but this compact was the wife's transportation. Anyhow, in the trunk I found a pair of pants—dungarees—and there was blood on them."

A memory stirred in Lenox's mind. The day of the

murder came back to him, little by little. He recalled the trousers left on the hall table. He remembered meeting Jerry in front of the rectory. The small car had been double-parked, with its trunk open. And later Mrs. Keller had said that the trousers had been collected by Mr. Gingerich. Christ! thought the minister. I'd forgotten all about that.

"But the best part," said the detective, "was that I found a five-dollar bill in the pants pocket. That really put the frosting on the cake. You probably don't know the significance of all this, Parson, so I'll explain. When the old geezer was autopsied, the M.E. discovered he had a corner of a five-dollar bill in one of his hands. Just the corner—it was torn off, you see." Again Quimby grinned. "Well, the bill I found in the pants had a corner missing, and when I put the two pieces together in the lab, they matched up a hundred percent. It was like in a Sherlock Holmes movie, on the Late Show. And that's the story. As I said at the beginning, one and one makes two."

Lenox gazed blankly at the clean gray blotter on his desk. What a strange denouement! he reflected. It was a bit like Sherlock Holmes, yes—but a Sherlock Holmes who had taken more cocaine than was good for him. This sleuth's reasoning was perfectly sound, all right, yet the result was nonsense. How odd that it should work out so neatly!

"Amazing!" he said under his breath.

"Thanks," said Quimby. "Naturally, I had them check the bloodstains, and it was type B—same as the corpse in the alley. The Gingerich family, including Jerome, all had type O, which is the most common classification for this part of the world. In Asia they usually have type B, the medicos say. Maybe Cavanaugh had a couple of Chinese ancestors, huh? But, anyhow, what I wanted to ask you was whether Gingerich ever discussed his money problems with you. I heard he used to come to you for advice a lot."

"Yes, he did. However, he never mentioned money, except to say that he couldn't afford to take a long vacation. Whenever he spoke to me in private, it was always about his mental difficulties. He was afraid he was losing his mind. I did my best to persuade him to go away for a while, or else to resume his psychiatric treatment—but obviously I didn't succeed."

"He didn't talk about his debts or anything?"

"No. Why?"

"And the subject of Cavanaugh—did he ever bring that up in your conversations?"

"Never. I had no idea there were financial dealings between them," Lenox declared, beginning to feel nervous again.

Quimby, his heavily veined eyes glinting with annoyance, stared across at his companion. "In case you didn't know it," he said, "Cavanaugh was worth around a million bucks—and after he died, it all disappeared."

"Mr. Tilbury told me the story."

"I used to think the money was hidden in the brownstone on Marlborough Street, but now I'm wondering if Gingerich didn't grab it. Maybe he ain't really nuts, Reverend. Maybe he's faking it. As far as I'm concerned, killing his wife and kids don't necessarily prove anything. Sane guys have done that before, too—and then run off and started a new life someplace. Did you hear he drove up to his hometown—Madison, Maine—the same day we found the bodies? Yeah—he visited his cousin and his aunt, and acted like nothing happened. But he was gone by the time the state troopers came looking for him. They believe he headed for Canada—sneaked over the border on one of those logging roads in the middle of the woods. That doesn't sound too crazy, does it?"

"I guess not," Lenox conceded.

At this point the detective commenced asking questions about Gingerich's church activities. He was particularly curious about the used-clothing rummage sales, which he had apparently heard of from another source. When the minister revealed that some of these things were stored in the church basement, he asked if he could see them.

Lenox dared not refuse, so they went across the yard, entered the staid old building and descended to the cellar. The stuff was in a large hamper. With surprising energy Quimby tackled the pile of clothing, but whatever it was he was hunting for, he failed to come up with it.

"Wouldn't that scald your balls?" he grumbled. "I had a kind of hunch I'd find a package in there. This has been a funny case, right from the start. Most of the homicides we get these days, though, are weird." He shook his grizzled head. "You never know what the hell to expect. I had one back in February that almost wrecked my digestion. And just this past week there was a real doozie, over near Copley Square. A guy and his wife were beaten to death. Maybe you read about it. Anyhow, when this cop climbed through the window and found them, the woman was still breathing. Not only that, as soon as she saw him she started gabbing away like a regular chatterbox. She was telling the uniformed man what happened, who beat them up—everything. But the trouble was, she was talking in a foreign language—Hungarian, they discovered afterwards. The cop, of course, was some Irish kid who wouldn't know Hungarian from Cherokee, and a few minutes later the woman stopped talking forever. The doctor said the only reason she lasted as long as she did was because she was wearing a wig when she was attacked, and that cushioned some of the blows. They took an awful beating, the two of them. And let me tell you, the boys handling that case are going to want wigs too—because they're tearing their hair out. I'm glad I got nothing to do with it."

Lenox, feeling the need of a little support, leaned against the wall.

"But this here deal is bad enough," Quimby continued. "I hoped that because Jerome left in such a big hurry, he might've neglected to pick up the dough. I figured he might've stashed it in with the old clothes, thinking nobody would look for it in a church. But you can't win them all. You got any ideas where he could've hid a bundle of money, Parson?"

"No," said Lenox in a dead voice. "None."

"Well, I better get back to Berkeley Street," Quimby said gloomily. "How do we get out of here?"

The visitor gone, Lenox sat for some time in his office pondering what he had learned. And as he reconsidered the story of Hofbauer's wife talking to the patrolman, the hairs on his neck bristled. Why hadn't he felt for her pulse before leaving the house? Had the woman spoken in English, a language she must have known, he'd now be pacing a prison cell and cursing his misfortune. But his luck had been potent that day—and since then, too.

Who could have imagined the police suspecting Gingerich of the Cavanaugh murders? Even more incredible—who could imagine them finding the bloody trousers to confirm their idiotic supposition?

Lenox laughed. It was almost as if a divine hand were protecting him, he mused.

What would Jerry say, though, when he was captured and they charged him with an extra crime? Would he remember where he got the trousers? Demented as he was, probably not. Mrs. Keller might recollect the incident, however. She seemed to forget nothing. Hell! Did it matter? All he would have to do was admit giving the florist a pair of pants—but firmly deny it was the pair the police found. The housekeeper hadn't looked at the pants herself, and as for Gingerich, the police weren't going to pay much attention to what he said, anyway.

There was little to worry about, the minister decided. Indeed, the entire situation had improved considerably. One murder more wouldn't cause Jerry additional discomfort. Besides, there was a strong likelihood that the poor fellow would kill himself before he was ever apprehended— which would simplify everything. Yes, Quimby had brought good news.

Lenox resolved to celebrate the occasion by having a hearty lunch at a restaurant.

38

The end of the week came without any new developments. The minister's feeling of contentment bordered on elation.

After a wedding rehearsal on Friday night, he had a couple of drinks with the prospective groom and his friends at the Harvard Club. He left the party at ten o'clock and drove to Marlborough Street, but Lucia was not at home.

Back in his car he changed his shirt, put on his dark glasses and went off to the cafeteria on Massachusetts Avenue. Cheeks was sitting in his alcove, reading the *Advertiser* and eating a plate of scallops and coleslaw. When Lenox joined him, however, he promptly laid down his fork and pushed the newspaper aside. Then, without even extending a greeting, he plunged directly into the story of the murder of Gus Vogel and his blond girl friend, lacing his recital with several harrowing descriptions and making frequent mention of the fact that "it all happened the exact same night I was talking to the guy out there on the street." Lenox learned from him that the police had a suspect in custody—and the knowledge made him uneasy.

"Yeah, they nabbed this drifter—caught him creeping

up a fire escape on Commonwealth Avenue," the gambler explained. "A punk kid he is—from Sarasota, New York. You know Sarasota—that ritzy track where the millionaires used to hang out years ago. He had blood on his shirt, but he alleges he got it mugging a guy in New York City last week. The dicks are trying to check on it, only it ain't easy because half the population of New York City gets mugged every day—if you can believe what you see on television. Poor Gus's head was really smashed in pieces, they say—busted like it was something made out of paper machete. And the whole house was wrecked, too."

"Where do you get your inside information?" Lenox asked him.

"Right out of the horse's mouth, Johnny. A very old pal of mine, Bernie O'Mara, told me all the particulars. Bernie's a cop—a sergeant over at Sixteen. Me and him's been boom companions for years and years. When we were little kids we stuck together like we was brothers. We were practically insufferable, him and me. Anyhow, I seen old Bernie in the cigar store this afternoon and he gave me the low-down on the case. Personally I don't think the suspect is the one who done it. He's just some shifty bum. The way I figure it, Gus was hit by a guy he finagled—a guy who turned out to be a tougher nut than he ever estimated. People can be tricky. You think a guy's a square John and all the time he's a soldier in the Mafia, only waiting to put you away."

"I suppose so. What else did your friend have to say about it?"

Cheeks replied to the question by delivering another spate of narrative—how Gus was using a phony name, how he had an electric bunko box in his cellar and how the cops were checking on a couple of the con man's former victims—but Lenox gleaned nothing of real interest from these supplementary remarks.

At last the horseplayer wound down, grabbed his fork again and resumed eating his now cold scallops. The minister went to the counter and ordered an English muffin and a cup of coffee.

Later that night he bought a morning newspaper and saw with relief that the New York drifter had been cleared of suspicion in the double murder.

39

That Sunday, Lucia failed to attend the morning service. Fearing the girl might be ill, Lenox went to see her after lunch, but though he rang the doorbell a number of times, there was no response from within. Mystified, he walked around the corner to the alley and peered through the iron gate in the brick wall. Weeds and wild shrubbery, however, prevented him from seeing any distance into the yard. Twice he called her name. He received no answer. He returned to his car and drove back to the rectory.

The day was hot and steamy. After changing into a pair of shorts, he spent the afternoon drinking cold beer and listening to a baseball game sprawled in a deck chair out on the patio behind the garage. Around six o'clock he re-entered the house, took a long shower, dressed in a tan batiste shirt and a deep-green tropical worsted suit, and went off to a French restaurant for dinner.

Three hours later he was in Tiny's Heat Wave on Boylston Street, sitting in a crimson leather booth with a buxom brunette named Sabra. They were drinking Scotch and trading lewd jokes. But at a quarter to eleven the girl left him to keep a date with a man who owned a television ad agency. Lenox, dejected, had a last Scotch, paid his bill and left also.

He drove to Marlborough Street. As he parked the car he noticed with satisfaction that a light was burning in a second-floor window of the old brownstone. When he climbed the stoop and rang the bell, however, no one answered the door.

"Damnation!" he said irritably.

Glancing at the Palladian window then, he saw to his surprise that Lucia was peeking out at him through a narrow gap in the curtain. She made a half-hearted effort to draw back—to conceal herself again behind the folds of blue velvet—even as he stared at her. But it wasn't possible. She was caught in his glance like a bird in a snare.

"Open up!" he demanded, rattling the knob.

The girl vanished from the window, and a moment later the rasp of a bolt sliding in its channel reached his ears.

"What's going on?" he asked, striding over the threshold. "Why didn't you answer the bell?"

Lucia closed the door with abnormal care and turned to face him. In her gray eyes, anxiety lurked. Her features were pale, while her long black hair, usually so neatly brushed, was matted and dull. She wore a wrinkled plaid shirt, the tails tied across her midriff, and a pair of soiled bell-bottom slacks.

"Let's . . . let's go inside," she said.

"I've been here three times," the minister declared, his voice husky from all the liquor he had drunk. "What's the idea? Are you hiding from somebody?"

She gave a strange little laugh. "Hiding? Yes . . . yes, I was. I've been afraid. For that matter, I still am."

They entered the living room, and she switched on the lights.

"Sounds weird," he said. "Who are you afraid of?"

She hesitated, looked directly at him, and then replied, "You. I'm afraid . . . afraid of you, John."

He halted in his tracks, raising his eyebrows. "What are you talking about? Why should you be afraid of me?"

Rubbing her temple with the palm of her hand, she said, "It's so complicated. Maybe it would be better not to talk about it." She frowned. "You're not wearing your church clothing. You're all dressed up. Why is that?"

"I went out to dinner. Believe it or not, I'm free to dress as I please," he answered, taking an armchair by the fireplace. "Tell me your complicated story."

"You've had some drinks, too—haven't you?"

"Yes. There's no canon that forbids me that, either. But why do you say you're afraid of me?"

She crossed the room and sat on the sofa. "The reason I'm afraid," she said, "is I think you might be a demon."

Lenox restrained an impulse to laugh. "A demon. You've been reading sacred literature again, I suppose," he said blandly. "You've decided I'm not saintly enough for a clergyman—is that it? Or have you had another vision?"

"No, John, it isn't anything like . . ." she began. Then, faltering, she swallowed and started over again. "It's a different thing altogether. Maybe I'm misinterpreting. I hope so. It would be absolutely wonderful if I was wrong. All right, I'll tell you. I'll tell you what happened."

Lucia paused, tugged the ends of her knotted shirttail and smiled timidly. A small cloud of apprehension began to form in the minister's mind, but his face remained impassive.

When the girl spoke again, the words tumbled quickly from her mouth. "I made the discovery last Sunday, exactly a week ago," she said. "I threw a book—a catechism I had bought at a Catholic church in Oakland—on the hall table, and it fell off. Ever since, I've been wondering if it was divine intervention—the whole accident, I mean. Well, I bent down to pick up the book and I saw a white envelope on the floor. The postman must have shoved it through the mail slot very hard, so it landed underneath the bottom shelf of the table. Strange, isn't it? For months the envelope had been lying there, and no one knew it. Of course, it was addressed to Uncle Amos, but I opened the thing because it was postmarked Switzerland. I thought it might be about the missing money, and I was right. The letter came from a bank in Geneva, and they wrote that they had received the signed directives giving John Matthew Lenox power of attorney over the account. It would take effect immediately, they said. I was going to call you, John, but I got scared. I became worried. I didn't know what you might tell me."

Though this news was quite disturbing to Lenox, he managed to preserve his composure. "Is that the awful secret?" he asked mockingly. "Is that what's caused you to bolt your door and hide behind the curtain? Ah, Lucia! You're much too romantic. I suppose, after reading the letter, you jumped to the conclusion that I was a cunning rascal, a thief, a foxy embezzler. Did you?"

"I . . . No, I just had a sensation of foreboding," she answered. "Things started coming back to me. I remembered the day I asked you if my uncle ever mentioned the subject of banks, and you said he hadn't. Also, I remembered how the two of us had searched in those dusty cartons, trying to find correspondence like this letter. I . . . got confused—tremendously confused. And I had bad premonitions."

"*O ye of little faith!*" Lenox admonished her. "Instead of going into seclusion, you should have come to see me. The explanation isn't nearly as sinister as you imagined. Your uncle did give me this power of attorney, true enough—but two weeks later he buttonholed me after church and said he had canceled the silly thing. He was close to eighty, you know, and a bit peculiar. Claimed he was taking all the money out of the Swiss bank and investing it in a mutual fund. I was delighted to hear it, since I hadn't wanted to get involved in the first place. He practically dragged me over here to sign those papers. I did it as a favor."

"A mutual fund, John?" the girl asked.

Had Lenox been less busy concocting his story, he might have marked a note of doubt in her tone, but as it was, he didn't. Blithely he prattled on: "Yes, a mutual fund. Mr. Cavanaugh had heard excellent reports of this outfit from one of his brokers. Their portfolio produced huge earnings, according to the prospectus he read. Unfortunately, your uncle never revealed the company's name, which is why I couldn't pass it on to you. In any event, I thought it best to leave the whole matter to Mr. Tilbury, who's a very shrewd man. I was confident he'd eventually track the money down. By the way, Lucia—did you show Mr. Tilbury that letter?"

"No, I didn't show it to anybody. I burned it in the backyard—in my hibachi stove."

"Good. That's that, then. Frankly, I'm not sure your uncle wanted Mr. Tilbury to know how he was disposing of his estate. The old fellow was rather secretive about his plans. He hated the idea of an inheritance tax, you know. I suspect he left his fortune to some charity, but in a way that enabled him to outsmart the Internal Revenue Service. Yes—and that was another reason why I didn't come forward with my information. You were wise to burn the letter."

"I did it because I thought it could harm you," she murmured, pulling on her shirttails again. "I burned it because I was in love with you, John."

He grinned and said, "You're sweet, Lucia. Come and sit on my lap. The letter couldn't harm me, though—not at all. Still, it's best to leave well enough alone. If Mr. Cavanaugh wanted to bequeath his estate secretly, I feel we should respect his wishes, don't you? And that being so, we better not say anything to Tilbury."

The girl, remaining where she was, looked at him intently. "I telephoned Geneva," she said, her lips trembling.

"What?"

"On Wednesday, I called the bank. My nerves were driving me to distraction, John. I was all chaotic. After I placed the call, it was an hour before it came through. Then this Mr. Picquet told me you had gone over there for the money, right after Uncle's death. He said you didn't know about the power of attorney being canceled, and that you were extremely disappointed. There wasn't a mutual fund. You're not telling the truth. You're lying, John."

His face suddenly rigid with anger, the minister leaned forward in his armchair. "What are you up to?" he asked. "Why didn't you mention this before? You think I killed him—is that it? And you've been trying to trap me."

Recoiling perceptibly, she blinked and shook her head.

"I suppose, Lucia, you longed to get your own hands on the million dollars, despite those humble pretenses of yours." Lenox scowled. "Have you told all this to Tilbury?"

Again she shook her head.

"I didn't kill Cavanaugh," he muttered as he attempted to re-form his thoughts into a new defense line. "It looks suspicious, yes—but that's precisely why I had to be careful of what I said. People often make wild inferences, just as you've done. The truth is, he gave me the power over his account so I could deliver the money to the Harvard Medical School—deliver it on the sly, to avoid the taxes. And what happened? After I flew four thousand miles to Switzerland, I found that the old imbecile had changed his mind."

The girl gazed at him in patent disbelief.

"It's true, damn it!" he exclaimed savagely. "Why would I want his rotten money? Anyway, it's irretrievably lost. Did Picquet tell you that? It's gone. No one can touch it. Mr. Cavanaugh, the stupid bastard, dropped his beloved fortune overboard—and now it's sunk into the murky, bottomless ocean of the Swiss Calvinist banking system."

Lucia, her voice stronger, declared, "The police say the murderer was someone who knew Uncle Amos. They say he wouldn't have gone into the alley with a stranger."

At this juncture Lenox might have won the argument by merely informing his opponent of Quimby's case against Jerry Gingerich, but he never thought of it. The many cans of beer he had consumed that afternoon, the bottle of Chablis he had drained at dinner, and the numerous Scotches he had drunk during the evening—all these, plus the shocks he had received since his arrival at the brownstone house, combined to anesthetize his powers of recall. The best he could do, therefore, was to sneer at her and say menacingly, "I'd be careful about making insinuations if I were you."

Ignoring his threat, the girl replied, "You're the one who spoke first of the murder, John. And you said I was trying to trap you too, but how can you be trapped if you're innocent? How? And you keep talking about his money as though it was yours, as though he cheated you out of it. Why is that?"

"Why are you raving like a lunatic?" he retorted.

"I'm not. I'm being very, very objective . . . even though it's all hateful and depressing. You're supposed to be a priest of God, and you've done nothing but tell lies. I can't believe you any more. You say my uncle was going to leave the money to Harvard. Where are the legal papers, then? There must have been papers."

"Sure there were—an envelope of instructions he gave me. But after I returned from my fool's errand to Geneva, I destroyed them. For Christ's sake, without the money the instructions were worthless."

"I could have guessed you'd make that kind of answer."

Lenox jumped up. "Listen, Lucia," he said in a strained voice, "whether or not you believe what I say doesn't mean a goddamn thing to me. As far as I'm concerned, you're a little weak in the head."

"And you're evil," she countered defiantly.

Clenching his right hand into a fist, he took a swift step toward her.

"Will you kill me, too?" she cried out, looking him straight in the eye.

Her response brought him up short. He laughed scornfully and opened his hand.

From another part of the house, the clock that he had first heard the night Cavanaugh had him to dinner began to toll the hour. Twelve tinny chimes, like the gasps of something moribund, drifted into the living room.

"I'm getting the hell out of here," Lenox said. "I'm going to a bar and buy a drink—a stiff one." He spun around and walked toward the door. "I might even find myself a scarlet woman—some easy lay," he added over his shoulder. "And I won't be very particular tonight, either— as long as she's not feeble-minded."

"A demon—that's what you are, John. You did it. Yes—you did it. I saw the guilt in your eyes," she called after him.

But as he opened the front door, he could hear the sound of weeping.

40

Not surprisingly, he awoke the next morning with a fierce hangover, and the recollection of his stupid behavior toward Lucia greatly added to his misery. He had acted like a donkey. If he had simply told her that the police knew Gingerich was the killer, that would have stopped her cold. Then, with a few soft words, he might have stifled the whole thing. Instead, however, he had babbled like a moron.

Finishing his breakfast, he got up from the table and started what proved to be a long and arduous day—one that left him no time to dwell on his own problems. At ten he met with the Bible-class teachers; at eleven he hurried to the Deaconess Hospital to visit Wilfred Dunbar, who'd had a kidney removed; at twelve-thirty he attended a seemingly endless lunch at the Commonwealth Christian Women's Guild; and when he got back to the rectory he found three parishioners waiting for him in his living room—each with a different matter to discuss. It was six-thirty before he was finally free to have his dinner.

Thoroughly exhausted, he went to bed at nine o'clock and fell asleep as soon as he closed his eyes. But, deep as his slumber was, it failed to carry him through to morning. A vivid dream about his dead mother awakened him at two-fifteen. His heart was pounding and his body was slick with perspiration. Though the little air conditioner could be heard toiling raucously, the room was as stuffy as a closet. Getting out of the damp bed, Lenox switched off the machine and threw open both windows, yet no cooling breeze entered to evict the oppressive atmosphere. The weather for the past week had been sweltering, and now the city lay drowned in a thick sea of simmering air.

He climbed into bed again, and discovered that he was no longer sleepy. While fatigued enough physically, mentally he was wide awake.

He thought of Lucia. Why hadn't she destroyed the note from the bank and let it go at that? Why the hell did she have to call Switzerland? Now she was convinced that he had committed the murder. Christ! Quimby might have his case against Gingerich, but then, he didn't know anything about the power of attorney. And if Jerry were found and interrogated, he would reveal where he picked up the bloody dungarees as soon as the question was put to him. The police would believe him too, since he had no reason to lie. And if corroboration was needed, Mrs. Keller could supply it in abundance. Those wretched dungarees! They were destined to become his winding sheet, it seemed.

Yet it all hinged on Lucia Pareto. He might still weather the storm if he could persuade her to forget what she had learned, persuade her to keep her mouth shut. Unfortunately, though, the girl wasn't stable. Her mind was a jumble of crazy fantasies, of half-baked notions about good and evil. How could he depend on such a dizzy creature? Sooner or later she'd succumb to a spasm of guilt and divulge the story to old Ed Tilbury. Then the fragile structure of his security would fall to pieces.

Growling like an animal, the minister punched his soggy pillow. In the darkness of the night, he contemplated his future with growing dread. The more he pondered his predicament, the worse it appeared. How long might Lucia keep quiet? A week? A month? He'd be living on a time bomb.

It was now five past three. He sat up and lit a cigarette, his mind still racing.

Perhaps she wasn't nearly as mad as she seemed to be. During their conversation he had accused her of wanting the million dollars herself. Was that really her game? If so, she would have no choice but to consult Tilbury. She might gush tender platitudes—might talk of love and virtue—yet all the while she could be planning to sell him for silver, like a damn Judas Iscariot. Good God! Why hadn't he grasped these perils the night he was with her alone?

"Treachery," he mumbled. "Treachery."

He snuffed out the cigarette and lay down again, but in his entire life he had never felt less like sleeping. The air in the room was motionless, warm, almost liquid in its density. Squirming on the rumpled bed he cursed the postman who had sailed the letter under the hall table, and Monsieur Picquet who had sent it.

Desperately he strove to rid his mind of grim speculation, but it was a futile effort. A ravenous fear had taken possession of him.

"She'll give me away," he croaked in the silence. "Intentionally or unintentionally, the silly bitch will give me away. Why did she have to call Switzerland? Surely she did it because she wants to get the old man's money."

At a quarter to four he turned on the light, poured a glass of Scotch, drank it and then got dressed.

A few minutes later he was down in the garage,

rummaging in a toolbox crammed with junk. He found a rusty monkey wrench. After wiping it off with a rag, he placed the heavy instrument on the front seat of the Volkswagen.

His muscles ached and he felt slightly feverish, but he was glad to be out of the bedroom. Now that he was up and active, the ferocity of his cogitation diminished and by degrees he grew more confident.

Driving from the garage, he saw white bolts of lightning crease the sky and realized that a storm was imminent. He must hurry. Rain would awaken the girl. Rain would send her scampering indoors.

He entered the alley, cut the engine and coasted the last hundred feet, coming to a stop directly beneath the brick wall. Opening the door quietly, he emerged and looked around. No lighted windows showed in the surrounding houses, and except for a brindle cat prowling among the garbage cans, all was tranquil.

Lenox got the car blanket from the back seat and tucked it under his arm. He then slipped the wrench in his belt, climbed on the roof of the Volkswagen and regarded the spikes of broken glass embedded in the top of the wall.

A rumble of not-too-distant thunder shattered the stillness.

He tossed the folded blanket onto the menacing parapet. It landed securely, covering an area almost three feet wide. He took a deep breath, extended his arms and leaped for this neutralized section. Thick as the blanket was, the jagged surface poked him cruelly in the stomach and chest, but he managed to scramble to a sitting position without sustaining any cuts.

After a pause to get his bearings, he spied a tree branch farther along the wall and inched toward it. Moments later he had dropped to the earth and was standing immobile on the yard's gravel path.

Had she heard him? It scarcely mattered, he decided. In such a confined place she could never escape him, anyway. A half-dozen quick blows, and his anxieties would be at an end. A minute or two of strenuous labor and his torments would cease.

The globe of the street lamp in the alley, though it was besieged by fluttering moths, threw an eerie saffron gleam on the masses of foliage. Using the silhouette of the giant oak tree as a guide, he started off for the clearing. He reached it swiftly. There, only just visible in the gloom, was the army canopy, and under it, the shadowy bulk of the sleeping bag. He pulled the monkey wrench from his belt and rushed forward, but before he had traversed a fraction of the intervening distance, he saw that the sleeping bag was empty. Flap unzipped, it lay on the twig-strewn ground as though patiently awaiting the girl's return.

Furious, the minister spun around, and when he did, something hard and sharp touched the very center of his forehead. He jumped back, frowned and raised his eyes. Almost directly above him, Lucia Pareto was hanging from a bough of the oak tree—hanging by a short length of braided rope, tightly knotted around her neck. What had pressed against his forehead was the toenail of her naked foot.

He gasped and dropped the wrench.

In the strange lambent glow of the street lamp the still figure, with its awkwardly tilted head, looked like a broken doll.

Lenox grimaced and retreated another step, nearly tripping over a clump of weeds. Like a blind man he groped in the darkness, found the camp chair nearby and leaned on it heavily.

"Ah, Lucia!" he whispered.

Then suddenly a streak of lightning rent the sky, transforming night into day. For an instant the scene was brilliantly illuminated. With marvelous clarity he could distinguish every detail of the girl's black-and-blue face. He saw the swollen tongue protruding from the gaping mouth; he saw the glittering, half-closed eyes leering down at him; he saw the sunken cheeks and the strangely wizened nose; he saw the rope-pinched flesh of the throat.

But as abruptly as the great glare burgeoned, just so abruptly did it expire—leaving the darkness deeper than before.

"Ah, Lucia!" he repeated hoarsely, unable to take his eyes from her limp, slender body.

Aloft, the thunder detonated in a series of crackling booms that reverberated hollowly from the row of houses on the other side of the alley.

Lenox shook his head in bewilderment. All his anger had melted away, and now in his heart he felt only a terrible grief, a numbing remorse. How could he ever have intended to do her harm? He must have been mad. The poor child hadn't planned to betray him—far from it. She was in love with him—in love with him! In order to save his life, she had taken her own. There on the tree was the awful proof of her devotion.

Again the lightning flashed, and again he looked upon the livid face suspended beneath the bough of the tree. Suddenly his mouth opened and he uttered a wail. His eyes enlarged in their sockets. The hanging girl was weeping! Huge tears, like fat black pearls, were slowly trickling down her cheeks.

"Lucia!" he bawled in astonishment. "You're still alive! You're crying!"

Frantically he ran across the clearing, raised his hands and grasped her ankles. They were cold and stiff—as cold and stiff as things of stone.

"My God!" he said, releasing her.

Then, hearing the patter of rain on the leaves and feeling some drops on his upturned face, he understood from whence the tears had come. His legs buckled and he fell on his knees to the ground.

Another deafening clap of thunder occurred at that moment, and immediately afterwards the wind rose. From the roiling heavens, sheets of slate-gray rain commenced to cascade down. The poncho canopy billowed, snapped one of its lashings and began to flap like a monstrous tethered bird while the little camp chair scudded off into the darkness. Shrieking insanely, the gale tore through the shrubbery. Branches and leaves whirled in every direction.

Gradually the body of Lucia Pareto started to swing on its halter. Back and forth it moved, rigid and rhythmic as a great pendulum, until at last it was describing long languid arcs in the turbulent air.

So swift and violent was the onset of the storm that Lenox was soaked to the skin in seconds—yet, head bowed, he remained on his knees. Though his eyes were open, they took no note of the wild events that were going on around him. Indeed, they held no expression at all. From time to time his lips would part, but what words they released—if any—were stifled by the howling of the wind. Occasionally, too, he would shudder convulsively, as if a stray tongue of lightning had flicked across his convex back.

The tempest, however, did not rage long. Having spent

its fury so lavishly, it was soon reduced to a soft drizzle and some impotent huffing and puffing.

The return of relative quiet roused Lenox from his trance. Lifting his head, he gazed for several minutes at the dripping, swaying corpse. Then he blinked and got to his feet.

The first pale rays of daylight had begun to penetrate the clouds. Close by, a pigeon cooed.

Noticing the monkey wrench glistening on the grass, the minister stooped automatically and picked it up. The urgent sound of a baby crying came from one of the houses. Lenox turned and went back the way he had come.

41

Ten days later, in the rectory office, Edward Tilbury said, "A melancholy affair, Reverend. It's as if the house were accursed, though I must admit the poor young lady was of an erratic temperament to begin with. A strange girl. The suicide note she left was scarcely coherent—full of references to evil spirits, and so on." Thrusting his thumbs in his vest pockets, the banker leaned back in the easy chair. "By the way, what did you think of that grubby little storefront church in the South End?"

"I thought it depressing," Lenox answered honestly. "However, she wanted to be buried from there, didn't she?"

"Yes, indeed. Her instructions on that point—if on nothing else—were most explicit. One of the Cubans informed me that she had been a member of their . . . congregation for several years. She joined long before she rambled off to California. Personally, I found the ceremony decidedly odd—a bit like spiritualism or voodoo. Did you know she left those people the house, too?"

"No, I didn't."

"It's a fact. Seems she made a will in a lawyer's office on Tremont Street, Monday morning—just hours before she put the rope around her neck. Now that brownstone—a property of considerable value—will pass into the hands of the Caribbean Church of the Radiant Cross. I can't help wondering what the neighbors will think when those chaps start pounding their bongo drums." Tilbury sighed. "Of course, the only aspect that still concerns me is the Cavanaugh money—which remains missing. Close to a million dollars, Reverend. What do you suppose the old schemer could have done with it? I've never been confronted by so baffling a riddle. Ah well—even if we find it now, there aren't any heirs to give it to. Lucia Pareto was the last relative Amos had. It's a melancholy business, all right."

"Would you like a cup of coffee?" the minister asked perfunctorily.

"No, no. I have to be on my way." Tilbury uncrossed his thin legs and stood up. "Tell me, Reverend—are you planning a vacation this year?"

"A vacation? Oh, I haven't really given it much thought. It's been a busy summer."

"All the more reason for you to take some time off. You've been looking rather worn-out lately, if you don't mind my saying so. How do you feel?"

"I feel fine," said Lenox. "There's nothing wrong with my health, though perhaps I do need a rest."

"Sure you do. Everybody needs a break in the routine once in a while. Take a couple of weeks in September, why don't you? We can get a young fellow to fill in for you. I've got that little cottage up near Bennington. You're certainly welcome to use it if you'd like."

"Thank you, Mr. Tilbury. You're very generous. Let me think about it."

The banker nodded and smiled. Lenox showed him to the door.

42

In telling Tilbury that he felt fine, Lenox had lied. The truth was, he felt altogether miserable. At night he suffered from insomnia, or what was even worse, ugly dreams, while during the day he was plagued by headaches, occasional stomach cramps, bouts of depression and periods of abnormal sensitivity to everything around him. Neglecting his duties, he would sit for hours in his bedroom or out on the patio, smoking cigarettes and sipping coffee. He was taciturn, moody, irritable. Seldom did he smile.

One morning after a particularly restless night, he went in to inspect the church, and finding it so peaceful and quiet there, sat down in one of the pews. Motes danced in the parallel beams of yellow light that fell obliquely from the medallion window above the altar. Bemused, he watched them for a while. Then wearily he lay his head on the back of the pew in front of him.

If only his mind could borrow some of this sweet serenity, he thought. If only he could relax—be as he was before. Why must he keep brooding about that foolish girl? He hadn't loved her—not at all. She meant nothing to him alive. Why should she rob him of his reason, now that she was dead?

Sitting up once more, he glanced at the ebony crucifix,

and as he did so, a keen and uncomfortable sensation engulfed him. He sensed that there was someone else in the church, someone lurking off to the left of the altar, perhaps behind the pulpit.

"Who's there?" he called.

His voice echoed from the walls, but the question was not answered.

He slipped out of the pew and walked hesitantly forward. When he reached the pulpit, however, he found nothing—nor was there anyone hiding in or behind the choir stall. Yet the feeling that he was not alone persisted.

Leaning against one of the Doric columns, he resumed looking at the crucifix. "Spooks," he said. "The dead rising from the grave. Ghosts and zombies. Disquieted spirits from the blurry beyond. Who knows? It might have been my saintly father, returning to the scene of his many triumphs." Lenox chuckled briefly. "Or maybe it was Amos Cavanaugh, coming back to collect his money. Ha! Or the sly Professor Hofbauer and his blonde from Hungary. Yes, why not? Or was it Lucia Pareto—the child with the passion for devils and self-destruction? She liked this church, she said. Amen. So be it. I have my weaknesses, but am I worse than other men? The things that I have done—they weren't innovations. They'd all been done before. It's quite impossible to commit an original sin—try as one might. And why should any of you complain? Wherever you are—hell, heaven or the Otherside—I'm sure you're sleeping more soundly than I am."

The rafters in the old building creaked softly, as if in protest. But Lenox, still contemplating the black cross, took no notice.

"Nonsense," he muttered. "Garbage—that's what it is. Evil, piety, love, hate, generosity, murder—they're just different ways of saying nothing. We're each of us alone in the world, and when we die, that's the end . . . the end . . . the end. There's no resurrection—no afterlife. How can there be? There isn't any God."

Scowling sardonically, he started back down to the nave, but as he passed through the gate in the chancel, the church was suddenly filled with a powerful roar. Beneath his feet the floor trembled. Pillars, walls and ceiling appeared to sway like painted backdrops in a draft. At the same moment the light from the medallion window was extinguished and the place grew dark.

Lenox stumbled and nearly fell. Grabbing the altar rail for support, he gaped up at the roof in alarm.

Then, as abruptly and mysteriously as it had made its appearance, the clamor faded away—and the light shone again through the medallion window.

For the space of a minute he remained exactly where he was, stupefied by what had happened. All around him the ancient timbers wheezed and whispered like gossiping women. At last, licking his lips anxiously, he turned and hastened down the aisle to the rear of the church, where he shoved open the main doors and stepped out into Pinckney Street.

Seated on the ledge of a basement window nearby was a shabby-looking man in a dirty purple nylon jacket. He had a pointed nose, a cleft chin and the rich ruby complexion of an alcoholic. In his grimy hands he held a grimy, half-eaten orange.

Regarding Lenox with sly bloodshot eyes, he remarked, "Ain't they something, Preacher? They'll be clipping the chimneys off of the houses pretty soon, them jets. Yes siree! Wouldn't be a bit surprised if that one got himself stuck on the Bunker Hill monument. Ha, ha!"

The minister gave the man a sickly grin, and then walked unsteadily toward the rectory.

43

"It's the third invitation you've declined. I don't believe I'll ask you to tea any more," Mrs. Gargan said. "What in the world is the matter with you lately?"

"I just haven't been feeling well," Lenox replied. "I've got a lingering virus of some sort, I suspect."

"Rubbish! You're not feeling well because you're not conducting your life properly."

"What exactly does that mean?"

"Oh, don't pretend ignorance, John. People aren't blind. Only yesterday, Ruth Delorry told me that she saw you late Monday night on Cambridge Street. She said you were very drunk, dressed up like a fop and had a red-headed demimondaine on your arm."

Lenox made a face into the phone. "What was Ruth doing on Cambridge Street late Monday night?" he inquired.

"You don't even deny it, then? Shame on you! The Delorrys were returning from a week on Mount Desert Island."

"Please, Geraldine—I have a terrible headache."

"No wonder," the woman answered unsympathetically. She then clucked her tongue and added, "Perhaps you should go to a psychiatrist. Your character is undergoing a curious metamorphosis. Cecily contends that that kind of thing occasionally happens to single men your age. There's a grim medical name for it, but I can't recall what it is. I know a splendid alienist. His office is in Brookline, on Clark Road. Do you want me to delve for his number?"

"Don't bother, my dear. Think how silly it would look if I went to a psychiatrist. Ministers are supposed to minister to others—not have others minister to them."

"You shouldn't be so flippant, young man. Some of your flock are beginning to view you with a jaundiced eye, you know. That's what I wished to discuss at tea. However, since you stubbornly refuse to behave in a civilized manner, I'll have to give you my news over the telephone. Listen closely, Reverend. This morning I received a call from Libby Sanders. She said that Mr. Spears—an old busybody if ever there was one—has been carrying on a private investigation into the financial affairs of the church. He's examined the bank accounts, made sundry lists and calculations, and come to the conclusion that there is a substantial shortage of funds."

The minister closed his eyes. "Is this a joke, Geraldine?" he asked, hiding his consternation beneath a breezy tone.

"Definitely not. Do you think I'd be as tasteless as that? Thomas Spears has a bee in his bonnet. Libby said he's talking of going to the district attorney's office about it."

"I see."

"Well, what action do you contemplate? You'll have to do something, won't you?"

"I'll speak to Mr. Spears on Sunday."

"Sunday!" Geraldine exclaimed. "That might be too late. Who knows what mischief the man might hatch by Sunday. I really can't understand your attitude. There isn't any money missing from those accounts, is there?"

"Not a penny," Lenox lied, "which is why I refuse to get excited. Let Tom Spears make an idiot of himself if he wants to."

"Pshaw! You just can't sit still in the face of such accusations, John. You must defend yourself. Go down and have a word with those people at the bank at least."

"Very well, Geraldine. I'll go tomorrow, when I feel better. Thank you for warning me."

"I do what I believe is right," said Mrs. Gargan, sounding pensive. Then she bade him good-bye and rang off.

44

The next evening, quite by chance, Lenox met Mary Urquhart. He had had a few drinks at the Congress Hotel bar and was wandering aimlessly among the back streets of Beacon Hill when he almost collided with the threadbare woman rounding a corner. Mary gave him a demonstrative greeting, and because he was wearing his denim suit, complimented him at length on his "mod, modish attire." Then, without waiting to be invited, she clutched his arm firmly and joined him in his jaunt. Preoccupied with worries about Mr. Spears and the depleted bank accounts, the minister made no effort to shake her off. Indeed, he found his new companion's torrent of chatter a welcome diversion.

They meandered down one street and up another. Though far from steady on her feet, the waitress set a lively pace, and the sharp rapping of her heels on the old red brick sidewalks provided a measured obbligato for her monologue.

After twenty minutes or so of this, they came to a halt. Lenox, who had been paying scant attention to his surroundings, suddenly looked up and saw that he was in a familiar courtyard, standing in front of a familiar door—the one belonging to Mary's basement apartment. However, he didn't protest when she flung the door open and elbowed him inside.

The living room was even more shabby, ramshackle and ragged than it had been on his previous visit. Out from behind the gibbous couch the rodentlike dog scurried, toot-toot-tooting as energetically as a calliope.

"Well, here we are—back at the lair," the woman said, slamming the door and kicking off her shoes. "Make yourself comfy, Reverend. No, no—don't sit on that awful wooden chair. The seat's as hard as an anvil. You don't want to get a blue behind like those baboons at the zoo, do you, silly? Ogadai, stop all that yapping. It's very rude."

She stooped, picked up an envelope from the floor, slit the flap with her fingernail and extracted a ten-dollar bill and a sheet of mauve paper. "Fan mail," she declared, grinning. "Let's see what the missive says.

"My dear Mrs. Urquhart,

Your letter saddened me greatly. Last night I didn't sleep a single wink. Please keep up your courage and have faith in God. I have said many prayers for you and I just know the operation is going to be a big success and that your polyps will be 100% benign. I also prayed for your poor epileptic sister, Cornelia. Tell her for me not to lose hope. Her rash is probably only poison ivy or something—but if she really thinks it is dermatomyositis, according to my medical encyclopedia she should see a doctor right away.

"Blah, blah, blah. All that sympathy, but she only contributed a paltry ten. I don't know what's happening in this country. Nobody is eleemosynary any more."

Mary crumpled letter and envelope into a ball and tossed it on the bamboo table. She then went to a corner of the room, dragged a huge bilious-green carpetbag from under a chiffonier, opened the thing wide and dropped the ten-dollar bill inside.

"But enough of this badinage and persiflage," she said, straightening up. "How about a noggin of grog, Reverend? Or, if you prefer, I've got some Latvian vodka that a sailor boy gave me. A nice chap he was, though fat as a sperm whale. Why do they call it a sperm whale, I wonder. Do you know? Because it was named by seamen, I imagine. Ha, ha. I was teaching him English. In the evening I'd read to him from the classics—*Fanny Hill*, *Lady Chatterley*, Frank Harris. It was amazing how quickly Wladyslaw grasped things—so to speak. But my educating him proved to be an act of folly. As soon as the chubby little bastard had learned the language, he deserted me. Ran off. Decamped. I couldn't stop the rascal. He was bent on leaving me. But he couldn't have been too bent, now that I think of it, because he said he was going to England to become a gamekeeper. Rum or vodka, lamb?"

Lenox smiled. "Vodka, I guess," he replied.

The waitress ducked into the closet and emerged with a half-gallon pottery jug and a couple of glasses. She put them on the gate-leg table.

Eying the bottle warily, Lenox said, "There's no label on that stuff. There's no identification at all."

"What?" she asked. "Oh. No, there isn't, is there? Isn't that funny? But does it matter, dear? You can't read Latvian, anyway, can you? Wladyslaw could, though. Wladyslaw was a Lett—the first one I ever had. I've had Finns, Lithuanians, Poles—but no Letts until he came along. When I was in my junior year at college I had a liaison with a Polish professor—Mr. Grescowiaki. He was a handsome blond brute with shoulders like a bridge. Came from Lodz. It wasn't a particularly happy affair, however. Mr. Grescowiaki was hopelessly vain, and a trifle sadistic, too. He loved to bite me. Of course, I don't object to a little nibble here and there, but when they start drawing blood—well, that's enough to disconcert anyone. And this man was an absolute omnivore. Whenever I got in bed with him, I felt as if I was taking part in some kind of Dracula spectacular. Uncanny, isn't it? It's people like him that give lechery a bad name, I think. Maybe he had a Transylvanian ancestor. Transylvania is in Hungary, if I'm not mistaken. But are Hungarians ghoulish? Ha, ha. What's wrong, Reverend? You appear a bit dazed."

"It's nothing, Mary. I'm all right," he said. "You've had some interesting experiences, haven't you?"

"Ah yes, I've had them galore," she said, handing him a brimming glass. "Here, darling—try this."

"Thanks. Brown vodka? I don't believe I've ever seen brown vodka before."

"It isn't brown. It's tawny. Drink it up like a good boy, or you won't get any dessert," Mary answered, showing him how by swigging her own considerable portion.

Lenox sipped the sorrel fluid and found to his surprise that it was quite palatable. Pleased, he offered his hostess a cigarette, lit one himself and settled back in his chair.

The threadbare woman, after refilling her glass, resumed chattering. "I can't help thinking Mr. Grescowiaki took advantage of me. He was a mature member of the faculty, while I was a mere nonage undergraduate. There was no real discipline in that school, though—and where teachers are slack, how can students be taught? Did you hear me, Reverend? You're not laughing. Don't you like puns? Oh, never mind. This Polish pedagogue, in addition to his other faults, was a snide son-of-a-bitch. He used to say, 'A woman, Mary, is only a glorified orifice.' Then he'd laugh in his quaint Slavic manner. That was his big joke. I must have heard it a dozen times. It got on my nerves after a while. One day when he pulled it, I turned to him and said, 'And a man, Mr. Grescowiaki, is only an unmitigated hard-on.' Believe you me, he didn't like that at all. Grew rather rancorous, in fact. He said I was impudent. Did I ever get chewed on that night! Later the villain went back to his wife—and later still, he flunked me in differential calculus."

The minister laughed and finished his drink. He had forgotten his anxieties, and now felt more light-hearted than he had in weeks. Encouraged by his evident appreciation of her remarks, Mary went on to relate a good many other amusing stories. Glass followed glass. At one point Lenox looked at his watch and saw that it was already after midnight—yet he didn't care. Tomorrow would arrive soon enough, he thought. As long as he was enjoying himself, what did it matter?

Gradually Mary's speech grew thick and she seemed to have trouble keeping her eyes open, but she kept on talking.

"Andrew, now—he was a peach, a nobleman, a sterling lover. My poor heart was smashed into shreds and shards the day he jilted me for another woman. And do you know who that other woman was? Do you? She was my best friend—Gwendolyn Zephyrius. She and I worked together at the Pago Pago Polynesian Village. We waited on tables, in the Papaya Room. Gwendolyn came from Macedonia. Used to brag that she was a direct descendant of Alexander the Great, on her mother's side. That's what she said, anyway. Personally, I think she was full of crap. In a magazine I read once it said Alexander the Great was queer, so how could he have descendants? It was in the *New Statesman*, I think. Said he was a raging queer. But, anyhow, she stole my sweetie—stole him forever. And you couldn't say she was pretty because she had the kind of mug you'd see in a tank down at the aquarium. She did have a nice slinky figure, though. That's what enticed my poor Andrew —which proves the old adage, eh? A man doesn't pay much attention to the clock on the mantel when he's busy poking the fire. Ha, ha! It's true, Reverend, absolutely true. I wouldn't feed a line to a Christian. But that's life—a few grins, a few groans. My bosom buddy, Gwendolyn Zephyrius . . . an ill wind that blew nobody good. Only—it didn't stop her from trying. She was a lousy waitress, too."

Mary showered cigarette ash on the skinny dog, Ogadai, at her feet. She coughed twice, put out her cigarette and sighed stertorously. Then she gulped some more vodka, dribbling at least an ounce on her wrinkled, faded, threadbare cotton dress.

"But I don't blame Andrew. No . . . he was as innocent as a pink babe in swaddling," she continued muzzily. "His only fault was that he was overly fond of tucking the bird in its nest. Ha, ha! And he was a grand tucker, too. Take my word for it—he could tuck with the best of them. I wonder where he is now, the poor dear. Did I tell you he liked to sing, Reverend? Did I? Hey—are you listening to me?"

"Yes, I'm listening, Mary," Lenox replied.

"Then how come you're not laughing, eh? And you're not drinking, either. If you finish your booze, it might make you a bit more frisky. I know what I'll do," she said, pushing herself out of the chair. "I'll play some music."

Four or five erratic steps brought her to the chiffonier,

on the top of which there was a portable phonograph. She opened the lid, and moments later a hermaphroditic voice burst loudly from the thing's speaker, filling the small room with clamor. Startled, the minister listened to these stirring words:

Some think the world is made for fun and frolic,
And so do I, and so do I.
Some think it well to be all melancholic,
To pine and sigh, to pine and sigh.
But I, I love to spend my time in singing,
Some joyous song, some joyous song.

Mary lowered the volume a little and declared, "He used to sing this, Andrew did. His voice was . . . was marvelously lilting . . . marvelously. Do you know what his favorite song was? Well, do you?"

"No," said Lenox, wondering whether she'd be able to make it back to her chair. "I have no idea."

"His favorite was a number entitled 'I Call My Sugar "Candy"'—'Cause She Makes My Peanut Brittle.' You've never heard it? That's strange. I'd sing you a few bars . . . but it always brings tears to my eyes."

"A few peanut-brittle bars?" he asked, chuckling.

The waitress leered at him. "Oh, you jolly quipper!" she said. "Underneath that . . . that staid and stolid exterior, you're a rogue, aren't you? I knew it the minute I laid eyes on you. Why don't you give me a kiss, eh? A tiny smooch to warm the cockles of my heart."

Lurching across the room, she took his head in her hands and began to kiss his cheeks. The resulting noise was like that of a plunger attacking an especially obstinate drain. Lenox managed to free himself, but not without a struggle.

Laughing gaily, Mary returned to her seat and swallowed the dregs of her drink. "You're a slippery one, Reverend," she said. "I'll bet . . . I'll bet you're positively lub . . . lub . . . lubricious. Why don't you stay tonight, eh? I'll put you up. Ha, ha, ha! Now, don't grin—I'm serious, lamb. Want to hear a poem?

> *"Mary found a woolly sheep*
> *She took it home with her to sleep;*
> *But . . . but it turned out to be a ram,*
> *So Mary had a little lamb."*

"Fleeced again—eh, Mary?" Lenox remarked puckishly.

"Ha, ha! Oh, you're a devil," she answered, filling her glass once more. "You're a rip, Reverend. You're a sly knave. Isn't he, Ogadai? You're a scalawag and a rake. I knew it the day we met. Yes, you're a rip . . . a rip. Ha, ha!"

> *Listen! Listen! Echoes sound afar.*
> *Listen! Listen! Echoes sound afar,*
> *Funiculi, funicula . . .*

the shrill voice from the record player chanted with determined brio.

Mary emptied her tumbler and placed it on the gate-leg table, then closed her eyes and began to snore.

Looking at his watch, Lenox was astounded to see that it was now a quarter to four in the morning. Where had the time gone? He stood up. As he did, his eyes fell on the green carpetbag that the woman had put the ten dollars in. It was partially open and appeared to be crammed with a multitude of small packages.

The singer wailed,

Ah me! 'Tis strange that some should take to sighing.
And like it well, and like it well.

Swaying appreciably from the effects of the vodka, Lenox went over to the bag and peered inside it. His eyes narrowed. The packages were stacks of money, each held together with tattered ribbons and rotting rubber bands.

"Jesus!" he murmured.

Funiculi, funicula—funiculi, funicula-a-a,
Echoes sound afar—funiculi, funicula.

He spread the mouth of the bag wide. In addition to the packages, of which there were a couple of dozen at least, there were many loose wads of greenbacks and uncashed personal checks. Fingers trembling, he picked up a package and examined it. The thing was as thick as a Bible and comprised of entirely tens and twenties.

A fortune! he thought. The satchel must contain forty or fifty thousand dollars. Look at it all. Did she get it just from writing those idiotic letters? A fortune—and it's sitting right here in front of me. Why . . . why, if I were to give the old doll a knock on the head, the bag could be mine. This time tomorrow, I might be in Paris.

Turning stealthily, he scanned the room for some sort of blunt heavy object.

"Ha, ha!" Mary chortled suddenly. "You've found that, have you? I saw you, Reverend. I . . . saw you slip your hand into my little reticule—you lewd lad, you!"

From beneath the bamboo table, Ogadai began to toot-toot-toot and jump around nervously.

"Do you need money, lamb? Do you, darling?" the waitress asked, ogling him with glassy, red-rimmed eyes.

Lenox gazed at her bleakly and nodded.

"Well . . . well, take some. Take a handful, you great silly! Take two handfuls . . . or three. Ha!"

"Do you really mean it, Mary?"

"What? Mean it? Of course I mean it. I've been shoving money into that damn bag for years—for years and years. Don't ask me why. All those letters—thousands of them. But I couldn't bring myself to . . . to spend the contributions. Once upon a time I dreamed of buying lots of fancy clothes . . . and shoes . . . and millinery—of coming home in a cab piled high with boxes of dresses. There's nothing like a good dress—eh, Reverend? Ha! Yes, yes. I used to think I'd go to Boylston Street and clean out Bonwit's. Now . . . now I know I never will—never, never, never. The trouble is, I like old clothes. I hate to part with things. They get to be like close friends. Or should it be clothes friends? Ha, ha, ha! Psychological, that's what it is. Goes back to my unhappy adol . . . adolescence. Take the money, lover. Take it all, if you want. I've got another reticule full of the stuff, anyway . . . bigger than that one . . . in a cold-storage warehouse in Cambridge. Oh, I'm so tired. Bushed. Beat. Pooped. Are you paying attention to me, you handsome devil? Do as Mary says. Take the whole thing—you hear? Use it for good works. Spread it around, you . . . sweet . . . lovely . . . charming boy."

With this final encomium, the threadbare lady shut her eyes again and resumed her tremulous snoring.

Lenox only lingered long enough to turn off the phonograph. Then he snatched up the carpetbag and went out the door.

45

It was a balmy night, presided over by a clear, spangled sky. As he hurried along Pinckney Street, he hummed the tune of "Funiculi, Funicula" to himself.

Never before, not even on the plane to Switzerland, had he experienced so great a sense of satisfaction. And that Mary had given him the money outright—had bestowed it on him as a gift—enhanced his joy a hundredfold. It belonged to him now. He owned it legally, and there could be no dangerous consequences to plague him later on. In the end, the breaks had finally fallen his way. After all his trials and troubles, he had it made at last. The long, long years of clerical servitude were drawing to a close. In the morning, his life would begin anew.

He dashed up the rectory steps, unlocked the door and entered. Switching on the lights, he went into the living room and sat down on the Empire sofa.

"The king is in his counting house, counting out his money," he whispered, smiling.

Then he reached for the carpetbag, but as he did, he heard a strange noise. It was quite close by, and sounded like someone breathing. At the same moment he smelled a sweet perfume. The thought of Lucia crossed his mind.

"Who's there?" he called, mystified.

Suddenly a bright flash swept in front of his eyes, and immediately afterwards he felt a thin, hard pressure on his Adam's apple.

Behind him a voice said, "The edge of the knife has been honed and honed. It's like a razor. I wouldn't try to get up, Reverend Lenox, if I were you. No, I wouldn't try to get up."

Despite this ominous warning, the minister started to lean forward. Instantly an agonizing pain seared the flesh at his throat. "Who is it?" he asked, quickly drawing his head back against the cushion. "Who is it?"

"It's me—Jerry—Jerry Gingerich. I've been waiting for you all night. Earlier I hid in the flower shop. It was nice to return to the old place. I got here around eleven o'clock, I guess. Had to break the latch on the kitchen door. I'm surprised nobody heard me. It made a loud noise."

Lenox raised his eyes as far as they would go, but he saw only the ceiling. He was afraid to move—afraid even to take a breath of air.

"Why did you come, Jerry?" he said. "Do you want me to help you? Is that it?"

"You help me? No, I don't want your help," answered Gingerich. "I don't trust you—not any more, I don't."

"But, Jerry, I've always been your friend . . . always."

"No, you haven't. You're lying. The real Reverend Lenox—he was my friend. He was a good, saintly man—with a heart of gold. But you're not the real Reverend Lenox. You're one of the others—one of the string cutters. You've robbed him of his brain. I knew it the night I called you and you didn't want to talk to me. I knew what was what when I came here and saw the lights on and rang the bell, and you wouldn't open the door . . . wouldn't help me. Sure. The real Reverend Lenox would have helped me, and then . . . then everything would've been all right. Working together, we could have stopped them. But the string cutters were too fast for me. They captured your brain, just the way they did with Vicki and Joseph and little Jerome."

"No, no. That isn't true," Lenox croaked frantically. "I'm still the same man, Jerry. I'm the real Reverend Lenox. Why . . . why don't we talk? You'll know right off that . . . I'm the same person. I really am. I swear it, Jerry."

Gingerich's face, upside down, suddenly came into view above him. Disembodied, it hovered there like a topsy-turvy painted balloon. The cheeks were flushed, though the large round eyes were empty of expression. Beads of sweat dotted the brow. After what seemed a long time, the lips on the face commenced to move. "I'm afraid to talk to you," they said apologetically. "You might pull some kind of trick. I have to be careful—so I can't talk any more."

"Wait!" the minister begged. "Jerry . . . wait . . . wait. Please. Only another minute!"

But even as he cried out, his head was yanked back by the hair and the knife entered his throat. He felt the blade tearing through his flesh, tasted the hot blood in his mouth, felt his mind dissolving in the awful, fiery pain.

Then it ended. It was all over—and in this world, Lenox suffered nothing more.

About the Author

Though born and reared in the Bronx, RUSSELL H. GREENAN has spent most of his adult life in Boston and France. Before beginning his writing career, he had been employed by a bank, a railroad and a variety of machinery-distribution concerns. He has also been an antique dealer—during periods of unemployment and at other opportune times.

Currently he is living in England with his wife and three children.